A man wearing a cowboy hat hunched over Claire, his features blurred.

"I called the dispatcher," he said. "The fire department's on the way."

She heard a wail in the distance and Claire wanted to shriek with it.

Her special day. Her anniversary. The last one spent cruising her hometown roads before they moved. Ruined. No. Demolished by this...this...

She squinted upward and focused. A dark swirl of hair brushed across the tall man's forehead; a light scar zigzagged down his square jaw.

It couldn't be...

"Tanner?"

"Hello, Claire." His mouth went up, just a fraction—the same ready-for-anything smile that had once undone her.

She closed her eyes, heart thudding. Ten years since she'd vowed never to see him again...and now here he stood, two for two in wrecking her life.

Dear Reader,

I have a confession. I almost flunked kindergarten. Had it not been for my "Tiger Dad" who insisted I really was smart, I would have started my schooling with a mark against me.

Why did I nearly fail? I couldn't concentrate. Couldn't sit still. Or pay attention for long...or at all. Nowadays, they have a label for it and medication that works: ADHD and Ritalin. Back then, we had lectures, time-outs and Fs on report cards. I couldn't even settle down to learn to read until fourth grade! If someone had said to me, "Karen, you see all of those books you're crying over? Someday, you'll write a few," I would have choked on a Tater Tot.

In *His Kind of Cowgirl*, Tanner Hayes also has ADHD, flunked a grade in school and was told by his frustrated teachers he'd never amount to much. Bull riding gives his energy an outlet. It's a profession he excels at and it gives him pride. In my research, I found that many bull riders shared my hero's story. Bull riding takes guts, skill and a smidge of insanity. Yet what it gives—a sense of accomplishment, pride and community—is invaluable. An organization that is dear to my heart, Warriors and Rodeo (WAR), funds veterans who want to bull ride. To learn more or donate, visit their home page at warriorsandrodeo.org.

Karen Rock

HEARTWARMING

His Kind of Cowgirl

—

Karen Rock

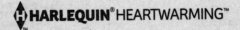

Recycling programs
for this product may
not exist in your area.

ISBN-13: 978-0-373-36779-5

His Kind of Cowgirl

Copyright © 2016 by Karen Rock

Printed in U.S.A.

Karen Rock is an award-winning YA and adult contemporary author. She holds a master's degree in English and worked as an ELA instructor before becoming a full-time author. Most recently, her Harlequin Heartwarming novels have won the 2015 National Excellence in Romance Fiction Award and the 2015 Booksellers' Best Award. When she's not writing, Karen loves scouring estate sales, cooking and hiking. She lives in the Adirondack Mountains region with her husband, daughter and Cavalier King Charles spaniels.

KarenRock.com

Books by Karen Rock

Harlequin Heartwarming

Wish Me Tomorrow
His Hometown Girl
Someone Like You
A League of Her Own
Raising the Stakes
Winter Wedding Bells
"The Kiss"

To all those with ADHD or other learning disabilities who've ever struggled to accomplish their goals. Your achievements are all the sweeter for the challenges you've overcome.

PROLOGUE

"Jonathan Riley Shelton, you're taking longer than a month of Sundays. Now get back in your seat."

Claire Shelton flipped another pancake then pointed the spatula at her wayward seven-year-old. He twirled beneath the living room's overhead fan, his freckled face pointed to the ceiling.

On the griddle, butter splattered and steam rose in vanilla-scented puffs. Her stomach growled, the traitor. She'd already eaten a peanut butter egg, a handful of jelly beans and the ears and tail off of Jonathan's Easter bunny this morning. When would she learn to resist? She and her scale would not be friends tomorrow. Maybe they needed a break…

"Goblins are going to eat your breakfast!"

A giggle floated from the cottage's front room. "You always say that!"

She peered at him through her galley kitchen's archway. Sunshine lit the air around Jonathan's small frame as he bashed through Lego bridges and elaborate battlefields of plastic soldiers.

Even the speed of light couldn't keep up with him, she thought, amused. Most days, neither could she…though she tried. And tried. And tried.

"Only when I see one."

He whirled and the gap from his missing tooth flashed in a pirate's grin. "Is it Guff?"

"Nope. Lottie. And she's dyed her hair purple. Come see. You might catch her this time."

"I want purple hair!" He grabbed his disheveled red mop and pulled, fingers tangling. Probably hadn't brushed it since he woke up. She'd have to lasso him to a chair and bribe him with Oreos to comb it later. When he turned away, his shoulder blades poked through a superhero T-shirt. She squinted at it and recognized the one she'd sneaked into the hamper last night, the same shirt he'd insisted on wearing all week.

Stubborn boy.

What would she do with him? Then again, what would she do without him?

A long breath escaped her when he rose on tiptoe and pressed his face against the window. Must be eager to get out in the warm spring day. Bolt down the road a piece before she noticed he hadn't picked up his room or done his homework.

She switched off the gas burner and let the inside of the pancake settle. Of course, she'd been just as mischievous at his age. She smiled, recalling her escapades growing up on her family's bull ranch. Momma saying she wouldn't sit still for any more of Claire's shenanigans. Her grin faded. What she'd give to hear those lectures again. She hadn't stopped missing Momma since she'd passed ten years ago. It was like waking with a stomachache every day.

She transferred the pancakes to the table and pulled open the fridge, hunting for juice. What advice would her mother give her now? Single parenting. Ten times harder than it looked, a hundred times more difficult than Claire had imagined. She was so busy she felt like twins.

If only she had backup. A husband at home instead of halfway around the world. Someone to remind Jonathan that peanut butter was for humans, not for dogs. That potatoes would grow out of his ears if he didn't wash them. Corn, at least. And that parents didn't negotiate bedtime with seven-year-olds, though she wound up doing it every night anyway.

She shook a near-empty carton of orange juice, filled Jonathan's glass and dribbled the rest into her own, topping it off with water. Breakfast of champions.

Thank goodness Kevin's year-long tour of duty ended this week. He never let new potato chip flavors distract him from buying the juice.

And he handled Jonathan better than she. Kevin disciplined; she caved, but that'd end soon. Her chest loosened. He'd be home from Afghanistan in a few days. Safe. Back to work at his auto repair shop. Their family intact again. Life how it ought to be. Sweet as stolen honey.

"Come on now, son. Time to eat."

Jonathan pivoted. Eyes wide. "Momma, soldiers! They're wearing Daddy's uniform. The fancy one with the shiny buttons."

The small hairs on her arms rose and she forced herself to put the cold syrup in the microwave. To stay calm. Breathe. This could mean anything. Or nothing. Not the worst thing. Not what kept her up most nights since Kevin's Texas National Guard unit deployed.

"On the road or in our driveway, honey?" She injected a casual note in her voice. No alarm bells ringing. None but the ones in her head.

She and Kevin just video chatted on Skype yesterday. Had talked about finishing his vintage truck restoration when he got home. That they'd cruise up and down Main Street for its first official drive then stop at Harrigan's for cherry-dipped vanilla cones. Her mouth had watered and Kevin had said he'd been dreaming about it…and her, his voice deepening.

She'd blushed at that, imagining…

And he'd mentioned a quick trip into a US-controlled town today (or was that yesterday his time—she never could keep it straight). He wanted to buy a gift for Jonathan…the son he'd raised from birth as his own. Nothing could be wrong. Nothing at all.

"One just stepped on our flowers! Can I open the door? Can I?"

Jonathan bounced on the balls of his feet, his T-shirt rising over his belly.

"No!" she wanted to holler.

"I'll get it," she said instead, and pressed her fingers to her temples.

Get hold of yourself, girl.

But her feet stuck to the ground. Forgot how to move. If she didn't answer the door, maybe the men would go away. Take their news with them. It wouldn't be real then. Her stomach tensed.

Kevin worked as a mechanic. Didn't see combat. Had a safe job, he'd reassured her when his group got called up. Any time Claire imagined losing him, a silent, primal scream would get trapped in her throat. She'd made a conscious choice, years ago, to avoid relationships that involved danger.

Maybe this had to do with the unit's homecoming…a date change. A delay. That was all it was.

Please let that be all this was…

The doorbell rang. And rang. And rang.

"Momma!" Jonathan yanked on her tank top.

Her fingers trembled on the knob. When she swung it open, the hat-holding officers' sober expressions said everything she didn't want to know. An icy thread of fear curled in her gut.

"Jonathan, go to your room." She tried to smooth out the jagged edge in her voice.

Her child peeked around her waist and looked up at the men. "Do you know my daddy? He fixes cars, only now he does humzees. I have a picture."

"Humvees," one of them corrected, a man with fair hair clipped short enough to show his reddish scalp. He swallowed hard and looked sideways at his partner.

The other, older man folded his arms and studied Jonathan with sympathetic eyes, muscles in the corners of his jaw knotting. "We didn't have that honor, son. Heard he was a good man."

Was.

Was.

Was.

Was a good man.

Not is. Not present tense. Past. As in no longer existed. As in… Claire's entire body felt hollowed by the bright white light of a nuclear blast. Yet she didn't shake. Her legs didn't give way. She remained perfectly still. Funny how that could be.

"Jonathan, go on now," she gasped.

"But, Momma…" he wheedled, his admiring eyes running over the uniformed men. Their stripes. Medals.

"Now," she snapped, and remorse jabbed her when he flinched, unused to that tone from her. But he'd get familiar with all kinds of pain now, she thought, dazed. He just didn't know it yet. Her mind raced. Poor baby. Poor her. Poor Kevin. Oh. No.

Jonathan scurried to his room, slammed the door, opened it again, then shut it properly, his attempt to behave making her eyes sting. Like that mattered.

Like anything mattered anymore.

"May we come in, Mrs. Shelton?"

She nodded automatically and stepped back, letting the large men inside. A bitter taste curdled at the back of her throat, as if she'd spent the morning drinking old coffee out of a rusted can. Her eyes felt gritty. Her body numb. Or was that her heart? She couldn't tell.

They studied each other for a long moment before she gestured them toward a flowered sofa and collapsed into Kevin's mammoth recliner.

"I'm Army Chaplain Edward Caston and this is Corporal James Finkly."

She opened her mouth and started to say "nice to meet you," only nothing came out. It wasn't nice to meet them. In fact, she wished she'd never laid eyes on either of them. That she was dreaming this, and that the buzzing in her head would morph into her alarm clock, waking her up.

The officers exchanged glances and the younger one rubbed his hands on his thighs. "We regret to inform you…"

Claire watched his lips move, her peripheral vision growing dark, tunneling, until the soldier grew smaller and more distant. With a blink, she could make him vanish. Disappear. Dissolve this nightmare.

A hand gripped hers and she shook her head clear.

"Ma'am. Did you hear what I said?"

She dragged in slow, deep gulps of air from her diaphragm, as she did when she led her yoga classes. It didn't help.

Calm down, she scolded herself, as her thoughts careened in hot, helpless circles. Be strong. Kevin had always been her rock. The man who carried her through the minefield of her old life. She needed to be that for him. For Jonathan. Claire took a deep, shaky breath and pulled herself together with all the strength that she had, as if she were heaving herself back up from a cliff edge.

"How did it happen?"

"His vehicle passed over an IED. He and another member of his unit were killed instantly. Take comfort that he didn't suffer."

Pain seared the center of her chest and she pressed her palm to it. The chaplain fell silent. Was that supposed to ease her agony? Did he think some kinds of loss were easier to bear than others?

"His remains?" she managed.

"Will be here tomorrow. Another officer, Captain Traynor, will help you make the funeral arrangements."

"Funeral," she repeated, trying the word. It tasted like dirt. She wanted to spit it out.

The younger officer shifted on the sofa and leaned forward. Earnest. "Ma'am, we deeply regret your loss. Kevin's commanding officer wanted us to share his and your husband's fellow guardsmen's condolences with you."

"But they're alive," Claire murmured, trying to imagine how they could be sorry when they still lived. When they would be coming home soon, like Kevin. Only…not like Kevin. He'd be in a box.

She shivered, her skin shaking over her bones at the image. She replaced it with his kind, honest face that broadcast "what you see is what you get." And what you got was the sweetest, most honorable, bravest man she'd ever known. A childhood friend who'd stepped up when she'd been left pregnant and brokenhearted by a callous ex. A hero who'd made her feel wanted again. Safe. Loved. And in return, she'd given him her heart. Forever, they'd promised when they'd married just after Jonathan's birth.

She gritted her teeth.

Death didn't change anything. She'd never stop loving him. Only now he wouldn't be here to love her back. The thought dropped straight into Claire's head with a thud.

"May we call your pastor, ma'am?" The chaplain's eyes scanned her face, his gaze assessing. "Someone to stay with you?"

How many times had he done this, she thought wildly. How many more? She pressed two fingertips to her forehead and closed her eyes, unable to look at him any longer.

"My father. I'll call him."

"If you're sure. We're more than happy to—"

She shook her head, suddenly needing them gone. The sight of their gleaming, intact uniforms made her ill. What did Kevin's uniform look like? Claire opened her eyes and felt a hard ball of fury lodge at the back of her throat, almost choking her.

"Please go."

She nodded stiffly at their murmured apologies and goodbyes as she stared at her lap, grateful when the door clicked shut behind them.

The refrigerator hummed in the sudden quiet. Outside the house she could hear the soft weekend sounds of her neighborhood: the twitter of sparrows, the far-off buzz of someone's lawn mower, the slam of a car door. In the distance, children's laughter bubbled. Life went on. Except Kevin's. She'd never hear his voice again.

The thought shoved her to her feet and hurled her down the short hall to their bedroom. She jerked open Kevin's sock drawer and yanked out the letter she'd discovered ten months ago. She stared at the front, mouthing his scrawled words. The ones she'd hoped to never read again.

To Claire: Open if I don't come home.

A wet splotch fell from her cheek and blurred his handwriting. She carefully slit the envelope and unfolded the page, the paper shaking. Her eyes raced over the lines.

Sweetheart,
If you're reading this note it means I'm gone and this is my last chance to say how much I love you. Maybe that makes me a little lucky. Not everyone gets to tell the

person they love how they feel before they go.

I'm not much of a writer. But you know that. Always was better with my hands. If I could build something to show you how I feel it'd be the Eiffel Tower. Then I'd take you all the way to the top and give you everything as far as we could see.

Remember how we'd do that when we were kids? Put our fingers over the top and bottom of the sun, or a cloud, or a mountain and give it to each other? You gave me everything, Claire, and I gave you my heart, young as it was. Didn't matter that I was a kid, I always knew you were the only one for me. Even when someone else came into your life for a spell, I never lost hope.

And I was right not to give up because you came to love me back. Even more, you gave me a son who's mine in my heart, where it counts. Jonathan is our boy and I know you'll raise him to be the man we'd want him to be. Please tell him his daddy is always proud of him, even when he sticks up for himself but gets knocked down, even when he drives his first miles and dings up one of my trucks, even when a girl crushes his heart but he goes on believing because I did and look what it got me. Two of the most loving people a man could ever be blessed to have.

Sure, I'd wish for more years, but some people live an entire life and never find the love I found. Guess that's the luckiest part of my life. Having you and Jonathan at all. Know that I'll always be with you. I give you the moon, the stars and most of all, my heart.
Your loving husband,
Kevin
P.S. I hope they make potato salad as good as yours in Heaven. I'll miss you, baby girl.

She read it twice more before lowering the paper. A steel vise wrapped around Claire's chest and squeezed so hard she felt as if she was suffocating. She turned from the bureau and fell back on the bed, burying her face in Kevin's pillow. It would never hold his head again, and neither would she.

She was pure liquid loss then, sobbing into that pillow, the band around her chest tightening. Her husband. Gone forever. Though she could smell his cologne on the fabric she hadn't washed since he'd deployed. Someday she'd die, too, and that clamp of grief would still be around her. She didn't want it to go away. It'd be as if Kevin had never existed, and she couldn't bear that. Not after everything he'd done for her. Given her. The moon. The stars. The world. A second chance when she hadn't thought she deserved one.

Did you call for me, Kevin?

The thought was like the tip of a knife twisting and turning at her very core.

But the chaplain had said it'd been instant.

No suffering.

Not so for her. Nor for Jonathan. He'd now lost two dads, though she'd make sure he'd never learn about the first. Kevin would be the only father Jonathan knew and Claire's one true love.

They would honor Kevin that way.

Always.

She rolled onto her back and pressed the heels of her palms to her wet eyelids. Losing Kevin felt like an actual breach between her ribs, a tear at the bottom of her lungs.

"Momma?" Her son's voice quavered from the doorway.

She swiped her eyes, sat up and held out her arms. Time to think about Jonathan. She gestured when he stayed still, his short nose scrunched, green eyes wide, as if he sensed the bad coming his way.

"Come here, honey. Momma's got some sad news."

He glanced over his shoulder at a scratch against the back door. "Can Roxy hear it, too?"

Claire dug her fingernails into the soft fabric and nodded. "Of course. Go on and let her in."

Jonathan flew down the hall, one sock half off his foot, trailing from his toes like a streamer. A chasm cracked open in her chest. How to make sense of this to her son? Cushion its blow?

Their silver-haired terrier rocketed into the room and leaped onto the bed, lavishing Claire with tongue kisses. Jonathan hitched up his slipping shorts and climbed next to her and the squirming dog.

"How come I had to go to my room?"

Claire smoothed back his cowlick. Kevin loved—had loved, she painfully corrected herself—ruffling it.

"Is Daddy okay?" Jonathan grabbed Roxy and pulled the writhing dog to his chest.

Kids. Never underestimate them, she marveled. He climbed into her lap and buried his face against her neck. His little body was warm and heavy. She pressed her lips against the silken skin of his cheek and protectiveness surged. After this, she'd never let Jonathan hurt again. Would keep him safe always.

She took a deep breath and began explaining the inexplicable… How their life would be now, even though, deep down, she hadn't a clue.

CHAPTER ONE

Two years later.

"HAPPY ANNIVERSARY, DARLIN'," Claire murmured as she drove past a Route 36 sign just outside of Coltrane, Texas. A car's lights flared in her rearview mirror.

She adjusted the mirror, the only thing she ever changed in the vehicle. Everything in her husband's vintage truck stayed as he'd left it. All but the paint job. She'd added the teal body coat when he didn't return from Afghanistan to finish its restoration...or take her on that promised first ride.

Her eyes stung and she cranked the volume dial on her radio. An old country tune played and Claire hummed along, feeling as if she knew the heartbroken singer...or, at least, what she'd gone through. The years since her husband's death had been tough, and she still felt the need to commemorate their wedding anniversary and talk to him, strange as some might think her.

"Can you believe this would have been nine years?" She twisted her wedding ring then picked up her coffee thermos.

A sports car flashed its brights then sped past. Her gaze dropped to the speedometer. Thirty miles per hour in a forty-five zone. Slow, but not slow enough to make this annual trip last as long as she wished.

The countryside loomed gray wherever her headlights touched, bluebonnets waving in thick clusters from the roadside, their sweet fragrance carrying on the warm March wind through the open windows. The road unrolled in front of her and she felt its thrum in her bones.

"Jonathan's doing well. Got all A's in home-school. He's smart, like his daddy."

Her voice cracked at the end, evaporating in the back of her tight throat. She recalled Jonathan's hushed voice when he'd admitted to being bullied and had begged not to return to public school. To spend his days on her father's ranch, the home they'd moved to after she'd been widowed. He'd always been small for his age and she'd hated thinking of him being pushed around by the bigger boys.

Would Kevin have handled it as she had? Let their son stay away, even after the bullies were punished? Jonathan had grown so withdrawn after losing his father, and she was concerned that the lack of social interaction with kids his age kept him from maturing the way he should. He was different from the rambunctious child Kevin had left behind.

A night bird ghosted over the Chevy Apache's hood and vanished. Outside the windshield, the full moon ran wild with streaks of cloud, its light pouring down thick enough to drench her on this humid night.

"Dad's got his speech back but his left side's still troubling him. Can't get around like he wants and won't use the electric scooter. But he's dragging his foot less, so that's progress. Right?"

Silence unfurled in the space and she imagined Kevin nodding, his hand dropping from the wheel to cradle hers. He would have known how to help her father accept his post-stroke limitations with that quiet self-assurance that had once steadied her spinning world.

"We finally got an offer on the ranch. Mr. Ruddell, the neighbor who's been helping us, said he'll take it off our hands. He can't afford much, but it'll be a quick sale so we'll beat the bank foreclosure. Just."

Her father's grim face and terse silences around her lately practically screamed "traitor." As if she'd engineered the proposed sale. Had twisted his arm to accept it…

Well…she had, but how else to avoid bankruptcy? A total loss on their generations-old ranch? With her dad's health failing, he didn't need extra pressure trying to save a lost cause. The doctor said more stress could kill him.

Ever since she'd intercepted a bank call and uncovered the horrible financial news, Claire would wake up each morning in a panic, sure that she'd run out of air. Then the breath would hit her like a horse's kick to the heart. She couldn't imagine selling her childhood home, but what choice did she have? Even her older sister, Dani, a horse wrangler who managed a Colorado dude ranch, supported the decision. Although, she'd never been as attached to the ranch as Claire. She'd preferred wandering on horseback to rocking on a porch swing as Claire did every night with her father.

If her dad passed away, leaving her as Kevin had… The thought scared her so much she wanted to take it back, swallow it down in a great gulp and drive faster, flee the possibility before it caught her.

"Do you remember the time you stopped by to help Dad fix one of the tractors and caught me sleeping in it?" She took a sip of her cooled coffee. "I was such a mess then. You knew I was."

She could imagine her husband's firm head

shake. He'd built her back up when she'd been breaking down. Restored her as he repaired everything else, like this 1959 truck. Not content there, he always improved on the original. Even her.

Especially her.

"I miss you, babe." And she did, the stabbing loss as deep as the day the Army broke the news. "But I'm doing okay."

She envisioned the skeptical, downward slant of his eyes.

"Want to hear our wedding song?"

A yellow light in the near distance caught her attention. She attempted to replace her thermos in its holder, missed and grabbed for it before it spilled on the reupholstered front seat. Out of the corner of her eye, she glimpsed the top edge of the traffic fixture as she entered the intersection.

Everything happened at once and in slow motion.

A crushing jolt shuddered through the truck. Her wheels skidded sideways. She smacked against the window when her pickup rolled down an embankment, as if punched by something large and lethal. Glass rained deadly sharp. The earth tumbled around her, her truck in spin cycle. When a massive tree loomed, the Chevy slammed into it then stilled.

Winded and stunned, she hung upside-down in her lap belt, blood, metallic and warm, on her tongue, a rushing sound whistling in her ears. Her heartbeat changed and grew slow and rolling in darkness. Something hurt, a long way away. Then nothing.

"Ma'am. Ma'am. Are you all right?" A man's voice shouted, rousing her. She tried turning her head but pain held it in place. When she opened her mouth, silent panic flew out.

"Hold on. I'm getting you out of there."

Acrid smoke pierced her consciousness. She closed her eyes against the billowing grit.

This wasn't happening. It was a dream. No. A nightmare.

A tugging motion jerked her right and left, followed by a ripping sound. Large hands halted her sudden fall.

"Got you."

Her rescuer cradled her against his chest, his breaths heaving beneath her ear. After carrying her some distance, he lowered her slowly to the ground. Grass scraped against her stinging cheeks and she opened her eyes.

"What?" she croaked, then swiped at the trickle leaking from her mouth. A man wearing a cowboy hat hunched over her, his features blurred.

"You've been in an accident. We have. Our trucks collided in the intersection."

"My truck!" She bolted upright and clutched the swirling ground.

An arm snaked around her back and eased her down. "I called the dispatcher. The fire department's on the way."

She heard a wail in the distance and wanted to shriek with it.

Her special day. Her anniversary. Ruined. No. Demolished by this…this…

She squinted upward and focused. A dark swirl of hair brushed across the tall man's forehead; a light scar zigzagged down his square jaw.

It couldn't be…

"Tanner?"

"Hello, Claire." His mouth went up, just a fraction—the same ready-for-anything smile that had once undone her.

She closed her eyes, heart thudding. Ten years since she'd vowed never to see him again…and now here he stood, two for two in wrecking her life.

THEY WERE THREE miles outside of town. Tanner Hayes knew it was unlikely another car would be passing for a while. He peered anxiously down at Claire. The lines of her face, turned up to the sky, nearly broke his heart.

"What are you doing here?" she rasped, winded. Was she having trouble breathing? Punctured a lung? His pulse sped.

"I'll tell you later. Where are you hurt?"

"I'm fine." Long lashes swept her cheek and the paleness of her skin blurred its edges like watercolor. But her green eyes flashed the way he remembered, her delicate features still arousing his protective instincts. Was she going into shock?

He shrugged off his jean jacket and draped it around her shoulders. She looked frozen to the bone, too cold to even shiver.

"Wear it," he insisted when she shook it off.

Her hand rose when he made to resettle it on her. "No. Thanks." She pushed to her elbows and held her wrist.

"Can you move that?" He hunkered beside her.

She winced slightly when she flexed it and edged away. "Just a strain. Bruising I'm guessing."

"Anything else?" Headlights illuminated the night and his eyes ran over her lithe form, taking in the fiery hair that seemed to grab the color from her porcelain skin. She looked smoothed, luminous, as if her flesh had been stripped away and she were made out of something so clear it was almost glass, something that could shatter. She looked beautiful.

"You're bleeding."

She jerked from his touch and his pulse raced at the swelling lump on her temple, the red slash through her full bottom lip. He stuffed unsteady hands into his jeans pockets, assuring himself she was okay. In one piece. Not seriously harmed.

Not again.

In the tense silence, the siren grew deafening and a fire truck thundered by and jerked to a halt. An ambulance and police car sped behind it then pulled to the opposite side of the road. Blue, red and white lights illuminated the velvet night.

EMTs raced their way. Tanner refused their help and moved aside, watching closely as they checked Claire's vitals and examined her. One wound an Ace bandage around her ankle and handed her an ice pack. Less than twenty yards away, firemen hosed down her smoking truck, their walkie-talkies squawking in the still air.

"Talk me through what happened." A young, heavyset police officer flipped open a pad and clicked the end of his pen.

When Tanner finished, the trooper continued scribbling and asked, "So, you're sure the light was green when you passed through the intersection?"

Tanner opened his mouth but another voice answered.

"It was yellow on my end." Claire limped their way, pain tucked in the corners of those determined eyes.

"When it's your turn, I'll take your statement." The officer lowered his gaze to Tanner's license.

"Are you *the* Tanner Hayes? The bull rider?"

Tanner nodded curtly. This wasn't some meet and greet. Plus, the man had been rude to a lady. To Claire. That didn't go down so good in his books.

The official pocketed his pad and thrust out a hand. "What a heck of a surprise. Can't wait to tell the boys I met the PBR world champion. We watch you on TV every week. Say. Can I get an autograph?"

A throat cleared behind them. "I'd like to give my statement now."

Tanner narrowed his eyes at the fawning officer. "Happy to oblige once you've gotten Claire's statement."

The cop glanced between them. "You two know each other?"

Claire's head bent and her red curls obscured

her face. "Once," she whispered. "Not anymore."

Her words stung. She had it about right, but Tanner wished otherwise. That things could have gone differently. That there'd been another path. One that hadn't left her behind and him full of regret.

After she gave her statement, she refused further medical treatment and wandered closer to her damaged truck. Tanner trailed her, stretching his steps to catch up. Pebbles ground together.

The passenger side of her pickup was crumpled and her windshield was smashed. His lungs burned as he imagined the worst. He'd heard from her father that she had a son. A nine-year-old who depended on her. Why the hell had she been running a red light in the dark? And why hadn't he spotted her in time?

He eyed his own truck with the experienced eye he'd gained helping mechanics on his rodeo crew. A crushed bumper. Smashed headlights. Pushed-up hood. Otherwise, drivable. At least, he supposed so. Someone had moved it to the other side of the road.

"I'm sorry, Claire."

Her shoulder bones moved restlessly under his touch. "This was my husband's truck."

Her admission went through Tanner like

the punch of an electric fence. He knew she'd moved on. Married. Yet hearing it from her trickled cold oil down his skin. His pained gaze flew to her truck—her spouse's truck—again. He could see it now. What he'd done... Sorry wasn't enough.

"I need to get it fixed back to the way Kevin wanted." Her last words ended on a watery gulp that made him step closer.

The officer handed them both tickets. Tanner scanned his. Driving without insurance. He winced. Rodeo travel. Road work meant irregular mail. His renewal must have come last month when he'd been laid up in a hospital, unable to remember his name and sure his career with the top thirty-five elite was over. His future a black hole ready to crush him.

"Running a red light?" Claire's voice rose and Tanner glanced up at her. She was all patches of black and white, like an illusion. As though one blink would turn her into moonlight and grass.

The cop looked at Claire and pointed to a motorcyclist donning his helmet. "Got a witness statement. He rode up behind you and saw the red."

Confusion sharpened Claire's features.

Tanner moved, restless. He didn't want Claire ticketed. "Might have been a mechanical failure, officer."

The uniformed man slit his eyes at Tanner. "Are you taking back your original statement? The light wasn't green?"

Tanner shifted in his boots. He wasn't a saint, but he was no liar, either. "No," he admitted, then glanced at Claire's pained expression. How many wrongs would he do her before he'd make it right?

The cop's face relaxed into friendly lines and he held out a pad and pen. "Now, how about that autograph?"

"Sure." Tanner scrawled his name without looking and turned at a metallic squeal. A tow truck's chains hoisted Claire's pickup. It was beat up. Had some mechanical damage given the small fire…but it wasn't totaled. Could be fixed.

Her small exclamation had his gaze swinging her way, his concern growing. She looked scraped right out. When she swayed, he slipped an arm around her and held her tight. She could squirm all she wanted, he wouldn't let go.

"Where are they taking it?"

Tanner read the side of the tow truck. "Bob's Auto Body. Not far."

As their small town's biggest repair shop, everyone knew Bob's. Tanner had even applied for a job there, but had been turned down when, like most of the townsfolk, Bob had been leery of hiring the fatherless child of a drug addict who'd caused his own share of trouble growing up.

Good thing he'd been hired at a local ranch. The job had helped him support his single mother until he'd caught the rodeo bug. Found an outlet for the jittering energy that roamed through him like fire ants. Proved everyone wrong who'd sworn he wouldn't amount to anything; that he'd turn out like his deadbeat dad and junkie mother.

Now that he faced the real possibility of a career-ending injury, his old neighbors might be proved right after all. Unless his last-ditch plan worked out... The one that'd brought him to Coltrane in the first place.

Claire waved away the hovering rescue personnel and turned on him once the cop drove off, the ambulance following.

"If you weren't here, this wouldn't have happened."

"It wasn't my fault, Claire."

A wounded laugh escaped her. "It never is, is it? And you're right, it's not your fault. But somehow, whenever you're around, bad stuff happens to me."

Her slender back arched as she swung away.

"Let me see you home."

At his offer, she turned in a quick circle, noticing, as he did, the taillights of the towing company disappearing around the road's bend.

"I'll walk." Her uneven gait churned up road dust, her face wincing with each step on her wrapped right foot.

He reached her side then jogged ahead, stopping her. "Your ranch is miles away. Be reasonable."

Her jaw jutted. "I'll call home. My dad's helper, Marie, might still be there. She could pick me up." Her face froze. "My cell phone is in the truck."

He handed over his phone and waited as she dialed and asked for Marie, then listened as she made reassuring noises before hanging up.

"She's gone?"

"Yes." Claire twisted her hair, her expression faraway.

"You didn't tell your dad what happened."

"I didn't want to worry him." She stared over his shoulders, a line forming between her brows. "I don't have any other numbers memorized."

"Claire, I'm not letting you stand out in the dark figuring out a ride when I can drive you myself."

Her right eyebrow rose. "You stopped being able to 'let me' do anything ten years ago."

He blew out a breath. Patience. He'd left when she'd given him the ultimatum: rodeo or her.

Her ruffled feathers were justified. Still, he'd figured she'd have gotten over it by now. If he hadn't given her father his word, he'd leave. Then again, where else could he go? With his invested winnings mismanaged and lost, and a forced retirement possible, he needed a place to figure out a new future. Fast.

"Claire. Please get in my truck."

Her hands fisted on the slight flare of her hips. "And if I say no?"

"It won't affect the outcome either way," he said evenly, containing his rising temper.

Obstinate woman.

Her eyes roamed skyward and she spoke to the stars. "It's taking you out of your way. Why bother?"

He cupped her jaw and looked her square in the eye. Truth time.

"I'm heading to your father's ranch anyway."

CHAPTER TWO

"What? Why?"

Claire stared at Tanner, her mind careening through the night's twists and turns.

"I'll tell you on the drive." A broad hand gestured. "After you."

She shook her head. Tanner's take-charge attitude hadn't changed a bit. Or the recklessness that'd propelled him through an intersection before noticing she was in it, illegally or not.

Same guy. Same story.

Some things never changed.

And now he might see Jonathan. What if he figured out her long-held secret? One he didn't deserve to know. If he learned he was her son's real father and asserted his rights, he'd destroy the stable life she'd reconstructed for her and Jonathan after Kevin's death.

Tanner cared too much about rodeo—he wouldn't stick around long enough to be a real father to her boy. And when he left, Jonathan's shaky confidence would be damaged even further. She couldn't let that happen.

She studied Tanner from the corner of her eye as she limped slowly beside him. He was as lithe and powerful as she remembered, his back muscles shifting under the white T-shirt tucked into his Wranglers. He still moved with a predator's grace: coiled strength beneath a relaxed exterior. The chiseled planes of his face hadn't changed, either, or the level brows over watchful blue eyes. How much would that thoughtful gaze puzzle out when Jonathan came into the picture?

Suddenly the wind rose and the air around them pricked with electricity. Elm trees lashed to and fro as water dusted the air.

"Looks like a bad one," Tanner hollered when the clouds opened up and threw their first wet volley. A flash lit up the sky, the crash of thunder following close on its heels.

"We'd better run for it," he said.

She looked down at her throbbing ankle and before she could react, he hoisted her over his shoulder in a fireman's hold and raced across the road.

"I can walk," she protested, but he'd already reached his truck. When she pounded on his broad back, he turned, and his breath, barely scented with the tang of cinnamon, was warm on her face, his lips disturbingly close.

"Hold still. You'll hurt yourself more," he said

in the deep, soft voice he used to gentle two-thousand-pound bulls.

"Let me down."

"Once you're inside. Don't want you injuring that ankle more." His strong, one-handed grip held her captive as if she weighed nothing. He opened the door and lowered her onto the passenger seat.

She watched him jog around to the driver's side, wishing she was anywhere but here. She wanted to be alone with her thoughts and memories of a man who'd actually cared about her, not with the one who'd proved he couldn't care less. A person who'd left her, and an unborn child he'd thankfully never learned of, for what truly mattered to him: fame and fortune.

Tanner slid inside and tossed his hat and jacket in the back. Raindrops fell from his nose and chin. "Here." He reached behind him and draped a blanket around her. Her teeth chattered and she gathered the covering close. She wanted nothing from him. Not the blanket. Not even this ride. But, given the weather, she couldn't argue.

"So—so why are you back?" she managed through clenched teeth, her muscles straining not to shake.

"Your father asked me." He cranked the heat and headed back onto the road.

Confusion mixed with the dull pounding in her head. "Why would he do that? He just had a stroke."

Blue eyes flicked her way, compassion deepening their color. "He told me about that and the ranch. I offered to help him save it."

"Are you kidding?"

"Nope." His mouth and jaw looked as firm as ever. Definitely not joking.

"So you just dropped your career and came? Can't remember that being an option before." She pressed her lips closed, mad that she'd let him get her tail up. His leaving her was water under the bridge. It didn't matter anymore. Unless he found out about Jonathan...

"And you're too late. The ranch is sold." At least she'd be seeing Tanner's taillights soon.

His swift, sidelong glance made her jump and peer out her window at the writhing darkness, rain twirling through the black.

"Your dad said the sale wasn't final."

"It practically is," she insisted, infuriated at his unruffled expression. "He just needs to sign the papers."

Tanner made a noncommittal sound that she barely heard over the thrumming engine.

"It's going through," she vowed, falling into the same rhythm their old arguments used to take. The calmer he got, the more irrational she sounded…and it drove her as crazy now as it had then. Men. Were they born with a straight-jacket on their emotions? Or maybe it was just Tanner.

Tanner shrugged. "There's still time."

Her heart beat a strange rhythm, stopping then racing. "Why are you butting into my family's business? Don't you have bulls to ride, autographs to sign?" She shrugged off the blanket, steaming now.

A muscle twitched in his cheek. "Tore my rotator cuff and got another concussion recently. I need a place to rehab until I'm cleared to ride again."

She pushed down the sudden, unwelcome concern. He'd stopped being hers to worry about long ago. The wind kicked up and tossed a small branch at the windshield.

"We're not a spa. You're wasting your time. Worse, you're wasting ours."

In the split second his eyes flashed to hers, something shimmered and stretched inside, a dormant part of herself rattling its chains. There couldn't be an atom of her that actually wanted him around, could there?

"Coming here makes sense," he said obliquely, returning his gaze to the slick road. The windshield wipers swished ragged sheets of water back and forth, the purr of heat lulled her.

"None of this makes sense." Despite everything, she dropped her head back and closed her eyes. She had to keep Jonathan and Tanner apart, but how? It seemed impossible. With Tanner around, would her lies be challenged? Suspected? Her reasons for keeping quiet ten years ago still made sense. Tanner might have done the responsible thing and returned home, but he would have felt resentful. Tied down. Obligated. She wouldn't let him blame her and Jonathan for losing out on his dreams. That wasn't the kind of dad Jonathan deserved. The partner she'd wanted.

"Don't go to sleep, Claire," he commanded, his voice suddenly sharp.

Her lids flew open and she noticed the line of cypress trees that marked the start of the Bakers' land. "I wasn't."

An uneven breath escaped him. "I should drive you to the hospital." He started to slow the truck as they approached an intersection and she waved a frantic hand.

"I need to get home. My family will worry if I'm gone too long." She had to get to the bottom of Tanner's stay. Convince her father to change his mind. She couldn't let him get stressed again trying to save the doomed ranch with some crazy, reckless scheme of Tanner's.

The doctor had ordered rest. Calm. Two things Tanner knew nothing about.

"You have a son. Jonathan?"

She pressed her shaking lips together, fighting to keep her face neutral. Already, the questions…

They rolled up to a stop sign and idled. Out of the gloom bounded a pair of braying Labradors, breaking the potent silence that stretched between them. At last, her vocal cords unstuck. "How do you know that?"

His forearms flexed as his fingers tightened on the wheel. "Heard about him from your father."

Her stomach clenched. "Then he told you I married nine years ago."

It hadn't been hard to convince her dad Kevin had fathered Jonathan, since she'd truly fallen for the wonderful man who'd married her three months after Jonathan's birth. Her father couldn't have shared anything incriminating with Tanner…

"I'm sorry about Kevin."

His sympathy fired through her, making her uncomfortable in her own skin. He had no business talking about her husband. Or Jonathan. She leaned her head against the window and stared out at the dim roadside pastures as they flashed by.

"Dad should have mentioned your visit." She wrapped her arms around herself and rubbed the bumps on her arms.

Intensity deepened the light creases that bracketed his mouth. "I asked him to. Must have forgotten."

Claire thought over her father's recent absent-mindedness. It could have slipped his mind... Still, why hadn't he consulted her right away? If he had, she might have stopped this catastrophe. Tanner staying with her family? On her ranch? Impossible. He would be a bad influence on her boy and her fragile father.

"How are you two still in touch?"

"When my tour group passes by he comes to watch and we go out to eat. Talk on the phone around the holidays."

"Birthdays, too, I suppose?" Bitterness colored her tone. How had her father kept this from her? Then again, he'd hidden the ranch's desperate finances. They passed Mr. Ruddell's ranch, his pear trees flanking the wagon wheels at the start of the drive.

"Sometimes."

Her temperature rose at his offhand admission. She knew her dad wished he'd had a son to help with the bulls, and Kevin had been more interested in machines than livestock. When she and Tanner had dated, her father had treated

Tanner like family. Even trusted him to work with their prize animals, sorting their breeding stock, keeping the best for their program and selling the rest privately or at auction.

"How long is Dad's invitation?"

Tanner rubbed the back of his neck. "It's open-ended. I'll be gone once I get the all-clear, though."

A short laugh escaped her. "Sounds right."

"Claire—"

She waved off his appeal. "Look. Whatever my dad and you planned...please forget it. Tell him you stopped by to say hello, wish you could help, but another commitment came up."

"I didn't expect you still felt that strongly."

"I don't." The rise in her voice made her pause and swallow her agitation. She wouldn't give Tanner the wrong impression...let him think he still affected her.

"We just don't need your kind of help." *Don't need you*, she added silently. Her increasingly withdrawn son could use a father figure, but not someone like Tanner. Never him.

A muscle in his jaw twitched. "And what kind of help is that?"

"The type that ends with people in hospitals," she snapped, her control breaking. Lightning forked down the road. An exclamation point on her mood.

He blew out a long breath then said, "You know I wouldn't have dared you to try out that new barrel horse if I'd known her history."

Claire's head throbbed harder as she recalled the weeks she'd spent in the hospital and then at home with a shattered pelvis, fractured skull and broken ribs after a competition practice gone bad more than a decade ago. "That's the thing. You rush into everything. Don't consider safety. Worse, you push others, too. It's all about the thrill."

"Better than the way you've been hiding ever since the accident."

His words echoed in the pit of her stomach. Her mouth opened and closed. After her accident, quickly followed by her mother's death, Claire's world had spun out of control, her emotions as bruised as her body. Her priorities shifted, transforming her from a young woman who never considered safety to one who understood human frailty and the importance of family.

Dani's dude ranch only allowed her a couple of weeks off, and Claire hadn't wanted to leave her grieving father alone to follow Tanner. And even if she had, how would she have coped watching the man she'd loved risk his life every day? Impossible. No. She'd made the right choice in giving him that ultimatum, as painful as his answer to it had been.

At last, she whispered, "These have been the happiest years of my life."

He ran a hand through the flattened hair at his crown. "We're almost there."

He flicked the blinker and turned onto a road only a mile from her drive. The truck's leathery scent grew strong as rain drummed around them, closing them in when all she wanted was to escape.

"You're not staying here." The words came out of her mouth strangely, making a flat splat like the water against her window.

The truck signaled then turned again before Tanner answered her.

"Let's hear your father out."

Another turn had them swinging, at last, onto Denton Creek Ranch's long drive. When they stopped, his warm hand fell on her arm before she could bolt.

"I'm not playing some game, Tanner," she exclaimed, "This is my life. Not a competition."

His eyes tightened in the corners, small flares appearing. "You used to like competing."

She thought back to her old rodeo dreams, how she'd once imagined crowds cheering her name.

"That girl's gone. Some things matter more than winning. I wish you'd learned that lesson."

"Maybe I should have," he said beneath his breath, his voice so low she wasn't sure she'd heard him right.

He settled his hat on his head and ducked out of the truck, leaving her to stare after him.

Whatever his plans, she'd stop them. It'd taken a good man's love to reassemble her broken world. She wouldn't let Tanner Hayes smash through it again.

TANNER REMOVED HIS hat and thrust open the porch's screen door for Claire. He studied her, drawn, as he'd always been, by some intangible quality. Something in the way she moved, in the straight back and the swing of her shoulders, her quick-fire expressions.

"Dad!" she called. A small terrier charged them and sprang as high as Tanner's belt buckle, barking.

"Settle down, Roxy." Claire scooped up the yapping dog and kissed it on the nose.

He followed her into a large, adobe-style kitchen and spotted her father and a young boy seated at a long oak table, hunched over chocolate cake.

"Hello, Martin."

The man looked up, surprised, before one

side of his mouth twisted in a smile, the other frozen in place. Dismay filled Tanner to see his old hero brought low, followed by a fierce conviction to restore him and his ranch to their former glory.

"Hey, Tanner. Glad you made it, but…" The furrows in the old man's brow dug in deeper. "Didn't expect you for another week or so."

"Why didn't you tell me?" Claire's sundress dripped as she crossed the room and placed her hands on her father's rising shoulders. She'd always been a loving daughter. Had been devoted to Tanner that way once. What if they'd never split? Would she be caring for him now, too? Helping him figure out his bleak future?

Martin peered up at her. "Thought I had more time." His deep-set green eyes narrowed, disappearing inside heavy lids. Under the harsh light, the extent of Claire's scrapes made Tanner suck in a fast breath. It unsettled him. Seeing her hurt. Knowing he'd caused it. Again. A reminder that he was no good for her.

"And why are you banged up? Are you hurt?"

The freckled young boy watched Claire under pulled-down eyebrows, rabbit-gnawing absently on his cake. Tangible proof that Claire hadn't really loved Tanner. She had a child whose age meant Claire had moved on to another man fast. Had found love, marriage and a family—

everything she'd wanted that Tanner couldn't give. But what if he had…he wondered, eyeing the youth. If he'd chosen Claire over rodeo, this could be his son.

"Are you okay, Mom?"

Claire scooted around the table to kiss his cheek, their sunset-colored hair mingling. "I'm just fine, honey. I had a little accident and Mr. Hayes drove me home. Why don't you and Roxy go upstairs? I'll be up in a bit for a story. Guff and Lottie."

"Can I take my cake?"

His shoulders drooped when Claire shook her head. "You know the rules. Take a last bite and scoot."

The child shoved a fourth of the slice into his mouth and bolted from the chair, cheeks bulging as he chewed. When he neared Tanner, he skidded to a halt. "Cool belt buckle."

"Upstairs, please." Claire pointed. "I'll sing you a song, too."

The jittering boy froze, his eyes widening. "Do you have to?"

Claire's dimples appeared, deep parentheses around her lovely mouth. Tanner forced his eyes away. Shoved back the memories of kissing her tenderly, passionately… He hadn't come here to rekindle an old flame.

"Only if you don't hustle. I've been dying to sing more lullabies."

The boy made a gagging sound and clutched his stomach. "I'm going!"

She gathered him close and squeezed. "I'll be up soon, buster." The motherly gesture did something funny to Tanner's gut. Made him regret something he couldn't name.

Released, Jonathan returned Tanner's smile. Roxy barked madly as they dashed up the stairs.

"'Night." Tanner grinned after the kid. When he glanced at Claire, her features looked pinched, her eyes pained.

Martin cleared his throat. "I want to hear more about this accident."

Claire dropped to a seat and propped her elbows on the table. "I'll fill you in later, okay? First, Tanner can't stay. He's reconsidered."

Her father pinned Tanner with a sharp look. "That true, son?"

He pulled out a chair and sat. "Claire would rather I leave." The smell of strong coffee permeated the tiled room and suddenly he wished for a cup. His knee jittered until he clamped a firm hand on it. He and caffeine didn't mix so well this late at night. It'd been a heck of a day and seeing Claire again had unnerved him more than he'd expected.

Martin patted his daughter's arm, his clumsy

movement tough to watch. He'd always been Tanner's idol. A father-figure to a boy without one. He owed Martin more than he could repay, though he'd sure try. Sweat equity for starters, and changes that'd get the ranch back in the black. With luck, he'd find a way to save his own future, too.

"That's for me to decide, Claire Belle. Not saying I shouldn't have told you first. Maybe I got confused at the date." The man peered at a Barns across America wall calendar beside an encased, folded flag—for a brother lost in Vietnam, Tanner recalled. "Looks like I did. Sorry about that, Tanner. I promised you I'd warn her."

Tanner nodded. "Not a problem, sir."

Claire pointed a spoon at her father. "It is a problem. You agreed to sell Mr. Ruddell the ranch and his offer expires in sixty days. We don't have time to mess around with Tanner and his risky ideas, whatever they are."

Her father's palm thudded on the table, making the milk in the glass slosh. Tanner echoed the frustrated sentiment. Martin needed help and Claire shouldn't interfere.

"I was born here, Claire. Planned on living out my days here, too, then passing it down to you and Jonathan. Thought I'd lost the chance until Tanner offered to help. Plan on him being our guest for a few weeks."

"Weeks?" she gasped. Her fingers flew as she wound her damp hair into some kind of bun. The back of her neck looked burned and for a moment the crazy urge to rest his cheek against it seized him. To see if her skin felt as soft as he remembered.

"What have you two planned? If we miss the sale deadline, the foreclosure happens only a month after that. Then you'll lose everything, including the money you need to pay for a spot alongside Uncle Bob at the assisted living facility. Dani's going to chip in, but she can't come close to covering it all."

Tanner looked out the dark window. Yes, the stakes were high, but didn't she see how much her father needed this shot?

Martin wiped his mouth after another bite of cake. "Tanner's got contacts to improve our sales and ideas to strengthen our stock. Plus, he's got plans to make some money here for himself, too. Seems like a win for us both."

Tanner met Martin's eye, silently acknowledging Tanner's proposed business venture. Martin had said he could count on Tanner and that confidence felt good. Honest. Earned. Or it would be…because no matter what Claire said, he wasn't leaving when he was needed so badly. When he needed to be here, too.

"Dr. Ogden said not to let you get worked up.

And the assisted living facility has the rehab you need to make a full recovery. Don't you care about getting better?" Claire picked up her son's plate and strode to the kitchen sink.

"I'd rather go all in than fold, darlin'." When Martin reached for the pitcher of coffee, Tanner grabbed it and filled a cup.

Claire jerked around. Her eyes locked with Tanner's and he read the emotions washing through them. Hurt. Resentment. Concern. Most of all...love for her father.

"What about how I feel?" she asked, returning to her father's side. "What Jonathan wants? He's already lost a father and you're all he's got. You mean more than saving the ranch. A million times more."

The stricken look on Claire's face made Tanner knot his hands under the table to keep from going to her. She wanted nothing to do with him. She'd made that clear enough.

Her father patted her cheek, his weathered face gray under the yellow overhead light. "I want to provide better for you and Jonathan. Restore the ranch to what it used to be while I still have the strength to try. Give me that peace of mind before I meet my Maker."

Tanner nodded at Martin. That was exactly what he aimed to do. They both had to succeed.

"Stop talking that way, Dad." Claire twisted

a napkin and the shredded paper snowed on the oak table.

Her father lowered his chin and two more appeared. "Most times I think you'd be happier off the ranch."

"That's not true." Yet her denial rang false. Tanner knew how uncomfortable she'd become around large, untrained, unpredictable animals after her accident. How she'd pleaded with him to stop riding bulls. It'd been the sticking point in their relationship, the issue they couldn't get past, until it'd broken them apart.

"If you want more advice, we could hire a consultant." Her insistent voice rose and her skin flushed a dull red. "Tanner doesn't need to stay here."

He didn't flinch when her eyes swerved in his direction. There was a snip of silence. She wasn't running him off.

"With what money?" Her father sipped his coffee through a straw, then continued. "We can't afford what it'd cost to hire someone with Tanner's knowledge to turn things around, and Dani can't get time off from work now that she just got promoted."

"I'll do my best," Tanner affirmed. He'd promised her father and would see this through.

"Your best?" Claire pushed back her chair

and paced before the brick wall-oven. "How many concussions have you had, Tanner?"

"Four. No. Five," he admitted, recalling the doctor's warning that one more serious spill could cause permanent brain damage. Maybe kill him.

But to envision another career? Impossible. He didn't focus or follow rules well in regular jobs. Only rodeo's wild rides gave his nonstop energy an outlet. Ironic that controlling a bucking bull felt more manageable than anything else. Still, soon he'd be thirty and getting old for bull riding. He had to figure out next steps or end up an aging rodeo clown, hanging out at the local honkytonks, swapping stories of glory years no one cared about or remembered clearly...not even him.

"Five? You should have stopped after your second, or third. You don't care about danger, Tanner. I don't know what you'll come up with for the ranch, but I'm guessing it won't be safe. Could scare my..." A grim layer stamped on her voice as it trailed off, a hint of desperation a sliver below it. She glanced toward the stairwell then looked down at her hands, hiding behind her eyelids.

Jonathan.

She thought his actions might endanger her child. The thought startled him more than it should have, a shock like a splinter jamming under a nail. He didn't worry about danger. Couldn't perform at his job if he did. But he'd never put a kid at risk. When he stood, his head brushed the dangling light fixture, making it swing.

"I'm going to make the ranch solvent again with no harm done. I swear it. 'Night, Martin." He put on his hat and tipped its brim. "Claire."

He strode outside to grab his bags, letting the porch door bang behind him. The rain had stopped and water dripped from every surface. His boots sloshed through puddles on the way to his pickup. He'd take it in tomorrow and see about getting it fixed. As for Claire's truck... He'd find a way to repair that, too.

At the door, he turned and glanced up to see Claire standing in a window watching him. She whirled when he spied her, but not quickly enough to hide her tortured expression.

Like so many from his past, she didn't believe in him. Funny how once she'd been his biggest supporter. He leaned against his truck and squinted at the glow behind Claire's curtains. He pulled out a cinnamon stick and clamped it between his teeth. Times like this made him wish for the cigarettes he'd quit six months ago.

But he was twenty-nine now. Old enough to know better. About lots of things.

So why, when it came to Claire and him, couldn't he understand a single one?

CHAPTER THREE

CLAIRE STOOD ON the wraparound porch of their large, two-story farmhouse and zipped a thin sweatshirt over her tank top. A clammy, shivery sensation crept up her legs. Her father had changed his mind without consulting her or Dani, whom she'd called before bed last night. Worse, he considered Tanner their savior.

A bitter noise escaped her. Of all people, the man who'd once wrecked her life was now supposed to save it? Her hands curled. Like heck he would.

She lowered her thermos then strode beneath laden magnolia trees along a fenced-off grazing area on their 15,000-acre ranch. Beyond it stood a couple of red-sided barns that housed equipment and their show livestock. Farther away still milled a breeding herd in another of their twenty pastures, the tin loafing shed empty. A bull bellowed in the distance.

At least Tanner had a kitchen in his separate housing unit. Bulls to tend. No reason for him to visit the main house or stop by the horse stable she managed. He wouldn't see much of Jonathan or her. Still, she needed him gone, not just absent. Needed to remove the possibility that he'd learn the truth about Jonathan. Yet doubt lingered. Was she wrong to keep him in the dark about having a son?

She shook off the traitorous thought. Kevin was Jonathan's father. Tanner hadn't even stuck around long enough to know about her pregnancy. He'd wanted fame, not her.

On the other hand, didn't Jonathan deserve to have a father? And didn't Tanner deserve to know the truth?

She rounded a bend and emerged into dappled sunlight.

No.

She'd made the right decision not to include Tanner. It was senseless to question it now. Her spirits rose when she considered Tanner's short-lived interests and how seldom he focused on anything for long. Whatever had drawn him here would lose its charm and he'd leave. She had to make sure that happened before they lost their buyer and the bank foreclosed.

At least he hadn't come for her. Restlessness zip-lined through her. Not that it should matter…

She reached the horse stable and turned to stare at her family's two-story white country house, its lines old-fashioned but stately. Morning glory and moon vines twined around the porch's newel posts, peppering the building with bursts of color. It was beautiful. Most of all, it was home. Except for her seven-year marriage, she'd lived nowhere else.

How would Jonathan handle leaving it and returning to public school when she found a job and couldn't homeschool him anymore? Would his bellyaches return? Those nights when he cried himself to sleep?

Claire's head throbbed. Nobody ever told you that being a mother was all about making what seemed like thousands of tiny decisions, some as painful as broken glass.

She had to let the ranch go and so did her dad. No sense delaying the inevitable. Putting it off only made their situation worse. She'd block every change Tanner tried to make until she drove him away. The sooner the better.

A horse nickered and she stepped inside the dim rectangular building. Dusty, a dapple-gray quarter horse, arched her neck and eyed Claire, her black nostrils blowing. More horses appeared at their doors, nosy to see what Claire brought them today.

"Hey, Dusty." She stopped to pet the horse's velvet nose and slipped her a carrot.

Another horse snorted and bobbed its sleek

mahogany head. "Would I forget you, Athena?" She stroked the paint horse's corded neck and blond mane as it munched on its treat. Athena's similarity to her old barrel racer struck her again. How many years since she'd ridden? Ten. Not since her eighteenth birthday. The day of her accident. Still, she'd never stopped loving these gentle giants even if she wouldn't ride them. Fear trickled down her spine. Ever. It took all her willpower to simply lead these tried and true horses in the ring with her beginner students and give instructions to her more proficient riders without giving in to her anxiety.

To calm her nerves, she sang like always.

"Oh, give me a home where the buffalo roam, and the deer and the antelope play…"

She moved down the line, doling out her treats, getting a quick visual on each animal before beginning her chores. A wiry four-legged body dashed between her legs.

"Home, home on the range," she continued, glad only the animals could hear her. What had her son called her singing? A punch in the ear? Yikes.

Roxy lifted her muzzle and howled along, her tail beating the gnats out of the air.

Claire crouched to scratch her pet's scraggly chin. "You're so cute, even if you are the bearded lady of dogs. Thanks for the accompaniment."

After grabbing a rake, she set to work on her morning chores, the mindless tasks temporarily chasing her worries away. She had riding lessons lined up starting at nine and needed to hurry to get breakfast and a shower before then.

A couple of hours later, she trudged up her porch steps and nearly collided with a tall man wearing a T-shirt and jeans covering well-worn boots.

Tanner.

Vivid blue eyes flashed from beneath a brown cowboy hat. Her heart picked up tempo at the hard, handsome curve of his lips, the flecks of stubble along his square jaw. His nose was straight, his chin dimpled. Skin tan, hair brown and waving. Body wired with energy. Tanner seemed spring-loaded, as if he was searching for something. He was perception and grit. Ambition and strong coffee. She could have looked at him forever. Their eyes locked.

"What are you doing here?" she blurted, flustered and more aware than she should have been of his sculpted arms and long legs.

His eyebrows rose. "Stopped by to ask your father a question and he invited me for breakfast."

"So you're done? Leaving?"

"Haven't finished my bacon yet," he drawled and chucked her gently under the chin. "Don't worry, I'll be right back."

She sputtered, the spot where he'd touched burning like a brand. "Wasn't concerned about that."

He swerved on the bottom step and peered up at her, his eyes gleaming. "If you're anxious about my food getting cold, just put it in the oven for me. I'd appreciate it." His mouth curled in amusement.

"I think certain places might freeze over first."

He tipped his hat then strode to his quarters, chuckling.

Obnoxious, infuriating, arrogant, pestilence of a man.

With a groan, she dashed upstairs and jumped into the shower. If only she could linger and keep from running into Tanner again. But with a student scheduled, she had to rush. Plus Jonathan would be downstairs. She needed to stay vigilant around them.

After a quick towel off, she pulled on jean shorts and a T-shirt. She trapped her unruly curls in a fishtail braid and slid on her boots before clomping back downstairs.

To her dismay, Tanner sprawled in a chair at the table, seeming to take up more space than

anyone else in the room. His eyes dropped to
her feet then rose slowly to meet hers, and the
warm appreciation in them darkened the shade
to a deep blue. She flushed. He had no right
looking at her that way. But hadn't she done the
same when they'd been outside, a voice whispered accusingly.

"Morning, Dad." She kissed the top of her
father's head then returned Jonathan's hug, stu-
diously ignoring the man making her nerves
jump. "How'd you sleep, honey?"

"Good. Here, Roxy." He leaned down and fed
his scampering terrier a bacon slice.

"Honey. No feeding the dog at the table."

The antennae-like hair over Roxy's eyebrows
twitched as she hunkered on the floor and began
chomping, her jaw snapping open again when
Jonathan snuck her another piece.

"Jonathan. What did I say?"

He shrugged, eyes glimmering and full of
false innocence. "You said no feeding Roxy at
the table so I did it under the table." His mischievous grin made Claire's lips twitch. "I didn't
break a rule."

"You sure bent it. What am I going to do
with you?"

"Feed me to the dogs?" He flopped upside
down on his chair and dangled his wrist to
Roxy. "Want a bite?"

She headed for the stove and filled her plate with eggs and toast. "What are you going to do today…besides disobey your mother?" Marie, the housekeeper Claire's father hired after her mother's death, handed her a glass of juice. "Thanks." The dark-haired woman returned her smile. It hurt, imagining they'd be letting her go when they sold the ranch, but luckily she already had plans to move in with her pregnant daughter in Arizona.

"Finishing my Benjamin Franklin report then maybe work on my model plane." Her son kept his head lowered, but she noticed his eyes flicking toward Tanner.

Her father nudged Jonathan. "Let's get out today, son. Marie will drive us into town. How about an ice cream at Harrigan's?"

Claire held her breath, hoping Jonathan would agree. He loved ice cream as much as any kid, but he rarely wanted to go into town knowing he might run into some of his old classmates. His counselor had warned them not to push him into activities that heightened his insecurities, so Claire stayed quiet.

"No, thanks, Grandpa." Jonathan chopped the rest of his bacon with his fork, scattering it around his plate.

"How about riding with your mother?" put in Tanner.

Martin's spoon clattered to the table and Jonathan's eyes grew round. Claire's breath stalled. "Momma. You don't ride."

"She used to be the best barrel racer in the area. Could have been a champion." Tanner raised his juice glass as if toasting her.

"Enough, Tanner." Claire tamped down the old rush of excitement at his admiring expression. She wasn't that woman anymore and she didn't want her son's head filled with crazy ideas. Worse, Tanner made her remember a side of herself she'd let go. Wouldn't want back.

Jonathan scooted to the edge of his chair. "I want to learn to ride, but Momma won't let me."

"Jonathan," Claire warned, shooting the cowboy a glare over her son's head.

Tanner smiled wide, seeming to enjoy her ire, which, of course, only fired her up more. "I'll take you, sometime, if your mother gives the okay."

"She doesn't." Claire tossed her cold toast back onto her plate, her appetite gone. How dare Tanner overstep and interfere with her parenting? First the ranch, now Jonathan? He was getting under her skin in the worst way.

"How's your day lined up, Tanner?" her father asked in the tense silence. He wiped his mouth but missed the stiff side. Claire leaned over and dabbed at the egg in a move too fast for a man's pride to register. She hoped…

"Mostly I'll be looking things over. Did a bit of that last night with the breed stock. I've got a rep from Carne Incorporado coming up from Mexico City tomorrow. He's a fan and friend who's looking to improve the company's beef with better breeders. I've also got my eye on a couple of bulls that could go for six figures at auction. Revelation's one."

Her father whistled and leaned forward, the red veins on the end of his nose filling. "That's my top stud. And Carne would be the biggest company we've worked with, yet. What's the chance of us getting a contract?"

Tanner shrugged and poured himself another cup of coffee. "Hard to say."

"May I have a word with you, Tanner?" Claire shoved her chair back and stood. "Outside, please?"

He studied her for a moment before he nodded. Roxy bounded after them then leaped off the porch to chase squawking chickens.

"You're raising my father's hopes for nothing." Her voice was indoors quiet, falling through the wide sunshine. "We're not large enough to interest big players like that."

Tanner gripped the porch rail and his forearms clenched as if he braced himself against her arguments. "Your father's got great seed stock. Large corporations like Carne will want to buy it."

She swayed a little, and her mouth clicked open. A bigger ranch meant more pressure on her fragile father. No. This business connection could not happen.

"A corporation like Carne has no loyalty to Denton. Even if they made an offer, they could easily pull out and leave us in even more in debt down the road."

He pulled off his hat and a small breeze ruffled his hair. "Well, this is how I see it. If we auction some of our top studs and syndicate others, selling stakeholders exclusive rights to their semen, we can get buyers talking about Denton again. Attract even more investors than Carne. We'll use the cash to expand and fill bigger and bigger quotas."

"Too risky," Claire fired back, struggling to keep her voice down. "Selling the ranch to Mr. Ruddell is safer."

Tanner leaned a boot on the porch's lower rail and tilted his head, studying her. "And safer is always better."

"Of course."

"Sounds more personal than professional, Claire." Tanner's voice was soft and flat.

She flinched, knowing he referred to her

change of heart about rodeo…and dating a bull rider. "That's ridiculous."

"Is it?" He pushed off the rail, all tanned arms and square shoulders, his demeanor infuriatingly cool. "Guess that's for you to decide. As for the ranch, not taking risks is what has put it behind the times."

"Just stop," she pleaded, her voice rising despite herself.

"Stop what exactly, Claire?" When he sauntered close, she breathed in his familiar scent. Leather and livestock. It scrambled her thoughts for a moment.

"All of it. Why do you care?"

He resettled his hat and squinted at the rising sun for a long moment. "I care, Claire." He started down the steps, his words falling over his shoulder. "More than I should."

TANNER PEERED AT a worn, creased paper, light bouncing off the page. The late afternoon felt like summer, pails of sunshine spilling through scuttling clouds, brightening the whole pasture. Dandelion seeds drifted on a low breeze and spiky ragwort flowered yellow.

"Plank position. Drop the knees. Hands underneath the pecs not the shoulders."

He ripped off his damp T-shirt and tossed it onto the ground beside his hat. In a swift move, he dropped into the springy grass, stretched out for the fancy push-up and executed thirty. His healing rotator cuff ached but he forced another set. Yoga was no joke. It kicked his butt. Sweat ran down the sides of his face and slicked his back and chest. He'd been at his physical therapy for an hour. Almost time to quit.

He held up the paper again, scanned it and stuffed it back in his jeans for the last time. Knot pose. On his belly, he crossed his bad arm under his chest then reached forward with the opposite hand, a deep drawing of the muscle. Still felt tight, but looser than it had a week ago. His therapist was right about yoga.

Tanner had scoffed at first. Thought it wouldn't be a challenge. A smile crept across his face. What an idiot. These easy-looking moves worked him harder than any bull. And his hand, wrist, arm and shoulder muscles felt stronger...critical in his job.

After his last bad landing, he'd worried his career was over. At this rate, he might get into shape, after all. With no savings after a mismanaged investment, he had no other option but to ride...unless his idea to start a rodeo school, renting space and buying Denton Ranch's more aggressive, mixed breed bulls, worked out. It'd be the first time he put his mind, not his grip, to use, and he didn't have as much faith in the former… Not when his occupation had been so good to him.

He rolled over. Meditation time. He slowed his breathing and let his body sink into the earth the way he'd been shown. Cleared his mind and pictured a peaceful spot. Denton Creek. Where he and Claire had picnicked and swum while dating.

"Tanner!"

He blinked up into the blue sky. Had he imagined Claire's voice? It'd sounded real.

"What are you doing?"

Nope. Not a dream.

He leaped to his feet and sauntered over to the metal fence. As he watched her unlatch the gate and walk inside, his heart rate picked up a notch. There was no denying she was beautifully made, with long graceful bones and flat muscles that flowed smoothly from the curves of her torso to the dip of her waist. The sun skidded across her face when she looked up at him. Dark green eyes and a full mouth that didn't give an inch.

He breathed in the fresh scent of her as she passed by, a one-of-a-kind mix of wildflowers, horses and the outdoors, that brought on memories he'd better forget again in a hurry.

"Are you hurt?" Her eyes ran over his bare chest then lowered, a pink tint darkening her cheeks as her eyes lingered on the kidney-bean-shaped birthmark beside his navel.

"I was meditating. Yoga."

"That's a joke, right?"

Tart-tongued gal. Her sarcasm had always challenged him. Made him want to kiss the sting right out of her until she melted, sweet and willing, in his arms. No other woman excited him this way. Lit him up the way rodeo did.

"Not if I want to rehab this shoulder." He grabbed a handkerchief out of his back pocket and mopped his brow. "What can I help you with? Didn't think you wanted to see me much."

Wariness curled in her eyes like smoke. "I don't. But I called my insurance company and they're not covering the truck repairs because of my ticket. I wondered if you had any ideas."

His thumbs hooked in his belt loops. "A few."

Claire leaned against the fence and slanted him a skeptical look. "I called the auto body. They said it'd take time to locate the specific parts, and lots of labor. It's going to cost a fortune."

He rested a hand on the fence rail beside her shoulder. "Let me figure that out. I'm having it towed here in the morning. Already called a mechanic to see if he'd work off-hours to help."

She angled her head and the red curls that escaped her braid blew across her face. "And then what? You're going to fix it?"

The scoff in her voice sounded all too familiar. Voices from his past telling him to not even try. It only fired him up. "That's the plan. I want Jonathan to work with me."

Her mouth dropped open. "Jonathan? He would never. I would never…"

Unable to resist, he tucked a wavy strand behind her ear, his fingertips lingering on the soft flesh. She shivered, despite the sun melting all around them.

He forced his mind back onto the conversation. Claire was magnetic, pulling him in when he'd had no intention of getting close again. "You're coddling him. He should have gone out with Martin today. Be doing things. Working with his hands."

"He makes model airplanes," she exclaimed.

"Will he ever fly a real one?"

Her eyes shimmered. "Too dangerous. He wouldn't want that."

"He should. Let him work with me." Having grown up without a father, he felt for the kid, wanted to help Martin's bid to get the boy out into the world.

For a moment, Tanner caught a weakening in her resistance, in the rounding of her eyes, the softening of her mouth. He leaned in, drawn to this glimpse of the old Claire. After a moment, she shook her head and ducked under his arm.

Back at the gate, she whirled. "When are you leaving?"

His lips twisted. "Planning a going-away party for me?"

Her eyes rose to the sky. "Why did you come back? Really?"

"I want to help your father." The truth. Mostly. She didn't need to know he had to save himself, too. Or he didn't want her to know, he admitted. Then there was his growing preoccupation with Claire. Being around her messed with his head. Filled him with thoughts he'd had under control for years.

Claire's eyebrows lifted. "And...?" she prompted.

"That's it," he said firmly.

"So this isn't about us?" Her shoulders hunched and her words came out in a muffled clump he strained to hear.

"Do you want it to be?" The question leaped out of him too fast to lasso back.

Her eyes met his, the questioning expression making his pulse thud. Hard.

At last she shook her head. "We both made our choices."

He recalled how sure he'd been that she'd come around once he succeeded at rodeo.

Letting her down when she'd given him the ultimatum—her or rodeo—had seemed the lesser of two evils. She hadn't known him when he'd spent his after-school hours in detention and struggled to graduate after an extra senior year. Rodeo was the only thing he'd ever been good at, and he hadn't wanted her to see him fail at a regular job.

"The right ones," he muttered, hanging his head and raising his eyes.

Her shoulders squared as she examined him, green eyes dull, just a little too wide. "So, nothing's changed."

His nod felt heavy. Dishonest somehow. "Nothing's changed."

Without another word, she unlatched the gate and strode away, leaving him with an empty feeling that didn't sit right.

He'd been on his own for ten years. Had worked hard to finally put her out of his mind. And now here she was again, muddling a straightforward plan to help Martin and a gamble to save his own future.

He headed back for his shirt and hat.

Claire affected him more than he'd bargained for. She was a complication, but he was doing this in spite of her, not because of her.

He pulled his brim low and watched her bright head disappear down a small hill.

Best he remember that.

CHAPTER FOUR

CLAIRE SHIELDED HER eyes from the bright morning sun the next day and scrutinized the pickup bumping up the ranch's drive. The truck's tall tires kept the road grit from its polished silver exterior. Definitely someone well-off and not from around here.

Her shoulders rose and tensed. Life these days held a constant drumbeat of worry. And the grim bass percussion underneath it all: Money. Money. Money. Were these the Carne Incorporado reps Tanner mentioned? If so, she had to intercept them. Stop whatever deal he planned.

Claire stood up in the flower garden. When the truck crunched to a halt, she dusted her knees and headed to meet the stranger. Jonathan, stretched out on the porch swing reading, marked his page with his finger and glanced over.

To her dismay, Tanner ambled up, dark hat tipped low, square jaw emerging from the brim's shadow. Her heart took a tumble as it had done, irritatingly often, since they'd spoken yesterday.

Lately she couldn't stop looking at him. He was so handsome. So Tanner. She knew the arc of his lower lip, the strength in his shoulders. The way he meticulously tucked his shirt into his jeans, the way his boots were worn down at the heel, the way he touched that scar on his jaw without realizing he was doing it.

She shouldn't have sought him out alone in the pasture. Cracked open the container where she'd locked memories of him away. Now they leaked into her thoughts. A constant drip.

Two men emerged from the truck, slammed the doors and strode to Tanner with extended hands and confident grins. Her jittering nerves turned to flat-out irritation at Tanner's wide-planted cowboy boots and straight-backed stance. He exuded authority. Command. As if he owned the place. Already ran it. Her jaw tightened. Like heck he did.

Her sandals churned up pebbles and when she joined the two men, Tanner raised his voice. "Bill Sanchez and Rick Ortis, this is Claire Shelton, Martin's daughter. Claire, these are the reps I mentioned from Carne Incorporado."

The middle-aged men, dressed in well-cut suits that looked oppressive given the balmy temperature, tipped their hats. Pressure built inside Claire. How to handle this?

The one with a thick moustache and large

round glasses, Bill, grasped her hand. "Pleasure to meet you, ma'am. Nice country you got up here."

She put on a smile that didn't feel like one. "Thank you. Would you like some sweet tea? You must have had a long trip coming from—" Her voice trailed off. Her mind twisted until the place came to her. "Mexico City."

"It was worth the drive," the second man, Rick, replied. "We've been anxious to get up here since Tanner phoned."

Rick shook her hand, his moist palm pressed briefly to hers. She itched to wipe it on her cut-off jean shorts but checked herself. Tried to exude professionalism despite her Daisy Duke outfit. Her eyes traveled down her soil-dusted black tank top and bare legs. Why hadn't Tanner mentioned their arrival time?

"Tea would be nice. How about after we've toured the barns?" Bill pulled off his hat and waved it in front of his full, flushed face. "Something to look forward to while we talk business."

"Business. Yes. About that." Her chin jerked up. "I'm afraid our plans have changed and we're not interested in expanding our buyers list at the moment. My apologies that this wasn't communicated before your trip."

Bill scratched his balding head. Looked puzzled. "We've been hearing about your top stud, Revelation. Would be a pleasure to take a look at him while we're here."

"He's the biggest!" piped up Jonathan. He'd crept up behind them and ducked behind Claire's back.

Rick smiled down at her boy. "That's what we've heard. If he looks half as good as he does on paper, we're hoping to put in an offer on him."

Jonathan pulled at Claire's shirt. "We're not selling Revelation, are we?" he whispered.

Her fingers ruffled his soft reddish-brown curls. "No, sweetie." All of the livestock would transfer to Mr. Ruddell when they sold him the ranch.

Tanner shot her an unreadable look, then stepped forward. "We'll be happy to show Revelation to you. Follow me." Without a backward glance, he unlatched a gate and ushered the men inside the grassy pasture that butted against red, pitched-roof barns.

Claire heard an angry buzzing, as if a wasp had gotten trapped between her ears. How dare he.

A tug at her arm stopped her from scrambling after the group. "Can I go?"

"You know the rule about the barns, Jonathan."

"Yeah. You said I can't go without a grown-up. So if I'm with you, I can come." He peered up at her. "Right?"

Claire glanced between the disappearing men and her mutinous son. He had a point… and how rarely he asked for anything lately… still. She needed to focus on stopping Tanner's business deal and couldn't do that while keeping a close eye on Jonathan. She didn't like him to be around large animals, even when they were restrained.

"Another time, honey. How about we make cookies when I get back?"

His eyes narrowed and he crossed his arms over his chest. "Is this a bribe?"

"Yep."

A grin replaced his pout. "It's a deal…if we make the kind we don't bake. You know. With the peanut butter?"

She tickled his side. "You got it."

"I'll get the ingredients!" he yelled and a wistful smile crossed her face as she watched him bolt to the house. What she wouldn't do to protect him…

"Love you," she called after Jonathan when he bounded up the porch steps, Roxy hot on his heels.

"I know!" he called over his shoulder and disappeared into the house.

"Don't let Roxy lick the peanut butter jar!"

Her father stood in the doorway, his firm gaze fixed on her. She didn't have to hear him to know his thoughts. He wanted her cooperation. Her back starched. Well. That wasn't an option. Nevertheless, her heart softened at his determined expression. He wanted the best for her, even if he was misguided. She blew him a small kiss before turning and striding after the group.

Time to shut Tanner down.

SUN SPILLED THROUGH the open windows, lighting the cavernous space housing their sire population. Stalls, sixty Tanner had counted, stretched from onc, double-sized door to the other, and the sweet aroma of fresh hay mingled with the pungent dung and pelt smell of large animals. Charlie O'Dell, a hired hand headed to veterinary school in the fall, gave a short wave before he continued preparing the show cattle's feed mix. Overhead, embedded circular fans whirred near the high ceiling.

Several gray Brahmans raised their heads as Tanner ushered in the Carne reps. Others continued feeding or drinking from the troughs in front of their stalls as they waited their turn to rotate into pasture, their drooping ears and large eyes giving them a docile appearance that matched their obedient nature. A good selling point for the seed stock.

"Denton Creek is a CSS Certified facility." Tanner gestured to a framed document on a far wall above a hand-built desk holding an old-school rotary phone and a yellowed records book. He strolled down the walkway between the stalls, taking his time, giving these all-important buyers a good look at what he assessed to be prime studs. Revelation wasn't the only bull he wanted Carne to purchase.

His head shot around when the barn door opened and Claire appeared, her face as stiff as cardboard. He waited for her to join them before resuming his talk.

"Denton Creek's purebred Brahman herd consists of two hundred breeding-age females and sixty bulls with a large emphasis on embryo transfer. It's primarily a closed herd, with focus on linebreeding exceptional cow families since 1944."

"1944?" Rick stopped to examine Lucky Luke, one of their top sires, according to records. The majestic bull raised its head and stared them down, pendulous throatlatch and dewlap swinging. Rick ran his hand along the animal's large hump, over the top of its shoulder and neck.

"We're one of the oldest continually operating Brahman herds in existence in the United States," Claire inserted. At her proud tone, longing seized Tanner. Here was the fierce woman he'd once loved… Fearless. Strong-willed. Undaunted. Infuriatingly resistant when it came to him…

He gave himself a tiny shake. He'd come to help Martin, not make amends with Claire, no matter how much she felt like an electric presence beside him, her arm brushing his. If anything, she'd grown more cautious than when they'd parted. Not exactly relationship material for a professional bull rider.

Your career can't last forever.

The doctor's warning returned to him, but Tanner shoved it aside. He'd figure out next steps, like the rodeo school, later. For now, he had to clinch his first deal for Martin. Prove to his old mentor he'd been right to entrust this job to Tanner.

"Lots of muscular tissue covering the processes," murmured Rick before he backed away from the side-stepping bull.

Tanner nodded. "Denton Creek cattle are known for their conformation, muscle, fertility, breed character, carcass traits, efficiency and that signature eye-appealing style."

They continued down the causeway, Rick and Tanner in front, and Bill and Claire following.

"We only sell to southern and southwestern states," she put in. "An international partnership would be out of our experience."

Tanner turned to stare at her and her gaze turned flinty. Why was she so bent on crushing this opportunity? Martin would be miserable rotting in some old folks home and happier fighting to save his business. Claire might want to seal herself off from the world, but she shouldn't force that fate on her father...the way she'd tried to nail Tanner down once.

"Due to the owner's health issues, Denton Creek's cattle haven't been present at trade shows in recent years, but we plan to attend the State Championships in three weeks."

"What?" Claire gasped behind him.

Tanner stopped. Turned. "Emailed our registration last night."

Denton Creek had potential for lucrative sales once he brought operations up to date. Once it'd been a national-champion-producing bull ranch and he'd help restore its reputation. Martin might not have the vigor to go to trade shows and auctions the way he used to, but for the next month, at least, Tanner would do his best to attend them and help other buyers rediscover Denton bulls. After that, hopefully Claire would step up and get the ranch back on track instead of trying to get rid of it.

"We'll be there," Bill said, rubbing his hands together, his gaze locking on a massive bull penned alone at the end of the barn. "Sure would like to get a deal done before then, though."

"Happy to consider your offer, Bill." Tanner nodded toward the lone bull. "That's Revelation if you two would like a closer look."

Claire rounded on him as the murmuring reps moved ahead.

"We don't have money for competitions. Are you trying to make us go under sooner?"

He studied her. "Hardly. We're looking for new buyers and we can't get their attention without trade show presence and wins."

When she stepped close he found it impossible to break eye contact. "Why are you making commitments? We both know you're going back to rodeo."

"I'm here to help your father," he said quietly, voice pitched so the murmuring reps over at Revelation's pen wouldn't hear. This close he could trace the curve of her cheek. He stuffed his hands in his pockets when the right one rose, seemingly of its own volition.

"Look. I get it. My dad was good to you. But you owe me, too. And I. Don't. Want. This." She punctuated each of her last words with a finger jab to his chest.

Unable to resist, he caught her raised hand

in his. The feel of her soft skin made his pulse speed. He resisted the urge to press his lips against her palm, to see if she still tasted as sweet as he remembered. "Claire, I'm speaking for your father. Doing what he wants."

Her eyes glistened and something softened inside him. "You made him believe in something that won't come true. He's desperate."

"He loves you." He cupped her cheek and for a heart-stopping moment she didn't move away. "And he doesn't need the stress of seeing us argue."

Her eyebrows lowered and she considered him for a long moment. At last her rigid shoulders relaxed. "No. No, he doesn't."

"So—truce?"

"In front of him? I suppose." She shooed away a fly buzzing round her face and turned back to the approaching business reps.

He didn't bother holding back the grin that surged out of him. One small step toward civility with Claire.

He'd take it.

Though any more steps might bring them too close. Better keep his guard up around this spirited woman. Her fighting nature sparked his need to dominate. Made him want to vanquish when he needed to steer clear or risk getting penned down to a life with too many question marks.

"That's one heck of a bull," Rick said as he and his partner joined them.

Tanner ushered the small group through the front of the barn and back toward the house.

"He should be a contender for the Houston Livestock Show. I imagine you're taking him to Throckmorton next." Bill cupped the front of his hat, curling the brim.

Tanner lengthened his stride, hoping the fast pace would slow down Claire's interference. "We're thinking of auctioning him there if we don't get investors beforehand."

Rick matched him pace for pace. "We'd be interested in talking more about syndication on Revelation if you have time." Tanner tracked the man's gaze as it slid to a frowning Claire. He hustled them up the main house's stairs and there, just as he'd hoped, sat Claire's father reading the morning paper. She'd agreed not to argue in front of Martin. Time to put that to the test.

After making introductions, the men sat down to sweet tea offered up by Marie. Martin beamed under the compliments the men showered on his herd. Claire drummed her fingernails against the side of her bubbled glass, but otherwise kept quiet.

When the conversation began to head into hard numbers, Martin steadied himself and rose. "Won't you gentleman join Tanner and me in my office?"

Claire bolted to her feet. "I'd like to come, too."

"What about the cookies?" All eyes swerved to the young boy who looked far too pale for country living. The kid had to get out more, Tanner thought, and he'd make it a point to find a way.

"I—I—" Claire's head swiveled between her son and the group. At last she hugged Jonathan. "Of course. A promise is a promise. Enjoy your conversation, gentlemen," she said, her tone lighthearted, her eyes anything but.

Unfettered, Tanner steered the group into Martin's office and they sat around a large oak desk, discussing numbers that weren't living up to the praise the men had heaped on Revelation.

Martin's gaze darted between Tanner and the Carne Incorporado reps. Tanner could tell the desperate rancher didn't like the lowball bid, but felt pressure to accept. Time to gamble.

He stood and offered a hand to each of the men. "Rick, Bill, it's been a pleasure. We'll keep your offer in mind as we take Revelation to shows and possible auction."

Rick took the toothpick out of his mouth, suddenly looking less sure than he had a moment ago. "This deal's only good if we can secure a majority share before Revelation shows. After that, we can't guarantee this price."

"So noted." Tanner forced a confident grin and nodded briskly to Martin who followed his cue and shook the men's hands as they exited.

"We were hoping to conclude our business today," Bill protested, donning his hat as they stepped past a wide-eyed Claire back out into the bright noon sun.

Tanner nodded to a card in Rick's hand. "You have the number we expect for a majority share pre-show. If you want to make a serious offer, give us a call. In the meantime, we'll look for you in Houston."

"But—" Rick's sharp-eyed glare snuffed out Bill's protest.

"See you in Houston." Rick tipped his hat. "It'll be a pleasure negotiating with you further once you've been out in the market again."

"Same," Martin said firmly, his mouth a thin line, his features not unpleasant, but harder. Certain. Less the recovering victim. More the head of an esteemed ranch. The man he was born to be. Tanner grinned to see his old mentor get back his vigor.

They watched the truck roll away. At a low chuckle Tanner turned, surprised.

"You got those suits on the ropes," rumbled Martin, one side of his mouth hitching. "They didn't expect you'd shoot down their offer."

Tanner adjusted his hat in the sweltering heat. "Nothing like a little pressure to up the ante."

Martin met his eye. "You're willing to take a chance on Revelation getting a better offer at the Houston Livestock show?"

"Yes, sir. We'll get higher numbers once the public sees Revelation."

"I appreciate your help." Martin thumped Tanner on the shoulder and turned. "I surely do."

Tanner studied Claire as she stood in the doorway, her expression swerving from wonder at her straight-backed father to mutiny when her eyes lit on Tanner. He imagined her questions and veered instead for his own quarters. Martin would sort her out.

Better to focus on what'd brought him here. Not a woman he'd gambled on once and lost.

Odds with her would never be in his favor.

CHAPTER FIVE

TANNER SWAYED SLIGHTLY atop Guardian, a chestnut-colored quarter horse, and guided the stallion down another pasture's rutted trail. An afternoon blow looked likely given the dishwater-gray morning. Lucky break. It'd perk up the yellowing grass and end the heat. It'd been drier than the heart of a haystack all week.

He'd barely seen Claire, what with showing cattle to prospective buyers. Nearly one every day. Best of all, he'd made four sales: two heifers, a prime breeding cow and Revelation's frozen semen. It'd felt downright good handing those checks to Claire, seeing her flush, making her lose her speech. Wasn't often he flustered the assured woman. When he did, he enjoyed every last minute of it. No more objections about the Houston Livestock trip fee.

Martin even planned to join him. He stepped livelier these days. Had taken to accompanying Tanner and the customers in the show barn. Stayed up late, reeling off long lineage histories from memory that made Tanner's jaw drop.

With a light tug, he pulled up Guardian and surveyed the herd Martin called his breeding hobby. Longhorn and Brahman mixes, Tanner assessed. Bucking bulls Martin had planned on selling to rodeos before his health problems. Their muscular flanks twitched, tails slapping at buzzing flies as they grazed. Others drank out of a full trough. No issues with the automated water supply here, though he'd fixed a broken pump on another pasture an hour ago.

He studied the large animals with a professional eye and breathed in the deep, dark smell of dung and sweet grass. They looked good. Better than good. They looked like champions. Powerfully built and aggressive, based on the bellows and snorts aimed his way. Guardian scraped the ground and blew, not backing up from the electric wire and steel fence, even when a bull charged it.

Feisty stallion. Tanner grinned and patted the spirited animal's neck. He liked grit. Especially in livestock. Even more in women. Particularly Claire…

Seeing her every day fired him up. The loving way she cared for her recovering father and fragile son revealed a type of strength he'd never glimpsed in her before. Yet she'd go from sweet to sass in five seconds flat when it came to him, and he couldn't say which side of her he liked best. She tempted him to try again. Win back what he'd once lost…and he hated losing.

His competitive nature must be causing his nonstop thoughts about her lately. She hadn't loved him in years, if she ever did. As for him, he'd moved on, too. Or his career had, though it didn't keep him warm at night, he admitted. The road was lonely. Not the thrill he'd anticipated. No one waiting for him when he hung up his hat. Pulled off his boots.

Now that he'd jumped off rodeo's carousel, he'd started questioning his life. Was there anything better than to feel wanted? Was that all anyone needed? His mother had been out of his life more than in it, either getting high with friends or passed out on the couch. Who, other than Claire and Martin, had ever wanted him for anything more than a photo op and a sold-out arena?

Not a one.

And he didn't see that changing unless he changed.

One of the bulls charged another and the two tussled, their thousand-pound bodies hurtling and whirling. Tanner envisioned the kind of fast spinning, high kicking and belly rolling he'd need for his rodeo school's bulls.

With money that friends had agreed to loan him, he'd buy a few and would rent space on the ranch. In fact, given that this pasture abutted the front of the property, it'd be the perfect spot to build holding pens and a rodeo coral. Just through word of mouth, he'd already gotten emails from fifteen potential bull-riding students.

What's more, Denton Ranch could sell or auction some of the best bucking bulls. That would help Martin fulfill his side interest in becoming a rodeo stock contractor. It was a profitable business and a world Tanner could navigate easily for his friend. He'd mention it tonight at dinner.

But would he be here long enough to see it through?

He nudged Guardian and started farther down the trail, rounding a bend to get a better view of the herd. The stallion's hooves clicked on the pebbled dirt path and kicked up dust clouds. His view of his future looked just as murky. Staying on the ranch for long hadn't appealed until he got here. Did that have to do with working the bulls, Claire or both?

He pulled off his hat and a small breeze lifted the damp hair on his brow. Both interested him more than he'd expected. He'd planned on establishing the rodeo school, hiring an agent to sell it, investing the funds in a new retirement plan and rejoining the rodeo circuit once his shoulder healed.

Could he succeed at something besides rodeo, after all? And if so, would a future with Claire be possible?

He shook off the thought and clucked, setting his horse off at a fast trot. No sense imagining it. Better not to try and look a fool than attempt it and remove all doubt, Martin once told him.

As he approached the horse barn, a small face ducked behind a tree. Had to be Jonathan. Funny. He'd never seen the boy venture far from the house on his own. Especially with his mother gone.

She'd left just before Tanner started his pasture rounds. Mentioned something about a grocery shopping run to a supercenter fifty miles away. He didn't expect her back already, so what was her son doing out here? Alone?

Tanner gave Guardian his head and the horse made for the front of the barn. After a quick dismount, he glanced around and caught a flash of red hair disappearing behind a nearby oak tree.

"Jonathan?" Tanner called.

A chickadee sounded from a branch. Otherwise, silence.

Must be afraid to show himself. Every time he'd spoken to Tanner these past few days, Claire had shushed Jonathan, her disapproval plain. Yet here Jonathan was, in what could be his first open rebellion, following Tanner. Well, good. The kid needed to get out from under his mother's thumb. If spying on Tanner did the trick, then so be it. He'd just go about his business and let the boy come to him.

After loosening the cinch, he walked Guardian in a slow circle then led him inside the cool barn. A gray mare nickered and an Appaloosa bobbed its head as they passed. Tanner heard shoes shuffling through hay behind him but didn't turn. Instead, he unbridled the stallion and slipped on a halter, tying it to one of the hooks. Guardian sidestepped and strained for his stall, but Tanner stroked the animal's arched neck and whispered, "Whoa, boy. Easy."

When the horse settled, Tanner undid the cinch completely, walked around to the offside, placed it atop the saddle then lifted both up and onto a shelf. He pulled off the blanket, folded it and set it beside the rest of the gear. It didn't need washing though he couldn't say the same for Guardian. Sweat and dirt streaks marked his sleek back.

"Would you fill that bucket with water, Jon?" Tanner called. Casual. Like he'd expected Jonathan. No big deal. Then Tanner waited.

"Could use the help," he continued after a spit of silence, pulling out a sponge and some soap.

"I want to help," piped up a young voice and Tanner turned as slowly as he would around a spooked horse. Jonathan popped out of one of the empty stalls and grabbed the door's upper opening. He lifted his feet off the sawdust-covered floor, dangling.

When the boy's green eyes swung Tanner's way, his resemblance to Claire hit Tanner again. Which of Jonathan's features took after his father? A light-haired man with brown eyes posed with Claire in the wedding photo on Martin's mantel. Tanner hadn't lingered over it, avoided it, actually…but now he studied the boy. Wanted a glimpse of the man who'd shoved Tanner out of Claire's heart.

"This horse won't wash itself, son."

Jonathan's giggle mingled with high-pitched barking from Roxy, who bustled in, bristling and full of dog bluster. "Maybe he can. Like when we're not around. A secret."

A smile sneaked across Tanner's mouth. "Could be, but for now, let's lather Guardian up."

The boy let go of the door and leaned against the frame, one foot scratching the back of his opposite calf. "How come you want me to help? I'm small."

"I could use a hand and you look like the man for the job."

Jonathan raised his chin and puffed his chest. "You need me?"

"Wouldn't ask if I didn't," Tanner drawled, gathering a brush and cloth. Not pressuring. Kids and untamed animals had a lot in common. Push too hard, they won't come willing. Don't try at all and they'll retreat further still. He had to find the right balance. Tanner kept his eyes off Jonathan but listened closely until he heard footsteps approach.

Jonathan grabbed the bucket Tanner held out, then bustled to the faucet and turned the knob. A gush of water spewed and Roxy snapped at the flying droplets.

"Where would Guardian hold the sponge?" Jonathan chased a yapping Roxy as the bucket filled, easily distracted. Always in motion. Reminded Tanner of himself at that age. "In his mouth?"

"I reckon."

Tanner watched Jonathan heft the overflowing bucket and struggle forward, his tongue between his teeth, water spilling with every step. Still, he didn't ask for help and Tanner didn't offer any. Better the boy feel useful. Needed. Depended on instead of dependent. Pride for the child filled Tanner as Jonathan neared. The kid had spunk.

"How would he wash his back?" With a

sploosh, Jonathan dropped the bucket near Tanner's boots, sending much of what was left of its contents over the side.

"His tail could be another washer. The sponge gets the front, the tail swipes the back."

Jonathan punched the air and whooped, making the horse skitter. "That's it!"

"No quick movements around horses, son," Tanner said gently, his hand on the halter while the other eased Jonathan farther away. Guardian looked over his shoulder again, his brown eyes large, ears pricked forward, but otherwise calm again.

Jonathan hung his head. Stilled. "Maybe I'd better go home."

"And leave me with all this work? That wouldn't be neighborly of you." Tanner kept his tone light while he squirted some horse shampoo into the bucket and swirled the sponge in the sudsy liquid before handing it over.

"You ride bulls in a rodeo." Jonathan swiped the soapy water across Guardian's flanks then strained on tiptoe to reach the horse's neck and back.

Tanner nodded, his eye on Guardian. Checking. The horse looked unruffled. So far, so good.

"Have you won any medals?"

"Some." Tanner thought about his gold buckles and the championship cup from last year's

PBR Las Vegas World Finals. It'd been his third. Would it be his last? He tried out the thought the way he'd feel for a missing tooth. No pain. How much did that glory and fame amount to anyway? Looking at Jonathan, Tanner glimpsed a real accomplishment. Something he'd never achieve living on the road. Fatherhood. The thought slid through him. Cut him in a few spots.

"Cool! Can I see them? Are you a star?"

Jonathan dimpled, his smile so like his mother's that Tanner's breath caught. "They're at my apartment and I'm just a bull rider. No star."

"But you're famous."

They trooped to Guardian's other side while Roxy wove in and out of their legs. When a barn cat strutted by, Roxy lit out after it.

"Did your grandfather tell you that?"

Jonathan's hand stilled and their eyes met. "Grandpa records bull riding and we watch it when Momma goes out. She doesn't like rodeo."

Tanner took the sponge from Jonathan and finished cleaning off Guardian's face and poll. "Nope. She sure doesn't."

Jonathan turned away. Scratched his nose. "Is that why she doesn't like you?"

"She doesn't like me?" Tanner grabbed a comb and started removing the tangles from

Guardian's mane and tail, his brain turning over the boy's observations. Stalling.

"She never smiles at you. Doesn't say 'hey.'" Jonathan raised a slanted eyebrow. In that moment, he reminded Tanner of someone... Maybe one of Claire's relatives.

He checked Guardian's hooves then led him to his stall. "Me and your momma. It's complicated. A grown-up thing."

Roxy barreled into Jonathan and nearly knocked the boy off his feet. He grabbed the squirming dog. "Ugh. I hate that excuse. Momma uses it all the time. It just means grown-ups don't feel like explaining."

"Maybe so." Tanner held in a grin. After freshening Guardian's water and feed, Tanner latched the stall door. He gestured for Jonathan to follow him and squinted as they stepped into the returning sunshine, pulling his hat brim low.

When Jonathan jogged to keep up with Tanner, he shortened his strides. "Thanks for lending a hand. Sure made things easier."

The boy tugged at Tanner's arm and lowered his voice. "Can I tell you a secret?"

"Sure. Shoot."

They stopped under an oak tree and Roxy spun, chasing her tail. Jonathan ducked his head and peeped up at Tanner. "The boys at school picked on me and I never fought back. Not once. I'm not brave like Daddy."

Tanner batted away the sympathy that leaped inside. Wouldn't show the boy pity. Only respect. He squatted to Jonathan's height. Leaned in. "Well, I don't agree."

Jonathan's face worked. "You don't?"

"You washed up a horse twice as tall as you. That took guts." Tanner squeezed Jonathan's arm.

"My dad was brave but he still died." A shudder rippled through the boy's body. "Didn't do him any good."

Tanner held his expression in check, wishing he could help Jonathan connect with his father a little and replace his grief with pride.

"Now, listen close." He waited for Jonathan's quick nod then continued. "Bravery is the best quality anyone can have. You have it and your Daddy had it. It's what made him a hero."

"I'd rather be a star like you."

Tanner shook his head, feeling truth's bite. What did eight seconds of glory on the back of a bull amount to when compared to a soldier's sacrifice? "Much much better to be a hero."

A small hand slipped into his. "I like you, Tanner. You don't care if I'm puny."

Tanner smiled down at the boy, a strange sensation tugging at his heart. "I like you, too. And size doesn't have nothing to do with anything. They called me Tiny Tanner all through school because I never got big. Then one year I shot up six inches. Grew another four the one after that. Nobody calls me Tiny anymore."

Jonathan's eyes shone. "You think that'll happen to me?"

Tanner recalled Kevin's medium build in the wedding photo, but Martin was a big man. Jonathan could take after his grandfather. "Could be. But what matters most is skills, and you've got lots of 'em. Heard you build model cars and airplanes."

Jonathan nodded, his dimples growing. "Boats, too."

"How about helping me fix up your Daddy's pickup? I'm working on it tomorrow after supper. Could use your help."

Jonathan pulled Tanner to his feet then let go and jumped ahead. "Momma will say no," he called over his shoulder, then he grabbed a stick and threw it for a galloping Roxy.

"I'll talk to her."

"She's right over there."

Tanner peered across the back lawn at Claire. She stood on the porch, beautiful in a green sundress that revealed the flare of her hips and shapely legs. With her red hair blowing around her flushed face, she resembled a match in a storm. She burned right through him.

Her frozen expression, however, doused the flame.

Jonathan ran ahead and she staggered at the hug he threw on her. Roxy pulled at her sandals' leather tassels. As she gazed down at them, her lips curved.

"Tanner's going to fix up Daddy's pickup and he said I can help. Can I?"

Tanner closed the distance and stopped at the foot of the stairs. Her smile vanished and she seemed shaken.

"I'll think about it," she said at last. "Now go on inside and wash up for lunch before it's a 'no' for sure."

When the porch door squeaked closed, Claire whirled, her eyebrows crowding one another.

"What were you two doing together?" she snapped.

Tanner studied her. Stood his ground. "He followed me when I came back from checking on the pastures. We washed up Guardian together."

"Without asking me?"

"You weren't around."

With a yank, she pulled her sandal out of the terrier's mouth and threw a ball. Roxy raced after it with a joyful bark. "That doesn't matter. I'm his mother."

"Mother or jailer?"

Her head jerked back as if a bee had buzzed her ear. "Excuse me?"

"You're coddling him. He needs to grow up a man, not a momma's boy."

"I don't want him becoming a man like you."

Pain speared his gut and he ducked his head, leaving his face in his hat's shadow. He wouldn't let her see how much that'd hurt. "Noted. But no harm will come to him with me."

"Oh, yes it could," she murmured, her voice low and breaking. When she whirled, he glimpsed the fear contorting her features. "More than you know."

He stared at the closed porch door for a long moment.

What had her so afraid?

He needed a cigarette, bad, but popped in a cinnamon stick instead and turned at the sound of an approaching truck. Another client. He'd have to puzzle this out later.

Claire had lots of reasons to be angry at him, but none when it came to Jonathan...none that made any real sense if you took away old prejudices. Tanner lived by his instincts and something told him there was more to this story than she was telling.

He tucked in his loose shirt and strode to the driveway.

Whatever it was, he'd get to the bottom of it. You could hang your hat on it.

CHAPTER SIX

CLAIRE SWIRLED A tea bag and watched the curls of black spread through the water like ink. The moonlight turned the kitchen's tiled walls blue, the china in the hutch white, the hanging copper pots a dull, gun-metal gray. It matched her mood.

It'd been one in the morning when she'd given up on sleep, responded to an email from Dani and headed downstairs for a drink. As if that'd help. Every time she closed her eyes she saw Tanner and Jonathan, walking back from the stables, their gaits identical, faces sporting matching crooked smiles. It'd about stopped her heart. Still did each time she pictured it.

If her father saw them that way, he'd surely guess her secret. The possibility of it coming out seemed less like an "if" now and more like a "when." Somehow she needed to keep them apart without raising too much suspicion.

She pulled out the teabag, added cream and sugar, and sipped the scalding liquid. Jonathan wanted a male role model, and with his grandfather limited health-wise, Tanner seemed like her son's top choice. How to say no to them working together, especially when Jonathan begged to fix up his dad's truck? Instead of building models, he'd eagerly told her, he'd get to do the real thing. It did her heart good to see Jonathan bursting with enthusiasm about something again, and she had Tanner to thank for it, strange as it sounded.

In the front parlor, the grandfather clock, as old as the house, chimed on the half hour. It looked like a long night. And tomorrow wouldn't get any better. She slumped over her tea and cupped the warm mug. Crazy that Tanner planned to repair her truck.

She felt the warmth seep up her arm and into her heart at the nice gesture. He said people changed and maybe he had. Tanner cared about Jonathan, and seeing them together filled her with guilt about keeping her secret.

And she'd come at him like a she-cat this morning.

What a dust-up. She shouldn't have been so mean. Who knew she was capable of speaking with such hardness? Each word sounded like a falling block of concrete when she replayed them in her mind.

The pained expression he'd covered after she'd lashed out didn't bring her any satisfaction. In fact, it'd done the opposite. Made her feel like the family guard dog, snapping and biting at strangers. It stung.

Beware of Claire, she thought grimly, and walked to the window. Outside, the moon resembled a silver coin, illuminating the back lawn. In the distance, a light burned in a window. Tanner's unit. What was he doing up at this hour and should she take it as an omen? A sign that she should give him an apology? To be fair, she owed him one for hitting below the belt.

Her sleepshirt snagged on an open drawer knob as she turned. When she yanked it loose, she peered down then froze. Inside rose a mound of unopened envelopes, the top of the heap emblazoned with a debt collector's logo.

What? She'd never seen these bills before. Money owed on top of the mortgage debt she'd already known about, lost sleep over.

Her heart plummeted and she sank with it, papers in hand, into her chair. As she thumbed through the stack, the postal dates went as far back as three months ago. Before her father's stroke. He'd started acting weird then, his face closed off and tight, his answers never quite matching her questions.

Why hide these additional debts? Worse, ignore them?

She opened the first and her eyes burned at the threatening words.

This is your last and final notice of your outstanding debt. Unless payment is made in thirty days a lien will be placed on your ranch until such time as our fee has been collected...

The date revealed it was more than two months old. They'd already missed the deadline. How many more?

Her hands shook as she opened one after another and read each menacing word, shrinking under the weight of them, the burden of her family's debt far greater than she'd known.

Tanner needed to know about these bills. They proved that any attempts to salvage the ranch were beyond pointless. Once he understood that, he'd leave, eliminating one of her problems, at least. Alone again, she'd focus on ways to pay off the extra debt, though right now she hadn't a clue.

Something large and heavy settled in the pit of her stomach and her head dropped to the cool table. She had to see Tanner.

Before doubt stopped her, she dashed outside and raced on the wet grass toward his unit. It'd rained some this afternoon, but now the sky cleared and the moon tossed its beams at her feet. At the door of the double-wide she paused, uncertainty staying her hand.

Do it, she dared herself, just as she had as a kid when trick-or-treating. What would this visit bring? Hopefully no more tricks. If they could be honest with each other, maybe he'd finally see reason, understand how desperate things were and go. Though given his stubborn personality, it was a long shot.

"Claire?"

A light blazed on and she blinked under its glare. A broad-shouldered man wearing low-slung shorts over narrow hips stood on the threshold. When her sight adjusted, her cheeks blazed. She stood at eye level with his magnificent chest. Strong, smooth pectorals rose above tight six-pack abs and a lean waist.

She stared at his hard stomach.

What had she come to say?

"I'm thinking you didn't stop by to star gaze?" One side of his mouth rose in a crooked smile, his blue eyes sparkling.

She felt herself start to grin. Caught it. This wasn't a social call. Especially with him wearing next to nothing and her in a sleep T-shirt that barely reached mid-thigh. Good gravy.

"No, I—uh—"

"Come on in." With a sweep of his arm, he gestured her inside the tidy, compact space. "Have a seat."

She didn't sit down. Instead she turned and

examined the utilitarian furnishings, the single dish and cup in the drainer, the TV tuned to a sports news channel. It practically screamed *lifelong bachelor*, and for a moment she dropped her own worries and felt sorry for him. She might have lost Kevin, but at least she had their years of marriage and Jonathan.

"Can I get you something?" came his muffled voice through the white T-shirt he dragged over his head.

She breathed easier when he'd covered up. Could focus. She'd come here to tell him about the letters and apologize for being so mean, she remembered.

"I'm sorry," she blurted and looked him square in the eye. Big mistake. His wary expression suddenly turned warm and it melted her to her toes. "I was a little too harsh today."

One eyebrow rose, dark and slanted.

"Okay. A lot harsh. I don't think you mean Jonathan any harm." The words stumbled over each other in their rush to get out.

He exhaled and dropped his crossed arms. "Glad to hear that. I'd like to help him connect with his father a little." He stopped and his piercing eyes narrowed on her. "Kevin is his father, right? There's no chance that I—"

"No," Claire cut him off swiftly, her heart squirming and thumping in her chest. "Not a chance." *Not in the way that counts*, she added mentally.

Tanner's level gaze made it hard to hold still and not drop her eyes. "You've always been honest with me."

She said nothing. Couldn't if she wanted to, her throat felt that tight.

After a long moment he turned, his expression shuttered. "Okay then, how about some sweet tea?" He strode into the tiny kitchen just off the living area and pulled open the fridge. It was so close she could feel the blast of cold.

"Sure." She wandered over to his computer desk, relieved, and glanced at the screen. Then looked again.

"Is that Denton Creek?"

He turned from the cabinet, two glasses in hand. "Yep. I'm designing a website."

"Do you know how to do that?"

"I will."

She followed his finger point to a book titled *Web Design for Dummies* and a surprised laugh escaped her. He took do-it-yourself to another level. Always had. "You're teaching yourself to be a web designer."

Ice cubes clinked against the pitcher's spout as he poured. "We don't have the money to hire a professional and the internet's a good way to reach a broader market."

"How long have you been at this?"

After he cut a couple of lemon slices and dropped them into each glass, he sauntered from behind the open counter. "A week, but I've finally got a banner up. Or is that a header?"

When she laughed again, his rich baritone twined with hers, a harmony she hadn't heard in years, and it felt good. Steadied her jittering nerves.

"So you're confident you'll figure this out?"

He handed her a glass and raised it in a toast. "Or die trying," he drawled, then drank.

She shook her head, impressed and touched, despite everything. What was the point of a website when they'd be selling in a few weeks anyway? Or worse, with all these liens, the bank could foreclose sooner than expected. Tanner was a fighter. Not one to quit. Stubborn as all get-out. It's what made him a world champion bull rider and the kind of man who'd give her father his all, no matter the odds. She'd loved that about him once.

But now he needed an extra dose of reality. Some harsh truths that would send him packing.

"What's that?" He nodded at the envelopes she clutched and for some inexplicable, infuriating reason tears rose to her eyes.

In a flash, he set his glass down on the desk

and guided her to the couch, his hand firm on her waist.

"What's going on, Claire?"

When they sat, the sagging cushions pulled them close and his shoulder brushed hers. She handed him the letters, silent. She couldn't loosen her vocal cords to say a word.

As he read through the pile, his broad hand stayed warm and steady on her trembling back. His eyebrows lowered and his jaw clenched. After he finished, he glanced up and their eyes locked.

"You didn't know about these?"

"No. My dad must have been hiding them. I think maybe he's—he's—" She couldn't finish the thought. Her father had always been her rock. To think he might be losing his mind, as well as his physical abilities, frightened the breath right out of her.

"He's not letting go," said Tanner quietly. When she glanced at his handsome profile, his expression looked distant, eyes faraway. "It's hard for a man to give up his dream."

Tanner's eyes swerved to hers and suddenly she wasn't sure they still spoke about her father. Her pulse sped at the clean, soapy, male scent of him. The damp, curling ends of his hair suggested a recent shower. For a moment she envisioned it, then blushed.

"He has to understand this is over, Tanner. Don't you see that now, more than ever? Please stop making him think he can save the ranch."

Tanner stacked the envelopes, rose and set them next to the computer before returning. "This doesn't change anything."

She blinked up at him. Disbelieving. Was he losing his mind, too? This took over-confidence to another stratosphere.

"Don't you get it?" She shoved herself sideways when he sat, trying to put some space between them. "These debts will wipe out any sales profit, meaning he won't be able to afford the assisted living facility."

A shiver ran through her and she squeezed her eyes shut. She wouldn't cry. Pillows were for tears, her father always said.

Warm arms wrapped around her and pulled her close. Tanner whispered into her ear. "I'll fix this."

"How?" She pushed against his chest but he tightened his grip. Held on until her body relaxed against him. How could she resist what felt right?

"I'm going to sell some of those bucking bulls for a decent sum. Already got a rep from a PBR stock contractor coming out in a couple of days and I contacted a few rodeos. We'll use the money to get rid of as many of these bills as we can and, when we win Grand Champion at the Houston Livestock Show, we'll erase the rest."

She leaned back. Pushed her hair out of her face. Stared. "We can't go to the show now. Any extra money has to pay these off, not take a gamble like that." Was he insane?

"This is when we double down. Not fold. The stakes couldn't be higher."

"Why won't you see it my way?"

"Because I don't think like you. I have faith."

"And I'm a realist."

"There you go."

A moment of strange, loaded silence descended.

"Will you let Jonathan fix up the truck with me?"

She placed a hand on his strong wrist then jerked back, remembering what touching him had once done to her. "If you really want to help us, just leave after you sell the buckers. There's nothing anyone can do beyond that at this point."

He shoved a hand through his hair. Made the ends stand up at odd angles that gave him a messy, sexy look. "I can't do that." His deep voice thrummed in her gut. Tickled her ear. "I'm seeing this through."

When she turned to face him their noses

brushed and she sucked in a fast breath. Backed off.

"Please," she whispered, suddenly lost in those steady blue eyes.

He cupped her face, his calloused palms tender. Their roughness had always been at odds with his gentle touch, she thought wildly.

"Do you really want me to go?"

"Yes," she said, though she shook her head. Those bills frightened her. Made her want to lean on someone. Tanner. A part of her felt glad he wasn't quitting, she admitted. With his full lips so close to hers, she couldn't quite think straight. Her eyes lingered on his mouth.

Tanner studied her for a moment then nodded, as if he'd just been given an order. He pushed her gently back against the sofa and shook his head. "Claire," he whispered. Then he kissed her.

He ran his hand down her neck and along her collarbone. The moonlight from the door's half window shone down on them, and their kiss was electric and soft, tentative and certain, terrifying and exactly right. She felt the old love rush from her to him and from Tanner to her. They were warm and shivering, and young and ancient and alive. *It's true*, she thought. *I've never stopped loving him*. Despite the accident, Kevin, Jonathan, everything. How could it be?

It couldn't.

She shoved Tanner. Hard. Bolted to her feet, heart hammering. Her breath came and went too fast to catch.

"Claire, I—" Tanner stayed seated, and for that she was grateful.

"Stop. Just. Stop."

With her back to the door, her hand on the knob, her mind cleared. Pulse slowed.

"If you can't or won't leave, then just stay away. You're ruining everything."

Anguish filled her. How could she betray her husband this way? Kevin had come to the rescue after Tanner had nearly destroyed her. Yet here she was, back in his arms, only a week after he'd returned. As if Kevin hadn't mattered at all.

She disgusted herself.

When she opened the door, Tanner reached her in three steps. "Don't leave this way." He touched her hair, his hand shaking slightly.

"I shouldn't have come at all. From now on, keep your distance. Okay?"

He nodded slowly though she didn't hear his door shut until she'd made it back up onto her own porch. She'd forgotten how protective of her he'd always been. If he really cared, though, he'd leave soon. Give her peace of mind. Hand over the piece of her heart he'd stolen back tonight. Kissing him couldn't have been a worse mistake.

She collapsed in a kitchen chair and picked up her cold cup of tea, the liquid's surface trembling.

She'd gone to Tanner to solve her problems, not send them over a cliff.

What had she done?

Everything was falling apart.

Most of all, her.

CHAPTER SEVEN

IN A MEADOW by Denton Creek, Tanner balanced on one foot, the other resting against the inside of his opposite knee, palms pressed together overhead.

"You're doing that wrong," drawled a soft voice behind him. He lost his focus and dropped his foot.

His head shot round and he spotted Claire. She wore a light pink, curve-hugging tank top that left her midriff bare. His hands itch to span it. To pull her close as he had a few nights ago—big mistake that it'd been.

She hadn't spoken to him in three long, frustrating days. And as much as they bickered, he'd rather have her salt than silence. Wanted to be challenged instead of ignored. As promised, he'd given her space, though he'd hoped she'd come to him. Now she had. Why?

"That was a tree pose."

"Looked more like a sapling." Her lips twitched before she pressed them back into a straight line. She grabbed a yoga mat out of a shoulder bag and unrolled it on the ground beside him, looking adorably efficient.

"What are you doing?"

She shrugged, her shoulders toned and kissable.

"Helping you rehab." Her teeth clamped an elastic band and she wrestled her mass of curls into a ponytail.

"You're going to help me?" Was this a joke? He watched, fascinated, as she tamed her irrepressible locks, though a few sprang free and dangled around her heart-shaped face. Translucent, flawless skin. Clear green eyes. Heartbreakingly full lips. Looking at her was like looking at the sunrise. You never knew what lay ahead but you sure were glad to witness it.

"The sooner your shoulder heals, the faster you get back to rodeo. I heard you on the phone this morning."

Tanner nodded, though he hadn't realized she'd listened to his cell phone conversation. She'd been busy taking down laundry on the lines beyond the porch. In fact, he barely recalled what he'd said himself, he'd been so riveted by her deft movements as she'd unclasped, folded and stacked linens with just a couple of wrist flicks.

"My agent. He wanted to review my sponsor's

contract language." His eyes ran over the sweet curve of her back as she twisted and stretched.

"You have to return to rodeo once you're medically cleared, right? You'll lose your sponsorship otherwise." She pulled her heel up to her back, her long legs encased in black spandex shorts that left little to the imagination, though a man could dream. Especially him when it came to Claire.

"Right. They're sending out a doctor next week."

She broke out in the first genuine smile he'd gotten from her since he'd arrived. It started in her eyes and didn't seem to end anywhere on her face.

"Then let's get started. No time to waste." She handed him a wooden block.

He examined it. He'd seen foam ones like this at the physical training center. Never knew what they did since he'd left once Martin called. "So you're helping me heal to get rid of me? That's your latest plan?"

"Something's got to work." Her small chin rose. The low-riding, early evening sun bathed her in gold and created a floodlit path down the rippling creek behind her.

A chuckle escaped him. Stubborn, persistent woman. "You're that determined."

"As serious as the business end of a .45." Her

dimples made thumbprints on either side of her mouth. Knocked the wind clean out of him.

After a moment, he laughed again. Couldn't help it. Kept on when her smile faded and a small line formed between her wide-spaced eyes.

"This is a win-win for both of us," she insisted, stepping close enough for him to inhale the faint, sweet, wildflower scent of her. "You get your career back and I rein in my father."

"What if rodeo isn't all I want anymore?" He sank his eyes into hers as deeply as he could. Tried to pour fire into them. Let her see the havoc those hide-and-seek dimples created.

He wanted his old life back. Of course he did. He'd already missed five events. Much more would get him kicked off the Elite Tour, make him ineligible to compete in the PBR championships next year, and lose him a sponsorship whose next installment he badly needed. But another life had started appealing more, lately, and it featured Claire in every frame.

"But you have to go back."

A twitchy feeling took hold. That trapped sense he got whenever he felt cornered. Like the bulls he rode, he didn't go willingly unless he decided to himself.

"What about the liens? We need to sort those out before I leave."

Her eyebrows met and, for the first time, she looked unsure. As much as he enjoyed in-your-face Claire, seeing her uncertainty roused his protective streak. He wanted to fix all her problems, even though this lady could more than handle them on her own. Would do a fine job, he admitted, if she'd stop letting fear get in the way.

She handed him a towel and dropped another beside her water bottle.

"A good offer for the bucking bulls will help. Thanks for reaching out to the tour's stock contractors. And I contacted the creditors. We got a thirty-day extension from a few but others are threatening to pressure the bank to foreclose."

She popped the top off her water bottle and drank. When she lowered it, her face looked tight, as if her ponytail scraped back her skin. "Worse, the bank called again today. They wanted reassurance that our sale's going through. An escrow, letter of intent…but Dad won't consider it now that you're here."

She ducked down to pull another block from her bag, but he glimpsed the red tips of her ears. Spotted the tremble of her jaw.

"And he shouldn't. Trust me, Claire."

"That ended when you boarded the rodeo bus ten years ago." The resignation, rather than the heat in her voice, packed a right hook to his jaw. Made his face sting.

"Look. This will work. And on the slim chance it doesn't, once I'm gone, your dad will give in and sell. But for now, let him fight while he can, have his dignity."

"I'd rather he have his life." She looked at him seriously, almost pleadingly.

"This *is* his life."

Their rising voices evaporated in the quiet glade and the passion faded from her eyes. Turned them hollow. The thought of hurting proud, caring Claire made Tanner feel ill. But he'd promised Martin. Needed this last ditch chance for himself, too.

"Please work with me. Let me get your shoulder back in shape." She'd steadied her voice again, but the inflections in it sounded wrong and her eyes were still bruised and hurt.

"Tell you what. If you let Jon—"

"Jonathan," she interrupted without looking up from untying her shoes.

"Jon," he countered. "It's a man's name and he needs to see himself that way."

She peered up at him and made a frustrated sound. "Is there anything you're not the authority on? Including my child?"

He smiled wide. "Not that I've found yet, but, hey, you never know."

A long elastic band biffed him on the shoulder.

"What are we doing with those?" he asked, suspicious. They looked like torture devices. He could handle pain. Just wasn't about tearing any more muscles.

"Afraid?" she challenged, her eyes sparking again. With pieces of hair blowing across those lush lips he wanted to kiss her. Badly.

"Terrified." His mouth hooked up on one side and her gaze slid out from under his.

"They're going to increase your flexibility."

"And you know this because you're some kind of yoga guru…"

"I prefer master. You can call me that." Her eyes slanted sideways at him, her dimples cheeky.

He snorted. "That'll be the day."

"A girl can dream. So, are we doing this?"

He eyed her gear and considered. "If you let Jon work with me on the pickup, you've got a deal."

The color drained from her face and she bit her lip. Tanner crossed his arms and waited. And waited. And waited. A butterfly lit on a purple wildflower stalk. A breeze bent the reeds lining the tinkling creek. A toad slipped off a rock and under the water when a blue heron stalked by.

Silence.

He started to give back the block, but she put up a hand. "Okay," she murmured, shoulders hunched. "But we're going to do yoga every day at dawn."

Relief washed through him. He hadn't realized until just now how much he wanted this time with her. And the truth was, that actually did frighten him.

Still. He couldn't resist. "So show me how to do a real tree pose. I'm no sapling."

Her eyes sank to his feet and rose slowly along his body until they reached his mouth and lingered. "Nope. Definitely not that."

His pulse sped. Did she have any idea how much her teasing revved him up? No matter how much she drove him crazy, he kept wanting more.

An hour later, he lay on his back, drenched in sweat. He tried slowing and deepening his breathing the way she'd taught him, though he wanted to pant like a dog. And he was dog-tired, too.

He slid his eyes to the serene woman beside him, her tank top as dry as when she'd started, only a faint sheen setting her face aglow. With her eyes closed and her chest slowly rising and falling, she could have been asleep. They called him a world champion and this rancher's daughter had just knocked him into next week.

She'd always been strong. Self-assured. While it'd scared off some guys back in the day, especially when she'd outright rejected everyone, he'd wanted a shot. Had kept asking her out until she'd finally said yes. It'd been one of the happiest days of his life.

With enough persistence, could he win her back again? No other woman grabbed hold of him this hard.

For a long time, he'd thought memories of Claire were just fantasy. Exaggerations. Working with her now, seeing how she'd grown stronger than ever, brought back old feelings and then some. Especially after kissing her.

Her mouth. That sassy, tell-it-like-it-is mouth. He wanted it on his, telling him off, making him laugh, smiling tenderly at her son or father, maybe even him someday...though he doubted it'd ever happen.

Even if he saved her ranch, he'd never be good enough for her. He'd failed at everything except at the one thing she hated most—rodeo. And when she found out he'd lost all of his earnings, she'd see he was a failure there, too.

"Time's over." She sat up beside him and most of her thick hair fell down around her face. Soft and full. He wanted to bury his face in it. "What'd you meditate about?"

When his eyes dropped to her lips, color crept into her cheeks.

"Something nice," he said, watching, fascinated, as her tongue darted out the way it did when she got skittish.

"Feels like it's getting hotter, not cooler." She waved a hand in front of her face and stowed the gear. Watching the elastic bands disappear, he had to admit that they'd helped. His shoulder ached, but in a good way. This actually might work.

So why didn't the thought cheer him? He planned to set up a school here and reestablish funds for his retirement. Beyond that, he needed to return to rodeo—the world that'd been good to him.

But Claire was good to you, too, once...

The thought caught him off guard. When he pushed it back, it didn't retreat much. Barely budged, in fact.

"Let's dunk our feet in the creek."

He rolled up his jeans, not exactly yoga gear but about as close as this cowboy got, and headed down the embankment. "You coming?" he called over his shoulder.

She shook her bright head, her busy fingers trapping her ringlets again. "Better get back. Make sure Jonathan's taken his bath."

"He hasn't."

A sigh escaped her. Then a rueful smile. She joined him on the flat rock and sat. "Of course he hasn't. What was I thinking?" They laughed together in the softening light, and a sense of camaraderie stole over him. Was this what being a parent would feel like? It filled him with a wistful sensation. A keyhole glimpse into a world he'd never thought about joining.

"Jonathan's been going on about Guardian. How horses can wash themselves with their tails. That maybe Guardian will stop by one night and give him a bath. However did he get that idea?"

Heat crawled up Tanner's neck. "I might have given him that impression. We play-talked when we washed Guardian. Silly, I guess."

Claire turned, her eyes considering. No disdain in them...more like wonder. And approval. It carbonated his bloodstream. "No. Not silly. I do that, too." She held out a finger for a hovering dragonfly but it zipped away. "I tell him goblins will eat his breakfast if he doesn't hurry up and come to the table."

Warmth spread in his chest as he imagined it. "Goblins?" When he hadn't gotten to breakfast fast enough, if there ever was one, his mother would have been more likely to swat him than speak to him.

Claire nodded. "Guff and Lottie. Guff—

well—he doesn't take any...and Lottie likes attention. She's always dyeing her hair or wearing some crazy outfit. Doing something naughty."

Caught up in her topic, she leaned closer and her hand brushed his, her delicate fingers glowing in the fading light, so close they could wind in his, her softly curved mouth electric with remembered kisses.

"I pretend they don't let kids see them so it makes him hurry to try and catch them. He's pretty old to believe it now, though. I think he just plays along to humor me."

"You're a good mother." Claire drove him crazy with her overreaction to danger, but seeing her with Jonathan made him admire a new side of her.

The fearful, bullied boy needed the strong support she gave because, even when the whole world threw rocks at you, if you had your mother at your back, you'd be okay. Some deep-rooted part of you would know you were loved. That you deserved to be loved. His mother hadn't given him that gift and the fact that Claire gave it to her son impressed him deeply.

"Sometimes I wonder." She plucked the tall grass sprouting beside the rock and plaited it.

He skipped a rock over the water. Tossed in a twig. Anything to keep his hands busy and from touching what he really wanted. "I shouldn't have called you a jailer. A man doesn't like to be held back, but I went too far. You love him. That's plain."

"Yes. But is it enough?" She dropped her feet into the water and swirled it with her toes.

"What else do you think he needs?"

She was silent and she continued braiding the grass, and he wondered if she thought of her husband.

"Lots of kids are raised by single mothers." His convincing tone wavered and he pictured his mom. Passed out on the bathroom floor. Staggering home past three in the morning. Calling for aspirin while she lay on the couch, a pillow over her head.

He didn't need her. He'd taught himself not to need anyone. And without even knowing he was doing it, he'd waited. He'd waited for anyone who got close to him to see something they didn't like in him, something they hadn't seen initially, and to grow cold and disappear, too, like summer dust. Like Claire. Because there had to be something wrong, didn't there, if even your own mother didn't really love you?

Rodeo had given him the affirmation he'd needed growing up, he realized.

"And that was hard on you," she exclaimed, and chucked the grass braid into the current.

"That's the past." Her concern took him

aback. How long had it been since anyone cared about him that way? When Claire loved, she did it as she did everything. All in. With her whole heart. Once he'd had her heart and he'd tossed it away. For what?

He thought of his trophies and awards and felt nothing. Wasn't as if they could feel anything for him, either. After pulling his dripping feet out of the water, he glanced around for his boots then remembered leaving them behind.

"Have you spoken to your mother?"

Her question was a punch to the gut. "Not since she showed up at a rodeo five years ago, drunk. She had more holes in her arm than Swiss cheese. Introduced me to a boyfriend younger than me."

Claire touched his arm and his tense muscles relaxed. "That's terrible."

"Some things never change."

She heaved out a sigh. "No. Some things don't."

"Did I know Kevin?"

Her head jerked at the abrupt topic change. "You might have seen him around. He went to our school and was my childhood friend, but he never liked rodeo."

"Sounds like you were perfect for each other." He tried and failed to keep the jealous note out of his voice. Darn it. Claire had once loved rodeo. If she'd given it another chance...maybe she would have stayed. Been with him.

The waking night sounded around them. Thrumming frogs accompanied crickets who'd been waiting for the lavender light to strike their notes. Rattling cicadas kept time.

At last Claire shook her head and her silky hair brushed his shoulder. "He was perfect. Me, I was a mess."

"Because of me," Tanner blurted and pressed his palms against the stone. Guilt rocked him when he imagined his young, foolish self. He'd thought winning a fortune would impress a girl like Claire. How little he'd known her, he now realized. She was much more than that.

"It wasn't all about you. I had things to work out on my own."

"Like...?"

She bolted to her feet, her body rigid and features tight. "I'd better see to Jonathan."

What?

Before he could react, she dashed up over the embankment. By the time he sprinted to the crest, her pumping legs had carried her halfway across the field, her speed impressive.

CHAPTER EIGHT

CLAIRE STIRRED THE chili bubbling in the stockpot the next evening. Her stomach growled at the spicy beef and bean aroma. Chili was a family favorite and she often cooked it on Marie's nights off. She sneaked a taste with a clean spoon.

"Cheater!"

She smiled over her shoulder at her son. He was dressed in last year's Halloween costume—fringed chaps over his jeans, spurred boots and a ten-gallon hat that kept slipping on his forehead. Too cute.

"Lottie dared me to."

He bustled up next to her and peered around the room. "Never listen to Lottie. She's trouble." He cupped his hands to his mouth and turned in a circle. "You hear that, Lottie? Trouble." His thumbs hooked into his belt loops. "She won't be bothering you anymore."

Claire sprinkled grated cheddar cheese atop the chili and turned down the flame. She pretended not to see Jonathan sneak some. "Thanks for taking care of that, partner."

He patted his plastic gun holder. "Anytime, ma'am," he drawled in a low twang, his best *Bonanza* imitation, and it made her giggle. He loved watching the reruns with her father.

"You're my hero, Little Joe." She fluttered her lashes at him which set them off again. When her father and Tanner walked into the kitchen, Claire and Jonathan were bent at the waist, howling along with a yipping, jumping Roxy.

"What in the Sam Hill are you two up to?" boomed her father, his voice growing stronger by the day. She stopped laughing but kept smiling at him until she caught a strange look on Tanner's face. He looked paralyzed. Stricken. She followed his gaze to Jonathan, who now teased Roxy with a squeaky squirrel. Had he glimpsed himself in their son?

"Hope everyone's hungry for corn bread..." she blurted. Anxious to distract.

"Looking forward to it, darlin'." Her father leaned on a few surfaces to steady himself, but made it to the table under his own steam. Pride filled her at her strong-willed parent, and relief to see him recovering. And Tanner's arrival had spurred on the change...

"Looks like we need the butter, though."

"I've got it!" Jonathan buzzed to the fridge while Tanner ambled up behind her.

"Anything I can help with?" His low voice rumbled near her ear and goose bumps rose on her arms.

"Nope. All set," she said briskly, untying her apron and moving away. It was tough to ignore the dashing figure he made in a crisp plaid shirt tucked into slim jeans with boots poking out of their cuffs, his dark hair wet and slicked off his handsome face. Since their kiss, she'd been more aware of him than ever. When he'd appeared on the porch yesterday, she'd barely been able to focus on the laundry.

What luck that she'd overheard his contract conversation. Knowing his sponsor pushed for his return tipped the balance—instead of avoiding him she could help him heal. Her passionate response to his kiss had been an anomaly. He'd caught her off guard. With her wits about her, she wouldn't let old feelings creep up again. Ever. Yet she'd been disarmed when Tanner had told her about his whimsical play with Jonathan. A horse that washed itself? Amazing that tough, competitive Tanner had a soft, silly side with kids. Even more surprising, he'd met her at dawn today and thoughtfully brought an extra cup of hot coffee.

Slowly but surely his interest in her son, support for her father, dedication to the ranch—a website?—and the flashes of his old self and their former relationship, chipped at the wall she'd erected between them.

Even Dani seemed to be on Tanner's side. In their recent conversation, she'd argued he was good for the ranch, just not for Claire. In that moment, she'd nearly confided the truth about Jonathan to her older sister. How she needed to talk to someone! If Kevin hadn't come along when he had, she would have told her distant sister long ago. Now, with the issue fresh again, it became more tempting every time they spoke.

When Claire grabbed for the pot holders, Tanner beat her to it and lugged the stockpot to the table. He held up the bright red lobster mitts encasing his hands. "I'll get the corn bread."

Jonathan dropped the butter dish on the table and the ceramic top rattled. "Lobster man!" He pointed at Tanner. "Watch out. He'll claw your eyes out."

Tanner grinned and Claire's pulse shifted up a gear. "No." He planted his feet wide apart, raised his chin and pointed, looking more like a superhero than a supervillain. "You'd better watch out, young man. With these claws I shall take over the universe...or at least this ranch!" He threw back his head and let out an evil-sounding laugh that made her father chuckle and her smile.

He snapped a claw in Jonathan's direction and lunged. Squealing and laughing, her son raced around the table. "Never! Your pinchers are no match for this." He drew his plastic gun and pointed, making a *pow-pow-pow* sound.

With a stagger and a chest clutch, Tanner reared back and crashed to their rag rug dramatically. He was insane, but in the best way, Claire admitted. Roxy leaped at his face and ferociously licked every inch.

"I know I'm supposed to be dead," he sputtered as the dog continued her manic affection. "And I'm the most evil villain in the universe. Or at least at Red Lobster...but can someone get this spit machine off of me? Her saliva is neutralizing my powers."

"Get him, Roxy!" shouted Jonathan, fist pumping the air. "You've defeated a master villain."

Claire's father guffawed. "Who said you can't keep a good man down?"

"Me!" Tanner pulled Roxy away and held her above his chest so the dog dangled, her little legs pumping, tongue flicking the air. "I'm putting you in puppy time out." He got to his feet and set down the dog. In a flash, she bounded after Claire's sandal tassels. "Sheesh. Fickle girl."

Tanner's eyes sparkled at Claire and she smiled back, charmed despite herself.

Shoot. If she wasn't careful she'd start wanting him to stay instead of go.

"Come get it while it's hot," she announced, pouring glasses of freshly squeezed lemonade. She'd made it special this morning after she'd finished giving riding lessons. The fact that it'd always been Tanner's favorite didn't factor in one bit.

"Where's Guff and Lottie?" Tanner asked, his eyes wide and innocent-looking. With his hair off his strong brow, his face resembled that of a model for a cologne or jeans campaign. She looked away, ordered her lungs to work again and took a seat.

"You know about them?" Jonathan jumped on the balls of his feet and held out his bowl while Claire tried ladling chili into the moving target.

"Of course. Lottie's the one with the crazy hair and Guff is stern-like."

"Where did you see them? They always run away from me. Wonder why?" He rolled his eyes at Claire, his mouth twisting up on one side, skeptical. Tanner poked her son's side as he sat and chili spilled onto the table. "Maybe if you'd stay still they might come out."

Jonathan jittered in his seat, as close to not

moving as he got. "I try. Real hard. But my body won't let me."

"Ants in his pants," put in her father. He slid his spoon into his bowl and carefully raised it to the good side of his mouth. "Good batch, honey."

"That's what my grandmother always said about me." Tanner nodded his thanks when Claire handed him a full bowl, their eyes meeting and bouncing away. Magnets repelling... only they weren't...not by a long shot. What was going on?

"What about your dad?" came Jonathan's innocent question.

Roxy's nails scratched on the tiles as she trotted around the table. The rest of the room grew silent.

"I never met him," said Tanner at last. He dropped a cherry in his lemonade and took a long drink. "Mmm...my favorite. Thanks, Claire."

"It's—uh—nothing special." Despite her words, she pulsed with pleasure at the compliment.

Jonathan's chair scraped as he scooched closer to his idol.

"Never ever?"

Tanner nodded. He buttered a piece of corn

bread and passed it to Jonathan. Claire did the same for Martin.

"Why's that?" Jonathan asked through a mouthful of crumbs.

"He left when I was born." Tanner kept his head down and shoveled in chili. Claire's heart went out to him. She remembered how he'd always carried a picture of himself as a newborn in his father's arms—the first and last time they'd been together. His daddy had lit out the next morning. Joined a carnival, they'd heard. Others said he sailed the gulf, netting shrimp. No one really knew. And, besides Tanner, no one really cared. Mr. Hayes had been a drunk, and a mean one, at that.

"My daddy left me, too, only not on purpose."

Claire looked away and blinked the sting out of her eyes.

"Of course not, son. What father wouldn't want to come home to you?" Tanner wrapped an arm around Jonathan and pulled him close. Rubbed his hair until the curls spiraled in every direction.

Claire busied herself back at the stove. Pulled out another pan of corn bread and fussed over straightening the kitchen towels. If Tanner knew Jonathan was his son, would he mean those words? Forgo weekly rodeo appearances and stick around to watch his son grow?

"My dad would have...he even bought me a present before. Before..." Jonathan rubbed his eyes on his sleeves and reached up to finger Tanner's bolo tie, turning the silver arrow over. "Will you come back to visit me sometime?"

A lump formed in Claire's throat at the desperate, hopeful sound in her child's voice. She wished her love was enough to fill Kevin's void. Tanner chucked Jonathan lightly under the chin. "Well. I've gotten kind of attached to you, Lottie and Guff."

Jonathan leaped and Claire caught his glass just before it tipped over. "What about Momma?"

Her father lowered his full spoon and Claire forced down a mouthful of corn bread. "Anyone want more chili?" She held up the ladle but no one moved.

"Your momma, too." Tanner's deep blue eyes swerved to hers and they locked gazes.

She looked for a sarcastic slant or a mischievous glint but saw sincerity, instead. He couldn't care for her again, could he? She wasn't the bold girl who'd taken the kinds of risks that'd impressed him once.

"Better eat your chili before Guff snatches it."

Jonathan scooted back to his spot and dunked his corn bread into his bowl, jaw working fast.

"So, how are things going with that rodeo school of yours?" asked her father.

Claire's spoon fell from her fingers. "What school?" She picked it up again, then placed it back in her bowl. Suddenly she didn't feel hungry.

Her father and Tanner exchanged looks and her father stretched out an upturned palm, his expression apologetic.

"Dad, what school?" Her head swiveled. "Tanner?"

"We might as well tell her, Tanner." Her father reached across and patted Claire's hand. "Nothing to worry about. Tanner here's going to buy some of the bucking bulls and rent that front pasture for a bull-riding school."

Claire thought about a time her parents had vacationed on a gulf beach. How she'd ventured farther into the water than her mother allowed. Waded out even more. Then a wave rolled in, curled over her. Swept her off her feet and sent her tumbling, head over heels, over and over until her lungs burned and her father had grabbed her out. His hollering had hurt less than the dread of never breathing again.

She'd forgotten how that had felt until now.

"That means new construction. Modifying the ranch. Our buyer didn't agree to that. He could back out just when the bank wants proof of the deal."

"I'm not planning on selling just yet, darlin'." Her father smiled in that new, uneven way that made it impossible to be cross. Besides, she wouldn't upset him. Worse, she and Tanner had agreed not to argue in front of him.

"Cool!" Jonathan tucked his heels under his hips and bounced on them. "A rodeo school. I want to go. Momma, can I go?"

"No!" Claire gathered up the empty bowls, but when her foot caught on a chair leg the stack dropped with a ferocious shatter.

She sank to her knees and started gathering the ceramic shards with shaking hands. "Stay back," she ordered when her son's shoes appeared.

"I want to help."

She closed her eyes and sat back on her heels. Pressed her fingertips to her lids. "Please go upstairs."

"I'm supposed to help Tanner on Daddy's truck."

"You can start tomorrow."

"No. Tonight!"

"Jonathan." She and Tanner spoke at once and she looked up at the cowboy who held out a hand to her son. "How about we do a puzzle?"

"Fine."

Claire focused on cleaning up the broken bowls. Bull riding. Here? Around her son? No. No. No, no, no.

Jonathan's chatter receded as he and Tanner disappeared upstairs. Claire dumped the pottery in the trash, her world rocking hard enough to make her motion sick.

She'd been wrong to think she and Tanner could reach some sort of truce until he left. Tanner wouldn't go softly into any good night. He'd rather light it up. Explode and fizz like firecrackers on the Fourth of July. Stupid of her to think otherwise.

"Claire," her father began but she held up a hand.

"How long have you known about this?"

Her father patted the seat next to him and she slid into it after mopping up the last of the pottery remnants. "We discussed it before he came out here."

"Why didn't you tell me?" She untucked the napkin from his shirt collar. Smoothed the fabric.

"I planned to."

The air spun out of her. "I know. You mixed up the dates. But why didn't you tell me when he got here?"

"He wasn't sure he'd be able to do it. He

needed—" A coughing fit turned her father's nose red.

"Needed what?" It couldn't be financing. Tanner must be a multi-millionaire. The PBR World Championship alone was a one-and-a-half million dollar purse, plus his sponsorship deal and possible thirty- to fifty-thousand-dollar wins each week. Money couldn't be an issue, so why the uncertainty?

Her father clamped his mouth shut. Shook his head. Looked mulish. "Not for me to say. All you need to know is it's going through."

"This is my home, too. And Jonathan's. I don't want him around bull riding. What if he gets interested?"

Her father's weak hand dropped into his lap and he used his other one to place it back on the table. "What if he does? The kid needs more things to feel good about."

"You want a nine-year-old on the back of a bull?" Had Dad lost his mind?

Her father's extra chin wagged when he shook his head. "No. But I'd like to see him outside. Getting involved. Socializing with other people besides family."

"Not that way."

"Then how, Claire? He's a rancher's son. This is his blood. His heritage."

"Times change, Daddy. Why won't you accept that?" Her leg started to jiggle involuntarily.

"Because I'm a stubborn old dog."

When he smiled, her heart softened. "You can still learn new tricks."

"Tanner's teaching me some. Syndicating bulls, rodeo stock contracting, now the school. I thought my ranching days were over but I feel like I've got a new start."

She touched his cheek. Felt his flush. "I hope you're right, Dad. I do. Just don't let it go so long that you lose everything."

"Darlin', I'm doin' my best not to."

Her father kissed her then stumped out onto the porch. The swing creaked and she imagined him looking out over his land. Turning over Tanner's wild ideas.

She'd thought getting rid of him would be tough but doable. That she could stop Tanner before he inflicted much collateral damage. Wrong. Wrong. With a bull-riding school on the property, rodeo and all its hazards would be close, its lure tempting her child, triggering her worse fears.

Whatever softening she'd felt toward Tanner ended immediately. Now that he'd brought rodeo to her front door, a win-win solution wasn't possible. He'd upped the stakes into an all-out war.

She'd block everything. The stock shows, the rodeo school and, most of all, Tanner...

Her mind flashed with a million possibilities. Settled on one that could work if her family's lawyer agreed.

Her father wanted to go all in? Well, he had no idea just how all in she could get.

CHAPTER NINE

"AN INJUNCTION?"

Claire's family lawyer, Mr. Redmond, raised his gray, tumbleweed eyebrows and stopped rolling a gold-trimmed pen on his desk blotter. His fleshy jaw was unshaven and peppered with white, unlike the pitch black of his combover. He obviously didn't shave on the weekends. Hadn't expected her emergency call this morning, but had come into his office anyway. He'd always been loyal to her family. Hopefully that wouldn't stop now.

"Yes. A man is trying to start a business on our property that poses a threat to my child." She stared down at her twisting hands. Tried to keep her expression neutral. Professional. Her mother used to tell her she had the world's worst poker face: her feelings floated across her features like reflections on a still pond. She would blurt out a confession within hours. Or she would go crazy with the tension and start chewing her fingernails into nubs.

"And your father approved this venture?" Mr.

Redmond smoothed the rumpled edge of his shirt collar. He was a big lump of a man, but still cut a dashing figure in Coltrane. Set the church ladies aflutter to see whose cake he'd take the largest piece from during socials. Once he'd confided that he flew to New York City every fall to order his tailor-made suits. Bought his expensive cologne there, too. The spicy kind that made Claire sneeze.

He handed her a tissue.

"Thanks." She dabbed her nose. "And my father doesn't know I'm here."

His perfectly shaped, shiny nails drummed. Must be those rumors of him dating Carol Lynn, the town's eccentric salon owner, were true, she mused.

"How's your daddy?" Mr. Redmond's chair squeaked when he leaned back and grabbed a cigar box from a shelf behind him.

"Doing better, thank you. I'm trying not to stress him, which is why I came to you instead of him. He thinks a rodeo school may help save the ranch."

Mr. Redmond bit off the end of the cigar and delicately spit it into his wastebasket. "And this has nothing to do with some grudge you're holding against Tanner Hayes?" His eyes closed as he put the cigar between his lips, flicked his lighter and held the flame to the tip.

"What?" She about came out of her seat. Rose an inch or two before she got hold of herself. Small towns equaled long memories. No sense getting riled by that. "No. Having bucking bulls ridden near my home poses a danger to my impressionable son."

Mr. Redmund exhaled a puff of cherry-and-hickory-scented smoke. "You're worried that Jonathan will get hurt if he has easier access to the bulls if they're penned closer to the house. Secondly, you don't trust Tanner to safeguard against that?"

"Tanner?" she asked, dubious.

They exchanged a long look and Mr. Redmond smiled slowly. He'd never been a fan of her ex. Had blamed Tanner when, as a teen, he'd organized the backfield racing derby where Mr. Redmond's son had crashed his father's vintage Mustang.

White smoke curled out of the lawyer's nose. "That boy's always been trouble. Surprised your father let him come around. Glad to see Tanner hasn't fooled you again, Claire."

She flushed, the old resentment she'd had at Mr. Redmond, and most of Coltrane's "respectable folk," for treating Tanner like a second-class citizen returning. How they'd whispered about him. Claimed he'd end up no better than his momma or daddy. She'd defended him, then...

Unease filled her. Finally she had an ally, though she didn't feel good about it. "Dad didn't tell me about Tanner. I thought we were selling to Mr. Ruddell until Tanner showed with all these crazy ideas."

When Mr. Redmond shook his head, his sprayed hair didn't budge an inch. "You've got only ten weeks before the bank takes possession. I've stalled them as long as I can, but if you don't sell before then, you'll be evicted."

Claire nodded, her gut sour. "I know. That's why I need this injunction. Hopefully it'll convince Tanner to leave before it's too late."

With a flourish, Mr. Redmond pulled a yellow pad from his desk drawer and twisted his pen so the tip appeared. "Then let's get started, young lady. This will be a prohibitory injunction forbidding Tanner from operating a business that relies on aggressive animals within..." He paused and glanced up at her, his brown eyes assessing. "No. On any property upon which you and your son reside. I can't promise you anything. However, a temporary injunction will halt the school from opening until a hearing date is set. Hopefully it will dissuade him from continuing."

Relief took the starch out of her spine. She

sank farther into one of the plush chairs set before Mr. Redmond's replica French Renaissance desk. "Sounds perfect. So, can I deliver it today?"

Mr. Redmond's pen paused, but he didn't lift his head. "Not for another week. It needs Judge Durrell's approval first. I'll mention it when I see him on the golf course this afternoon and send it to his chambers Monday. When it's ready, I'll call."

He waved a hand, Claire dismissed.

She dawdled by his desk, counting the strands that traipsed across his expansive, bald head.

At last, he stopped writing and looked up, impatient. "Yes?"

"Thank you, Mr. Redmond. My father's not himself these days and your help's appreciated. If there's anything I can do…"

A gleam entered his eyes. "You could bring your momma's pineapple upside-down cake to tomorrow's Founder's Day."

"Founder's Day?" Shoot. She'd forgotten about the annual town picnic with all the craziness back home.

"You promised Carol Lynn you'd be in her wig show."

"Tell her I'll be there…with the cake."

"Now don't forget the cherries, you hear?"

he called when she reached the door. Her hand rested on its fancy side-scrolled handle.

"And homemade whipped cream."

He puffed his cigar, closed his eyes and smiled. "Looks like we've got a deal."

Claire stepped out into the bright day, feeling hopeful for the first time in a while. Then, like a cloud passing in front of the sun, her mood dimmed.

What would Tanner think of the injunction?

And why did she care so much?

Too late now. She'd deal with the fallout when it happened.

TANNER SHIFTED IN the metal folding chair positioned beside the white fabric runway for Lady Bird Salon's wig show the next day. A country band played from a distant bandstand, the driving beat making his boots tap. Food trucks selling everything from pulled-pork sandwiches to funnel-cake-dipped fried Oreos lined the bustling thoroughfare, the smells of fried, salty and sweet food mingling in the warm afternoon.

He pulled at his shirt collar and wished he hadn't dressed up for the occasion in the eighty-five-degree heat. It bugged him that the townspeople's opinions still mattered. That he wanted to impress them with how far he'd come, though strangely few had asked him much about rodeo.

Instead, many had greeted him warmly, welcomed him back and inquired after his health. Asked how long he'd be in town. Said how good it was to see him. They'd been downright sincere.

A head scratcher.

He'd gotten so used to offering up autographs and rodeo anecdotes that he'd forgotten what it felt like to just talk to folks. And of all places for that to happen—Coltrane. Had he imagined the town-wide censure all these years?

He glanced at the banner hanging over the bandstand that read "Welcome Home, Tanner. Coltrane's Champion!" and felt flush with pride. Seemed as if he'd let the comments of a few color his view of his hometown.

Though some things hadn't changed, of course.

Malcolm Durrell, now the local magistrate, still talked loud enough to be heard yards away. Tanner made out something about fracking and political meddling. Kim Middleton, the local art teacher, painted the same unicorns and rainbows on kid's faces while an ex-minor league baseball player, Frank Stallman, organized the traditional T-ball game in a distant field.

It struck Tanner that there was something oddly comforting in continuity. A deep connection with people whose lives wove with yours and colored who you were. No matter how far he'd traveled, he realized, he'd always carried Coltrane with him.

Even Mrs. Purdy, the local floral shop owner, played a role. She'd been one of his worst detractors and now she buzzed from group to group, her red slash of a mouth moving fast, her eyes darting his way. A few folks followed the direction of her gaze, but just as many, or more, glanced away, looking bored. Nice to see that most people couldn't care less about rehashing old gossip.

A burly young boy tugged on his shirt and snapped him out of his thoughts. "Can I have your autograph?"

He glanced from the sandy-haired kid to Jonathan who suddenly turned in the seat beside Tanner and hugged his knees to his chest—as if he wanted to disappear.

When Tanner glanced from the boy up at the man resting his hand on the child's shoulder, he figured out Jonathan's discomfort. Like father like son. Zach Sully. The leader of the group that'd bullied Tanner through most of his school years.

"How are you, Zach?" Tanner drawled. He stretched out his legs and crossed them at the ankle.

"Wow! You know him, Dad?" The blond

boy looked from his heavyset father to Tanner. Where were those muscles that'd scared Tanner into eating his lunch beneath the bleachers every day? Now the guy looked soft. Easy to take...if he was worth the effort. Which he wasn't.

"Yeah." Zach shifted uncomfortably in his boots. "We went to school together."

"Did more than that," Tanner added. Casual. Easy. "We spent a lot of time together."

Jonathan made to leave, but Tanner put a hand on the boy's arm. "Remember all those times you gave me pink belly on the playground, Zach?"

"Hah! That's funny, Dad. So you were, like, friends?"

"Shut it, Tucker," hissed Zach. "Let's get some food."

"I want an autograph!" Tucker stamped his foot and Jonathan braved a look before lowering his head again. Tucker stepped closer. "What else did you two do?"

Tanner tapped his chin. Pursed his lips. Pretended he struggled to remember, though the memories loomed stark and hard. Each detail had flooded back the moment they'd passed his old school while driving to town.

"Well, your dad gave me a lot of wedgies in the locker room." Out of the corner of his eye,

Tanner noticed Jonathan's head snap up and Tucker's mouth fall open. Tanner kept his eyes dead on Zach. "Then there were the swirlies in the bathroom when he'd try to flush my head down the toilet every day before homeroom. Now that was fun."

"That's not fun," muttered Jonathan. The boy now sat up straight and faced the father-son team. His small hand slipped into Tanner's and squeezed.

"Sure was fun for Zach, though, wasn't it?"

Zach pulled at his son, nearly yanking the boy off his feet. "I said, let's go."

"Did my dad beat you up?" Tucker demanded, digging his heels in, and his eyes darted to Jonathan.

"Split lip, black eye, bruised cheek…yeah… he whupped me a few times, when he caught me."

"But we watch you every week on TV. Dad doesn't miss a show. He cheers for you."

"Guess things have changed."

"You should apologize, Dad." Tucker's lower lip stuck out and his raised voice quieted the nearby crowds.

"Maybe you should apologize to Jon."

Zach lurched forward and Tanner stood just as fast.

"How dare you?"

Tanner stared into his old nemesis's face, seeing that same snake-eyed mean streak. It didn't intimidate Tanner anymore. And he wasn't ashamed of whatever slurs against him and his family Mrs. Purdy spouted. Tanner had made something of himself, and as far as anyone knew, he was still a success. He would be one again, he vowed, his resolve to succeed at the ranch growing.

Tanner pulled out a pen and turned over the Founder's Day program. "Do you want me to sign it Tiny Tanner?"

"That's what your dad called my—called Tanner!" Jonathan put in, the skin between his freckles bright pink.

"We don't want nothing from you," Zach said, turning.

But Tucker whirled around. He hung his head, then blurted, "I'm sorry, Jonathan."

Jonathan gripped Tanner's fingers so hard he winced. "I accept." He grabbed the program Tanner had signed properly and passed it over to Tucker.

"Thank you, Mr. Hayes. Jonathan." Tucker looked down at the program and let out a whoop before letting his father drag him off.

"You're welcome, son," called Tanner to the departing pair.

"That was awesome!" Jonathan jogged

around his chair, jabbing the air like a boxer until he subsided again. "Tucker pushed me off the top of the monkey bars."

"I figured something like that."

Jonathan leaned close as the band swung into a rockabilly tune. "Can I tell you something, Tanner?"

"Anything."

His toes scuffed the dirt, then he peeked up and grinned self-consciously. "Even if it's lame?"

"Especially if it's lame."

"You're my hero." Tanner peered at Jonathan's flushed face and his heart tumbled. Grew. Stretched. Made room for this fatherless boy who reminded him of himself more every day. It didn't match the fired-up rush after a great bull ride. No. It was better. A full, satisfied sensation that seemed as if it'd never wear off the way adrenaline did. A built-to-last feeling.

Would it continue after he left... An eventuality that held less and less appeal. Yet with his sponsors pressuring and his need to restore his finances, what choice did he have? At least he'd quiet them temporarily when he did the photo shoot for their ad campaign at next week's rodeo in Oklahoma. Get them to release his next contract payment so he'd have all the funds he needed to pay the contractors who would build the rodeo school.

"You're my hero, too." He pointed at the boy's shirt button, and when Jonathan looked down chucked his chin. "Made you look."

"Okay. Now you're just embarrassing me." Jonathan's saucy expression made Tanner smile.

"Never claimed to be cool."

Jonathan nodded slowly, then grinned. "Yeah. Who wants to be cool?"

"Not the really cool people."

"Like us!" With his shoulders pushed back, the boy already looked taller.

Tanner carefully wiped a caramel stain off Jonathan's cheek. "Exactly."

"Ladies and gents," boomed a voice. "Welcome to Lady Bird's first annual wig show."

A woman who looked as though she'd barely come up to Tanner's chest appeared from a curtained-off area. She was wearing a fire-engine-red jacket with a diagonally striped skirt. With her short, permed purplish-gray hair and apple-pink cheeks, she looked like a brightly wrapped lollipop. Carol Lynn Bird. She hadn't changed a bit, either, Tanner thought wryly.

The crowd burst into enthusiastic applause and Martin stopped conversing with another rancher to beat on his leg with his good hand. His excitement to see Claire matched Jonathan's, who stood on his chair and waved his hands until Martin ordered him down. Tanner kept his own interest from showing. No reason to give the eagle-eyed gossipmongers anything else to cackle over. If they really knew how eager he felt to see Claire…

Since the rodeo school announcement, Claire had retreated into tight-lipped silence again, putting him through his yoga paces, but avoiding him otherwise. At least she hadn't fought him over the school. A nice change. Maybe she was coming around. Starting to trust him. He wanted her faith again, he admitted. A lot.

"I'm proud as punch to introduce my very first wig line that, if y'all can believe it, has been picked up by QVC. It's called Fairy Dust."

The crowd jumped to its feet and applauded again while Carol Lynn beamed. She made a dramatic sweep with her arm and backed off the runway. "Enjoy the show."

"Go, Momma!" Jonathan piped up, then lowered his voice when Martin put a finger to his lips. Jonathan knelt on the chair. "Do you like my momma?" he asked Tanner quietly.

Tanner's pulse sputtered and his eyes swerved from a model's fuchsia tresses. "Of course I do."

"Then how come you fight so much?" Jonathan scratched his peeling nose. He'd gotten a sunburn following Tanner around the past few days. "You never said why she doesn't like you."

Tanner kept his eye on the next wig, a silver tinseled thing that resembled a glittery version of Raggedy Ann's hair. "We don't fight," he said out of the corner of his mouth. Low. Not that they needed to keep it down much. Between the loud Star Wars sound track—what did it have to do with fairies? he wondered—and the exclaiming crowd, he could barely hear anything.

"Yes, you do," Jonathan murmured. "Just 'cause I don't see it doesn't mean it's not there."

Tanner stared down at the small boy, wise beyond his years. Kids. Never underestimate them.

"Your momma and I have some stuff to work out. That's all."

"But you liked her once, right? I heard grandpa say you were her boyfriend."

Tanner pinched the bridge of his nose. Where were these questions coming from? Another model sped by, her pink hair fashioned into a cotton-candy cloud. "Yes."

"Did you love her?"

Air rushed out of him as did the answer. "Yes."

Jonathan slid off his chair and tried catching a cricket darting through the trampled brown grass. "Then how come you don't like each other no more?"

"Anymore," Tanner automatically corrected. Stalling.

"Anymore," sighed Jonathan. "So why don't you like her *anymore*?"

Time for the Texas two-step side-step. "Your momma married your daddy."

Jonathan gave up on the bug and scrambled back into his seat after a stern look from his grandfather. "But *you* didn't marry anybody so you must still love her."

Tanner put his foot over his opposite knee. Dropped it. Crossed his ankles. Shifted to the left then straightened again. For a nine-year-old, Jonathan made more sense than most adults and hit too close to home.

"It's more complicated than that."

"Adult stuff again?" groaned Jonathan.

Tanner nodded. "Adult stuff." He grinned down at the boy and ruffled the cowlick that reminded him of someone…he couldn't put his finger on it…but that counterclockwise swirl on the left temple. Who did he once know who had it?

Before he could complete the thought, the curtain swished open again and Claire appeared. She looked tall and ethereal with iridescent blue hair that turned her green eyes to emeralds and brought out the natural pink of her lips. He couldn't take his eyes off her as she walked slowly down the runway, her wig caught back from her face with some kind of rhinestone tiara that turned her into something magical, otherworldly, untouchable...at least, to him.

He ached, suddenly, to make it different. To rewind. Change the past so that he'd attended Founder's Day picnics each year, Claire by his side...but then Jonathan wouldn't be here. Tanner stared down at the wriggling boy and smiled. He wouldn't change a thing of the past if it meant Jonathan wouldn't be around. Things had happened the way they were supposed to.

Besides, would Claire have been content with a ranch hand on her arm? Worse, an unemployed one if his lack of focus got him fired? He looked up at the sky and grimaced. Even if she had, it wouldn't have been acceptable to him. The small town had changed, but in some ways, at its core, it stayed the same. And so had he.

If he stuck around this time, would he only end up getting restless, losing interest and mucking up the rodeo school and overseeing the ranch? A short-term stay was manageable but any longer and he risked failing—something he'd never let Claire see.

She stopped and pivoted, her soft, flowing

white gown drifting around ankles wrapped in silver bands.

"Momma's a fairy queen," breathed Jonathan, miraculously still for once.

"All she needs is a wand," Tanner murmured back, staring.

"If she waved it, would you love her again?"

"It's not that simple, Jon."

Jonathan plucked at his frayed T-shirt's hem. "I don't get it."

Tanner's gaze lingered on Claire, radiant amidst the applause.

"Neither do I, son." He followed her graceful walk until she disappeared behind the curtain. "Neither do I."

CHAPTER TEN

"JONATHAN'S BEEN OUT there awhile," observed Claire's father the following night. He leaned against the carved post at the top of the porch stairs and nodded to the old barn that held her damaged truck. His voice carried in the still evening, the air potent with the fragrance of newly blooming roses.

"Must have lost track of time. I'd better get him." Claire started down the steps, but her father's hand on her shoulder stopped her and she turned. He'd gained weight in the past few weeks, she noticed. Had filled out the skin that'd bagged around his large frame. Lately he'd even begun combing his white hair back into his trademark pompadour and replaced his potbellied slump with a straighter spine.

"Why haven't I been getting the mail lately?"

Claire toyed with the string that tied the waistband of her shorts. "You have, Dad."

"Not all of it."

She shoved a curl under her headband and

peered up at him. "What do you think you're missing?"

His lips firmed and he shot her the stern look that used to make her quake as a teenager. Still did.

"You found the bills in the kitchen drawer."

"Yes."

She took his hand and led him to the porch swing. When they reached it, he held the wicker back, waited for her to sit, then dropped heavily onto the seat. It swung forward with a metallic creak and the dim, humid air whispered against Claire's face. "Why did you hide them?"

Her father squinted at grazing, distant bulls. "I planned on getting to them. Kept thinking I'd turn things around." In the quiet, the swing rocked and Claire held her tongue. Sensed her father had more to say.

He exhaled slowly then patted her arm. "I failed you and your sister, darlin'. Worse than you thought."

A lump rose in Claire's throat and she rested her head on his shoulder. Pressed a kiss to the underside of his jaw. "Never, Dad. Your body gave up is all. Faulting yourself for that would be like saying I failed you because I wasn't born a boy. Didn't want to take over the ranch. Or Dani for wanting to go north and work on a dude ranch. Do you blame us?"

He patted the top of her head. "Wouldn't change a thing about either of you, honey. You girls and your mother were my pride and joy. Just wish I'd done better by all of you."

She swiveled to face him, aching that he felt this way. "You did great. We grew up on an amazing ranch and had a storybook childhood. Some days I never even wanted to come inside. And Dani—she'd set out on horseback at dawn and not come home till sundown. Remember the time you and Momma found me asleep in the rabbit hutch?"

He snorted. "Keeping track of you two was like trying to bag flies, but your momma never quit. Miss that woman. Glad she's not here to see how low I've sunk."

"Dad. Stop. I miss her, too, and if she was here she'd be proud of how hard you worked… but then she'd knock some sense into your thick head about moving to the assisted living center."

A chuckle started in his belly, low and rumbling. "Always was a bossy little thing."

Claire smiled fondly, pleasure and pain mingling as she remembered her feisty mother. "And you listened to her. Why won't you do the same for me? Or Dani? She agrees with me." Claire didn't mention how she'd made her sister promise not to encourage their father with Tanner's ideas.

"If I leave, I can't give Jonathan the memories you have. And Dani, she won't have a place to come home to if she changes her mind about Colorado."

"Do you think that matters more than your health?"

Her father's head lowered and his chin rested on his breastbone. "Yes. Yes, I do."

Claire hugged her father, hard, and felt the tremble in his shoulders. Proud, obstinate man. Obviously she wouldn't convince him with Tanner around to give false hope.

"Nothing matters more than that. Not to me and not to Jonathan."

"He's coming around, that boy." Her father lifted his chin and smiled. "Been dogging Tanner's boots these past couple of weeks. Even bikes after Guardian during the pasture rounds."

Claire scooched to the edge of the seat. "While I'm giving riding lessons?"

Her father nodded. "Yep."

"I don't want him anywhere near the livestock without you or me close. You know that."

"Thought since you were letting him work with Tanner it'd be okay." He slapped a mosquito on his arm.

"That's with the car. Not animals."

"You sure it's not Tanner you want Jonathan

away from?" Her father's shrewd eyes leveled with hers and stopped her heart.

"What do you mean?"

"It's what I'm suspecting, but I'll keep that to myself for now." Her father rested crossed arms atop his stomach.

"Are you suggesting something?"

"His ears. Ever notice how Jonathan's lobes are attached directly to his head?"

She gazed at him, pulse quickening, blood cells drag racing in her veins. "Pixie ears."

"Tanner's got them, too."

"Dad!"

He held up a hand. "Look. I'm not going to talk about this anymore until you're ready to... but when you are, just know your Pa is here."

Her chest burned and she clasped her hands in front of her. If Dad could guess her secret, then Tanner might, too. The urge to get her son out of that barn and back home in bed seized her.

She bolted to her feet then leaned down and kissed her father again. "Thank you, Daddy, but whatever you're thinking, Kevin is Jonathan's father. The only one he'll ever know."

"Well that'd be a darn shame," her father called as she sprinted down the steps and out to the barn. "Tanner's a good influence."

What on earth was he suggesting? That Tanner would make a good father? Insane. Easy to see how kids would like a cowboy who charmed and entertained them. No wonder Jonathan had fallen under Tanner's spell. But fatherhood took real commitment and it wasn't glamorous. It meant sticking around, not chasing after fame and fortune the way Tanner did.

She skirted a pasture and picked up her pace. What if her father slipped and told Tanner? Or worse, Jonathan? Danger shimmied down her spine. They'd both be furious. Feel betrayed. Call her a liar or worse. And she'd never want to hurt her son that way.

Was she better off telling Tanner before he found out on his own? Her stomach lurched reflexively when she imagined the conversation.

Oh. By the way, Tanner, Jonathan is your son. Would you pass the salt, please?

She pressed on her aching gut and tipped her head to gaze at the shimmer of stars. What was the right thing to do?

Please let him leave before she had to decide…

A minute later, she nodded a quiet hello to their ranch hand, Charlie O'Dell, as he headed out of the barn. Then she slipped through the open door. Inside, her crumpled truck hunkered in the musty, lofted space. A thumping country tune boomed from a radio set on a table holding an open tool box and empty water bottles

along with a contraband bag of Oreos. Hmm…
how had Jonathan smuggled those?

She opened her mouth to call out, but shut it
again and stayed in the shadows when she spotted them by the front fender. Tanner squatted
next to Jonathan, their heads cocked at exactly
the same angle as they studied it. There was a
tender, teary feeling in Claire's chest.

"Normally we might be able to pound out
dents in a chrome fender like this, but it's too
far gone. Better to see about ordering another."
Tanner wiggled the hanging piece and it came
free in his hands. He put it aside with the other
car parts littering the floor.

"What if it's too much money?"

Tanner rumpled her son's cowlick, the gesture slicing through her since Kevin had done it,
too. "You don't have to worry about that, Jon."

Her heart swelled at her child's quick nod.
"Yes, I do. It's my dad's truck. Hey!" He leaped
to his feet and Roxy woke from her nap and
barked, sure, as always, there must be something worth getting excited over. Even the air
would do. "How about the junkyard? They got a
lot of old pickups. Might have one with a fender
like this."

Tanner sat back on his heels and studied her
little guy, his expression as proud and impressed
as she felt. A tingling started in her fingertips.

It spread up her arms and down her legs to her feet. She felt as if she'd been asleep for a million years and someone had just blasted her awake.

Tanner cared about her son. Their son. He wasn't just being charming or goofing around. He genuinely had feelings for Jonathan, and the realization filled her with some unidentifiable emotion…satisfaction? But that couldn't be right. Comfort? Joy? They had to be wrong, too.

Nonetheless, looking at the picture Tanner and Jonathan made felt like sipping tomato soup on a rainy day. Eating macaroni and cheese out of a bread bowl. It stuck to her ribs. Filled the cold, hollow spaces Kevin had left behind. For a moment, her loneliness receded as she witnessed someone else spot all the amazing things she saw in Jonathan.

The urge to confess the truth surged in her again, harder than ever, and her forehead beaded.

Tanner sauntered to the cookies, grabbed some and passed a couple to Jonathan. "Well, now. That's a fine idea. You just saved the day. I'll call them in the morning." He glanced down at his watch and whistled. "Hey, we'd better pack up. Your momma will be looking for you."

Claire stepped out of the shadows and stuffed her moist palms into her pockets. "She found him."

At her voice they turned, wearing matching surprised expressions. Emotions roiled in her gut. It touched her deeply to see her withdrawn boy coming out of his shell under Tanner's attention. He'd chattered nonstop yesterday about how Tanner got Tucker Sully, the ringleader of Jonathan's bullies, to apologize. Jonathan had been so excited he'd even called an old friend from school and they had their first playdate in almost a year set up for tomorrow! It'd made her so happy she'd only made Tanner hold the plank pose five minutes this morning.

On the other hand, the closer Tanner and Jonathan got, the more her anxiety grew. Jonathan was getting attached and Tanner seemed to be encouraging the relationship. A flame flared in her gut.

"Hey, Momma!" Jonathan buried his face in her stomach and wrapped his arms around her waist. She looked up and Tanner's unreadable eyes settled on her. What was he thinking?

"Hiya, honey. Time for bed."

"Do I have to?" Jonathan cast a longing look over at the pickup.

"Listen to your mother, Jon," Tanner said, his voice firm. He handed Jonathan the half-empty bag of Oreos.

"Aye-aye, captain." Jonathan crushed the bag to his chest and raced out the door. Roxy sprinted after him, stopping every few feet to scoop up the crumbs the boy trailed behind him.

Surprise spiked in Claire. Only Kevin and her dad got such immediate obedience. How nice to have backup. To get a break from bargaining, wheedling and bribing her son.

She glanced out the barn door and returned her father's wave. He stood on the porch, watching Jonathan and Roxy bounding home. Even from this distance, she could make out him pointing to his wristwatch and signaling her to stay. Putting his grandson to bed was something her father hadn't done since his stroke. Euphoria filled her to see him getting back to his old routines. She wouldn't ruin it and hurry home, much as she wanted to avoid Tanner.

She turned back to the tall cowboy. Today he wore a green T-shirt that contrasted with his deep blue eyes. It fit snugly over his broad chest and disappeared into the narrow waist of his jeans. "Looks like you two are having fun."

His eyes crinkled at her and he gestured to the truck. "Making a mess is more like it. Charlie's helping, but I'm calling Rick Granger from Bob's Auto Body to lend a hand, too. He does work on the side. Cheap if it's cash." He held out an Oreo. "Want one?"

When he handed her the cookie, the brief touch of his fingers sent an electric pulse fizzing through her. "Thanks. Look. I, ah, wanted to thank you for what you did yesterday."

He flipped off the radio while she chewed on the cookie and ran her hand along the truck's side.

Kevin.

"What'd I do?"

"I didn't know you'd been bullied in school."

Tanner ducked his head and bent to collect the tools. "Lots of kids get bullied." He placed them in the box and clicked the latch closed.

"Jonathan didn't know that. Wouldn't have believed a tough guy like you went through it. That meant a lot."

Tanner ran a hand through his thick hair, making the ends stand up. He shot her a rueful smile.

"You think I'm a tough guy?"

She rolled her eyes. "Please. You know what I'm saying."

He sauntered near and her skin prickled. Every time he stood close to her Claire felt as if she was a few degrees warmer than she should have been. "Let's go outside," she blurted.

They walked out, and he closed the barn door with a rattle then flipped the old-fashioned latch.

"Stars look pretty tonight," he murmured, his eyes on her.

She stared up at the brilliant lights studding

the ink-black sky. In the distance an owl hooted, and farther still she caught the faint trickle of Denton Creek. A small breeze ruffled the hair at her temples and carried the earthy smells of home.

"This is the prettiest place on earth," she said. Their strides synched up as they strolled alongside a pasture fence, back to her home and his unit.

"Don't know why you're so eager to get rid of it, then."

Her feet stopped at an old wooden wagon they kept mainly for show, a little in hopes Jonathan might play on it, too.

"I'm not eager. You think I want to lose my home?"

In the dark, his eyes turned navy, their expression considering. "Thought you wanted to be safer. Away from the animals."

"That's not it."

He peered up at the wagon then extended a hand. "Always wanted to sit up there. Would you do me the honor?"

Intrigued, she nodded. His hands spanned her waist and, as though she weighed nothing, lifted her onto the old-fashioned seat. In a bound, he joined her and toyed with the worn leather reins.

"So what is it? Really?"

She hugged her knees to her chest and gathered her thoughts. And courage. "Do you like steak?"

His brows rose. "Doesn't everybody?"

"Six weeks and five days ago, we had a barbecue."

He cocked his head and his eyes delved into hers. "Go on."

"We were talking about something on the news. Can't remember exactly. A local theft, I think. When I asked Dad if he knew the name of the guy they caught, he didn't answer. He just made this *huck huck huck* sound." She shuddered and Tanner's arm slipped around her and pulled her close. She rested her head against his chest. Listening to the sturdy drum of his heart steadied her. It helped her continue with a story she hadn't spoken out loud to anyone.

"Jonathan started laughing. He thought his grandpa was making a joke. When my father's eyes met mine, though, and I saw how scared he looked..." Her voice dried right up for a moment. Snuck down her windpipe and hid.

Tanner rubbed her arm, his strong fingers gentle on her skin. "That's horrible."

She nodded. "I've never seen my daddy afraid of anything in my life before."

"He was having a stroke," Tanner said, his words stirring the hair on her forehead.

"Turned out that way, though I thought he

was choking on the steak. He always ate it too fast. Always." Her eyes burned and her face worked as she strove to save her tears for her pillow.

She might have imagined it but she thought she felt a light kiss press against her hair. "You called 911."

"After I shooed Jonathan upstairs."

"And then what?"

"I tried saving Daddy's life. Got the steak out of his throat."

"But it didn't help."

She trembled and Tanner swept another arm around her, encircled her so she wouldn't fall into a million pieces after all. "He couldn't talk to me. I kept saying, 'Daddy. Are you all right? Daddy?' And he just stared." Her voice dropped and a choked whisper emerged. "I thought he was dying on me."

"How long before the ambulance arrived?"

"Twelve minutes. Least—that's what it said on the report. Felt like hours. All I could do was hold him. Never felt so powerless. Hopeless."

His thumbs brushed away the dampness that'd gathered beneath her eyes with an aching tenderness. "You were brave."

"I was useless," she quavered, the old futile, frustrated, panicked feeling zip-lined through her.

"You comforted him. Don't you think he

needed to see his girl at that moment? That you gave him strength to keep fighting?"

She rubbed her temples, considering. Was Tanner right? Had she made a difference? After her barrel-racing accident, she'd always felt inadequate in the face of danger, yet here was another view...

"I kept telling him to hold on."

Tanner took her face in his hands—one on her cold cheek, one under her jaw. "And he heard you. It made a difference."

Their eyes locked. "I don't ever want him going through that again."

"He won't."

"How do you know?" she exclaimed and moved away. "Those old bills prove the stress he was under. Now you're heaping on more."

"No. I'm giving him hope. Isn't that better than quitting? Being only half alive?"

"Half is better than not at all." Her mind flashed to Kevin's casket, her mother's headstone and her inert father. She squeezed her eyes shut. Wished she could blot out those memories forever.

"Ever think it's more stressful for him to lose his home? What will he have to live for then? He might give up."

She stared at him in wonder. Glanced up at the stars spinning above her, imagined the

Earth tilting like her own world. "Did he tell you that?"

"No. But I know how I'd feel."

"You've never wanted a home. Roots."

He repositioned her slipping headband and toyed with a curl. "Sometimes I wonder. When I die, who'll miss me? What will my legacy be?"

Jonathan's face flashed before her eyes and she pressed her lips closed, shaken at just how badly she suddenly wanted to tell him…though it'd destroy everything.

A strange, loaded silence descended.

"You've got your records," Claire blurted. "Awards. Plus you're rich. You could donate to charity. Have the wing of a college named after you or something."

His expression closed off and he turned away. "None of that matters."

She touched his arm. "It used to. More than me." As soon as the words slipped out, she gave herself a good solid mental kick.

"I was a fool."

"So—so—what are you saying? That you wish you hadn't become a professional bull rider? That you would have been happier staying with me?"

"Rodeo is all I'm good at," he muttered, his eyes on the rooster weather vane on the barn.

"How do you know that?"

He shrugged and she leaned around to put her face in front of his.

"Is this because of school?"

His nostrils flared. "What do you mean?"

"How you almost flunked out. Couldn't concentrate on the SAT. Go to college."

She felt him stiffen beside her and his fingers mashed each other in his lap. "So you knew about that."

A short laugh escaped her. "This is Coltrane. Besides, that didn't matter to me."

"Because I was good at bull riding."

She stared at his profile. The side of his face was calm. Eyebrows down, focused on the distant tree line. "I liked more about you than that. Remember Sam Wolkowitz?"

He turned and a crease appeared between his brows. "The little guy who mucked out the stalls?"

"I saw you helping him."

"What?"

"I'd heard his job was on the line unless he worked faster. When I saw you helping him, I knew you must have heard that rumor, too."

He stared at her intently. "I asked you out again that night."

"And that's when I finally said yes."

Tanner reeled. All this time he'd thought his skill on the back of a bull had won over hard-to-get Claire, not raking out manure with the clean-up crew. He'd believed she'd only wanted a winner and, for him, that could only mean bull riding. Now he wasn't so sure.

How much did he really know about her? He turned over her delicate hand, marveling. This wasn't the girl of his fantasies. Some remembered teenage dream. Claire had depths he'd missed when they'd dated. She frustrated the heck out of him with her stubborn temper, then laid him bare when she opened up and got vulnerable like this.

"Tanner, I should go." She tugged at her hand but he pressed a kiss to its center, seized by impulse. He wanted her in this moment...had for even longer, he admitted now.

"Please stay."

"Why?"

Truth time. "Because if you leave, I'm afraid I'll never get this moment back again."

"You? Afraid?" she scoffed, though her voice hitched.

He looked down into her lovely upturned face. "I'm never more afraid than when I'm with you."

"Oh." Her dark, wary eyes widened.

"So," he said softly, "Claire Elizabeth Shelton. Are you going to leave me here? Waste this moment?"

She studied his lower lip. "No," she breathed and leaned closer. Laid her palm on the seat between them.

"Excellent answer." He absorbed the feel of her hand against his hip. Felt suddenly joyous.

He dropped his head and kissed her. He kissed her, and it was a kiss of utter certainty, the kind of kiss during which monarchs die and whole continents fall without anyone even noticing.

She tasted like fresh picked strawberries. Drove him just as wild. At her low whimper, he brushed his lips against hers again. Soft. Gentle. The barest of touches, yet everything else went still and static and there was only the rush of his heartbeat in his ears. He wrapped her in his arms and kissed her harder so that she moaned in the back of her throat. Or was that him? He couldn't tell. Lost his bearings. Lost himself in her as she arched against him.

He traced her delicate jaw with his fingertips, giving in to every impulse he'd held back these past few days. It'd been torture working out with her every day. Laboring close enough to touch her. Keeping himself in check.

No more. Now he unleashed his feelings and gave her a blistering kiss. And she kissed him back. Every bit the firebrand who'd turned him to dust in her arms ten years ago. No one made him feel this strange mix of power and powerlessness like Claire. They commanded each other.

He wanted all of her. More of her. Every bit that she could give he would take. She clutched his shoulders and fitted herself into the angles of his body tighter still, her lips leaving his to nibble on his ear. When her finger dragged across his chest, he caught fire.

He wove his fingers in her silky curls. At last. Claire. Touching. Tasting. Holding her. It felt like coming home. And he'd stayed away too long, he realized. Needed to make up for lost time.

When her head fell back, he pressed kisses from her temple down to the arch of her neck, stopping at the sweet spot at the base of her throat. When his mouth rose to recapture hers, he held her snug, her body soft and pliant. He never wanted to let her go and his heart beat so strongly it felt as if his entire body pulsed.

A long, keening bellow sounded in the pasture behind them and Claire stiffened. When she jerked away, he released her.

Her hands drifted to her hair and touched her lips. Her unfocused gaze settled on him, then sharpened.

"This was a mistake," she gasped.

"God, I hope not," he breathed.

Her mouth worked before she sputtered, "Forget this happened."

"Sorry, sweetheart, but I don't think that's possible."

She scrambled from him. Slid the length of the seat away. "I don't mean to give you the wrong impression. But you and I. That can't work."

"Why not?"

Her eyebrows sort of twitched and knit over her beautiful eyes. "Because nothing's changed. I don't do stuff like this."

"You used to…"

"I'm not that girl anymore."

"That's up for debate."

She hopped off the wagon and peered up at him. "No. No more debating. No more kissing. I don't want Jonathan following you on his bike when you do pasture rounds. I appreciate what you did for him at Founder's Day. I do. I know you don't mean him harm, but that's the thing, Tanner. You don't mean to hurt people. You just do. Please. Leave us alone."

He crumpled inside as he saw her eyes glisten. He would never want to hurt her. Why couldn't she see that? "Not sure I can do that, darlin'."

She flung her hands skyward. "Why?" Her panicked gaze darted in a million directions before she turned and bolted home without waiting for his answer.

Claire left an aching hollow in her place.

He knew why. Because she was beautiful. And before that, because she was kind. And before that, because she was smart and bold and sassy. Because he could imagine spending the rest of his life with her without ever getting bored or restless. Because whenever he saw something new and interesting, or new and ridiculous, he always wondered what she'd have to say about it—how much they'd agree or, better yet, disagree. He liked their fights. Not the serious ones. Not the one that'd broken them apart. But challenges. Those were fun. Exciting. A thrill to see who'd come out on top...especially because, with Claire, he was never sure.

He sprang down off the wagon and trudged into the pasture, searching for the calving cow he'd heard. With Claire, uncertainty reigned.

When he got back from tomorrow's photo shoot in Oklahoma, he'd push her further.

Find out exactly how far they could go in their relationship.

But the bigger question was...could it last? If he failed to save her father's ranch, she'd never forgive him. And if he succeeded there but didn't figure out his own future, she'd never respect him as a man. If, by some miracle, he managed to accomplish both, would she take a risk on him again or repeat the same ultimatum she'd given him ten years ago? He wasn't ready to say goodbye to rodeo just yet…couldn't afford to, in any event.

Maybe the solution was within Claire. How to remind her of her old fun-loving nature? She said she'd changed, but he wasn't so sure.

He stopped a few yards away from the cow lying on its side, stomach heaving.

Everything looked normal, he thought as he circled the animal, but he'd keep checking through the night. Hoped she'd deliver before he boarded his 5 a.m. flight to Oklahoma. Eager as he was to get back to rodeo, even for a short while, he hated to hand this responsibility over to Charlie rather than see it through.

The sentiment stopped him short. Was he thinking like a rancher or a bull rider? Both took patience, hard work and passion.

The same could be said for winning a woman like Claire.

If he applied those principles to his own life would it help him to succeed outside of bull riding? To be the kind of man Claire might accept and he could live with? So far she'd opposed everything he'd suggested…all but the rodeo school. He hoped that meant she'd be okay with it, and if he succeeded in that, then anything was possible.

He glanced up at her house and caught her bedroom light wink out.

Maybe even he and Claire.

CHAPTER ELEVEN

"WHAT DO YOU mean he's not around?" Claire dropped the toast crust she'd dunked in her coffee and stared at Charlie.

He shuffled his work boots in the doorway to the kitchen before stomping inside, one strap of his coveralls slipping down his bony shoulder, strands of straw-blond hair floating around his face, a smudge of dirt on his left cheekbone.

"He told me yesterday he had rodeo business to attend to and he'd be back in a couple days. Didn't think it'd be a problem but Blossom hasn't dropped her calf yet. She's been laboring since last night." His close-set brown eyes darted between Claire and her father.

"A new calf! I want to see."

Claire caught the back of her son's jeans and halted his headlong rush out the door. "Settle down, honey. No one goes into the pastures without supervision."

He pinwheeled his arms and strained forward so that his heels lifted, his body leaning at an impossible angle. Claire hung on for dear life. Otherwise Jonathan would smash face first into the floor and crush Roxy on the way. She flushed at Charlie's raised eyebrows.

"Jonathan. Mind your mother," growled her father, and her son flopped to the floor and crossed his legs. When he threw a ball of Claire's yarn for Roxy, she didn't have the energy to stop it. Not when the meaning behind Charlie's words finally sunk in.

"Two days?"

"It's what he said. Mind if I grab a cup of coffee?"

Jonathan's worried face lifted. "Is Tanner gone for good?"

She stroked her son's hair. "No, honey." Darn Tanner for not giving her a heads-up so she could prepare Jonathan. He didn't need to have another man disappearing from his life without warning.

She looked at their hired hand. "Boots at the door, please." By the time Charlie joined them at the table, she had the steaming brew poured and cream, sugar and a spoon set beside the mug.

"Dad. Did Tanner tell you he was leaving?" As far as she knew, he'd attend his medical clearance appointment in two days. What bull riding business could he have? Or was this an excuse to get back to rodeo, even for a little while? He had to miss it. Maybe he'd decide to stay and not return to the ranch after all.

Was that why he hadn't mentioned anything after last night's kiss? Left without a goodbye? Did he suspect there was a chance he might be leaving her again? The possibility should make her happy, except it didn't. It struck her suddenly that she missed him. Had grown used to seeing him in the house…at meals…and the thought shook her.

Her father nodded a thanks to Marie when she spooned more scrambled eggs onto his plate then bustled back to the sink. "Can't remember. Suppose he must have. Seems I remember him saying something…"

"Did he say why?"

"I—I—" Her father's expression grew confused. Anxious. It tore at her.

"It's okay, Dad. I'm sure he's got a good reason."

She wouldn't let her father get upset over Tanner. Despite the changes she'd seen in him, he still thought of himself first. Considered others last.

Last night, she'd let her guard down. He'd made her feel safe. Comfortable. For the first time, she'd opened up about her father's stroke and faced her helplessness. Through Tanner's eyes she'd seen that she'd actually made a difference. It'd made her feel powerful. Maybe even a little daring. Willing to dawdle with Tanner despite the attraction she battled every day.

What's more, she'd thought he'd come to truly care for her son. Their son. Had almost told him the truth. Her hands clenched on her lap. Thank goodness she hadn't. Walking in and out of their lives on a whim would not fly in her family. She'd never let him join it, no matter how much being around him tempted her to reveal all.

"Have you called the vet?" Her father pulled a cell phone from the breast pocket of his plaid shirt and squinted at it.

After a sip, Charlie lowered his cup and nodded. "He'll be here soon, but he requested that a manager or owner be around." He helped himself to one of Marie's blueberry muffins and reached for the butter. "You know, in case there's any tough calls to make." His prominent teeth appeared and he took a massive bite.

Jonathan dashed to the window then turned. "Is something going to happen to Blossom?"

"Hope not," grumbled her father. "Had an offer on her a couple of days ago. Her and her calf. It'll pay the last of what we owe for the livestock show costs or we'll have to cancel."

After he finished chewing, Charlie nodded and grinned a smile full of crumbs. "Been selling a lot of stock, lately. Tanner's turned things around."

"Momma. I don't see Blossom," Jonathan exclaimed from the window. He opened the pane and craned his head outside.

"Her pasture's too far away."

"I'm going to check on her!"

Claire joined him at the window. Closed the sash to keep the air conditioning in. "She won't be up to visitors."

"Can't I just watch?" He put his hands together. "Please."

"No," her dad ordered in that firm voice that got results when she didn't. Jonathan slouched back to Roxy and played tug of war with a particularly expensive ball of iridescent wool. So much for the booties she'd planned to contribute to July's town-wide Secret Santa.

Her father stood, clutched the table and the color drained from his face. Heart in her mouth, Claire raced around the table and she and Marie helped him down to his seat.

"Are you okay, Dad?"

He shook his head. "I'm fine, darlin'. Woke up tired and felt a bit dizzy there. No need to fuss."

"I'm calling the doctor."

"Just need more sleep. Charlie, would you mind helping me up to bed?"

Claire tried to punch in their physician's number three times until her fingers cooperated. Her father disappeared up the stairs.

"Dr. Ogden's office," said the receptionist.

"I need to speak to the doctor immediately about my father. This is Claire Shelton."

"Is Grandpa okay?" Before she could answer, Jonathan hustled upstairs, calling, "I'm checking."

After a moment, a deep voice boomed through the speaker. "Claire. What seems to be the trouble?"

"It's my dad. He's feeling dizzy. Said he woke up tired."

"Any numbness? Slurred speech? Difficulty moving?"

"Not that I could see."

"Could be his metabolics are off. Low iron or potassium. Can you drive him in to my office? I'll have the nurse draw his blood here so we'll get the results quicker. Decide if I should admit him or not."

"We'll be there in fifteen. Thank you, doctor." She clicked off the phone, grabbed her keys and was stopped at the stairwell by a knock on the door.

"I'll get it," Marie called.

"Thanks." Claire took the steps two at a time

and found her father already tucked into bed, his lashes fluttering.

"Dr. Ogden says to come to the office now, Dad. I'll drive you."

He raised his good hand an inch above the covers and made a flicking motion before dropping it. "Just need sleep."

Was he slurring? Her heart clenched. "Dad. No." She forced her stern voice and even Roxy stopped her restless pawing at something beneath Mom's hope chest. "I'm calling an ambulance if you won't cooperate."

"But—" he blustered, and a bit of color returned to his face.

"No buts. So which do you choose?"

"Oh, hell in a handbasket, help me back up, Charlie. With all this clucking, how's a man to get some peace?"

A minute later she and Charlie maneuvered her father downstairs and stopped short at the sight of their veterinarian.

"Is everything okay?" Dr. Frank's expert eyes ran over her father then darted to her.

"Claire making a fuss is all. Won't be able to join you with Blossom," grumbled her father. "We've got her and her calf sold for a good price, so don't lose her."

"Will one of you be on the premises? Or a manager?"

Claire thought of Tanner, living it up with his rodeo buddies and swore beneath her breath. "I'm sorry, but we've got to go. Charlie will assist and I'll keep in touch via cell phone, okay?"

Dr. Frank stroked his short beard then slipped the dark-rimmed glasses he'd worn as long as she'd known him up his long nose. "I've got your number. Good luck, Martin."

Her father grumbled as she helped him to the car, eased him inside and nearly slid into the driver's seat before she remembered.

"Jonathan!"

His bright red hair appeared from behind Marie. "You're coming with me." She wouldn't risk him giving their aide the slip and joining Dr. Frank.

"Can Roxy come?"

"Marie will watch her. Please, honey, I can't wait."

"I didn't finish breakfast."

"Bring the Oreos," she temporized and slid behind the wheel with a sigh. Mother of the year, she was not.

"Spoiling that boy."

"Dad." She didn't look up from the hurried text she fired off to Dani.

He shrugged one shoulder and squinted through the windshield to watch Charlie and

Dr. Frank head to a distant pasture. "I need to be out there."

"You need to be taking care of yourself. Top priority. Number one. Why won't you understand that?"

His hand fumbled across the space and he grazed her knee in an attempted pat. "Love you, darlin'."

Her throat swelled. "I love you, too, Daddy." She laid on the horn and lowered the windows. Sticking her head out, she hollered, "Jonathan!"

The back door opened instantly and he hopped inside.

"Seatbelt."

"I want Grandpa to have this." He held out a metal object between the seats and dropped it onto her father's lap. "It's to help him be brave."

Claire put the car in gear and drove. When she flicked her eyes sideways, she nearly slammed on the brakes.

Kevin's medal.

"Honey. Where did you get that?"

"You always keep it under your pillow."

Her father studied her and her fingers tightened on the wheel. "That'll sure help. Thank you, Jonathan."

"Do you want a cookie, too, Grandpa?" A bag appeared.

"Seatbelt, Jonathan," Claire repeated, her

eyes on their long driveway but her heart with her father who'd been turning the medal over in his hand.

"It's stuck."

"Put it all the way back and pull again. Slowly."

She glanced in the rearview mirror and re-laxed when she heard the click before they turned onto the road.

"Got it," hollered Jonathan. "You still okay, Grandpa?"

"All right, son." Her father dropped his head against the headrest and when she slid her eyes his way, she noticed his lashes lowering to his cheeks.

"Don't go to sleep, Dad."

"Told you that's all I needed. Some rest."

"Let the doctor decide. Jonathan. Keep your grandfather awake."

"You got it!" He leaned as far forward as his seatbelt allowed and began singing the national anthem in her father's ear.

Despite her involuntary grin, worry gnawed inside.

Please, Dad. Please. Be okay.

Three songs and an approximate performance of Little Joe teaching sign language on their fa-vorite *Bonanza* episode later, they screeched to a halt in front of the doctor's office.

Jonathan hopped out of the car and yanked open the passenger door. He leaned across and unbuckled his grandfather. "Did I do it? Did I keep you up, Grandpa?"

Her father rubbed his temples and half his mouth lifted in a grin. "That and you gave me a whopping headache. Good work, son."

Jonathan beamed. "I'm good at being annoying. It's one of my superpowers."

"Never works on me. Always like having you around. Guess that means I'm your kryptonite."

Claire smiled to see her father's humor return and responded to Dani's anxious text with a promise to call soon. Minutes later the nurse ushered them to a room, took her father's vitals and drew three vials of blood.

"She's a vampire," Jonathan whispered in Claire's ear as the woman bustled out.

Claire kept her eyes on her pale father. "Maybe the friendly kind."

"She looks like she drinks it." Jonathan poked around the sink area, lifting the metallic lids off cotton ball holders and long Q-tips.

"Not if she's going to test it. Now come away from there."

"What am I supposed to do?" He flung himself on a stool and spun.

"Why don't you tell me about those goblins?"

her father encouraged. When he tried sitting up, she gently guided his shoulders down.

Jonathan spun again and his red curls whirled like sparks off a firecracker. "Do you believe in them, Grandpa? That's the most important part."

Her father's struggle to smile yanked at her heart.

Please don't let anything happen to him...

"I believe. Go ahead, young man."

"Once upon a time..."

Jonathan's voice droned and Claire's phone vibrated.

She squinted at her father then slipped out into the hall, leaving the door open wide enough for her to keep him in view.

"Hey, Dani."

"You didn't call me."

"Sorry. We just got settled in. Dad had his vitals taken and some blood."

"What happened?"

Claire filled her sister in on the morning's events, pacing. "The doctor thinks his metabolics are off."

A long sigh came through the phone. "I hate that I'm not there."

Claire blinked back the sudden sting of tears as she imagined having her big sis close. "I wish you were, too."

"I should just come home."

"No. Don't jeopardize your promotion. I'm holding down the fort."

"You and Tanner. It's crazy to think he's back."

"Not for long."

"And that's a good thing?"

"Dani…"

"Okay. Just checking."

It sounded as though Dani clamped her hand over the receiver and her voice grew muffled as she promised someone she'd be along in a moment. "For the love of all," she said, louder now. "One of my excursion leaders called in sick and I've got to lead this group out. Worst timing. I'll call again as soon as I can, okay?"

"Okay."

"Give Dad my love."

"I will. Love you, Dani."

"Love you, Claire."

Before she could pocket her phone it buzzed again. "Claire here."

A bleating sounded through the line and over it came Dr. Frank's urgent voice. "Claire, we've got a dystocia."

Claire turned and wandered a few steps down the hall. She lowered her voice so far she could barely hear it over her pounding heart. "This is Blossom's first calf."

"She's struggling. Or she was. Now it looks like she's given up. Went back to grazing."

"No," Claire breathed. A very bad sign. She slumped against a wall. "What's the calf's position?"

"Posterior, and she's hip-locked."

A hand touched her arm and she straightened.

"Everything all right?" asked Dr. Ogden. He'd tucked a chart under his arm and she noticed a coffee stain on his red plaid tie.

Hold it together, girl.

She let out a breath. "Just something at the ranch. Are you heading in to see my father?"

He nodded.

"I'll be right there." When he disappeared through the door, she brought the phone back to her ear.

"Claire? Are you still there?"

She pressed her forehead against the cool wall. Still here? She had to be everywhere. She needed Tanner and of course he was MIA. Anger singed her gut.

Then her head reeled.

Kevin.

She always wished for him in a crisis, and this time she'd thought of Tanner, instead. The realization unfurled like dark smoke inside her. A threat.

"I'm here, but I've got to go. Do whatever you think is best. We trust you."

"The sack's ruptured so I've got to get the calf out fast. That means a C-section."

She thought of the cost but didn't hesitate. "Like I said, make the call and we'll support it. Thanks, Doctor."

When she rejoined her family, Jonathan zipped across the floor on the stool and stopped at her feet.

"Dr. Ogden says Grandpa's heart is super fast. Like a superhero!"

She stared down at her son's beaming face and tried to hide her anguish. He shouldn't be frightened and she needed to take him out of the room, yet then she'd miss the doctor's report.

Some days she needed a clone of herself. Today, she needed two.

The nurse stuck her head in the door and waved a lollipop. "I was passing by and thought maybe a boy might be around to eat this? It's the last blue one we've got."

Jonathan bounded out the door. "Yes!"

Dr. Ogden flipped open the chart again, rested his hip on the edge of her father's bed and patted his longtime friend's hand.

"Like I was saying, your heart rate's over one hundred, but it's steady, suggesting sinus tachycardia. It's causing you that fatigue and dizziness."

Concern fluttered in Claire. A trapped moth beating. "Are you going to admit him?"

The doctor nodded slowly. "I wouldn't normally. Sinus cases are usually treated by managing the causes, like stress and overwork. But given Martin's recent stroke, it's better to be cautious."

Claire nodded and her father groaned. "I've got to get back to the ranch. A calving heifer's in trouble."

"Dad, that's the last thing you need worry about."

"We need that sale."

Dr. Ogden paused in his writing and glanced up. "Thought you were selling the ranch."

Claire sighed. "We were until Tanner Hayes came to stay. He's got my father convinced he can save it instead. Has him worked up with all kinds of new schemes."

With a snap of the chart, Dr. Ogden straightened and loomed over her father. "Martin, you're acting like a fool. After a serious stroke, you need to take it easy, like I told you. No more stress."

Claire wanted to jump up and down and yell *hallelujah*. Finally. Someone on her side.

"I'm doing just fine," rumbled her father, already sitting up and reaching for his hat.

"Your heart rate is telling you to slow down. I'm ordering bedrest for the next two days, and when you get home I want you to stop acting like a twenty-year-old."

"He's been out in the pastures with Tanner," Claire spoke up, earning her a scowl from her dad. Full-disclosure time. Dr. Ogden needed to know her father had pushed himself lately.

A *tsk* sounded from the doctor. "A smart man knows his limits, Martin."

Her dad swatted the air then scanned the floor for his shoes. "Claire. Drive me home."

She shook her head, glad the adjacent hospital would have orderlies to wheel her father over once Dr. Ogden called in the admission.

"Not happening, Dad."

"Claire," he boomed and she gave him a hug as his physician hustled out, muttering about forms.

"You have to listen to the doctor. I'm going to protect you, even if you won't do it for yourself."

His eyes lost focus for a moment and he lay back down. "If we lose that cow, Revelation won't be able to compete in the livestock show. We'll have to take Carne's low offer and it's not enough to save the ranch."

"Not worried about that."

"Tanner would be."

Jab. Right to the heart. Another reminder she wasn't the son he needed.

"Well. Tanner's at the rodeo," she said, her words as bitter as they tasted. How had he kissed her like that then left without a word?

Her father passed a shaky hand over his eyes. "He'll be back."

She opened her mouth to express her doubts and shut it. Agitating her father was petty and wrong. He needed peace.

"We'll manage, no matter what."

Her father nodded and turned away. "Tanner wouldn't leave us in the lurch. Have faith."

She thought of her life's letdowns. Toward the top of that list: Tanner. "I try."

"I know you do, darlin' and I appreciate it. There isn't anything I wouldn't do for you."

"Same here," she answered, and thought of how she needed Tanner out of their lives more than ever. Their connection last night made her deception even harder to keep. She'd run when the kiss had ended, but it'd followed her anyway and kept her up all night wondering if Tanner could be the father Jonathan needed…the partner she craved.

Yet he'd left for the rodeo without mentioning it to her. Hadn't considered her feelings. Not promising at all.

And telling Tanner meant dishonoring Kevin. Diminishing his title as Jonathan's father and the love of her life. It wasn't right.

No.

However much confessing to Tanner tempted her, she'd keep fighting the impulse, for Jonathan's good and…possibly Tanner's. She had no proof he actually wanted a son. Living on the road was his life. Not the environment in which to raise a family.

"Please check in without a fuss, Dad."

Her father's chest rose and fell. "All right, so here's the deal. I'll go on one condition."

Claire leaned forward and helped her father sit up. Finally. Rational thinking. "Anything."

"Since I'm out of commission, I want your promise to take my place. Work with Tanner to save the ranch."

She opened her mouth to object, horrified. There wasn't a chance she'd agree. But looking at her father's slack face, his concerned eyes, she nodded anyway.

It took her a moment to find her voice. "I promise."

"You won't regret it."

An orderly entered with a wheelchair and guided her father into the seat.

Oh, yes I will, she thought, and tried to hide the sinking disappointment in her gut as she trudged after them.

"TURN THIS WAY, TANNER! That's it. Just a half smile. Look like you know a juicy secret."

A camera clicked around Tanner as he leaned against a tractor manufactured by his sponsor, one boot back and resting on a wheel.

"He's so handsome," giggled a couple of young women pressed against the rope that separated the area from his gathering fans.

"Marry me, Tanner!" shouted another.

He lowered his lids and gave the camera the smirk they wanted, earning him another squeal from the crowd. The sooner he got this over with, the faster he'd get back to the ranch. Jonathan. Claire. He missed them both, he realized with a pang. Martin, too. Strange that after a day of being feted with a fancy lunch, a meet-up with the other guys in the Elite group, and now this photo shoot filled with compliments and adoration, he just wanted the comfort of home.

He froze.

Home.

As in Denton Creek Ranch?

Since when had he thought of it as home?

He pictured Claire's flushed cheeks and determined chin as she labored through yoga moves with him. Jonathan's bright eyes and nonstop pedaling to keep up with him and Guardian. Martin's stubborn spirit and tough negotiating with recent buyers.

Yes.

That felt like home.

Even more, it felt like family. Something he'd never known.

But was it enough to settle his relentless energy? Hold his focus so that he wouldn't drop the ball on the rodeo school and succeed there rather than fail?

"Can we try the black hat?" one of the stylists asked.

He doffed the white one and donned the other. The photographer pursed his lips. "Now I feel like we need a lighter shirt."

"How about no shirt?" hollered a woman in the crowd, her comment earning her an appreciative chuckle from the rest of the female audience.

"Let's try the blue one with the green circle logo," shouted the photographer. When Tanner pulled his shirt over his head, more hoots rose from the gaggle that'd hung out this entire three-hour shoot, waiting for an autograph.

Nice of them, he thought, though he wasn't as excited to meet his fans as he should be. Didn't even want to stay and watch tonight's rodeo. Being in this high-energy world filled with bright lights, ceaseless action and pumping music should ease the restlessness that made him feel like a fish out of water anywhere else. Yet for some reason, he'd felt awkward at lunch. Couldn't muster up enthusiasm about returning for good when his friends hassled him.

And he certainly had no interest in the groupies who'd dogged his steps all day. The only woman he wanted was Claire. Since last night, he hadn't stopped thinking about her or their kiss. "Tanner would you climb into the cab, but sit sideways so your legs come out of the opening?"

"Sure." He clambered up, hoping this would be the last set. "How's this?" With his elbow on his thigh, he rested his head on his hand and stared broodingly into the distance.

"Yes!" shouted the photographer, moving quickly. "Just like that, Tanner. Hold it. Relax your mouth. Now close your eyes just a little. Squint, but not hard. Yes. That's it!"

Tanner's shoulder ached as he maintained the pose. It was stiff, he'd noticed earlier. His body had gotten used to those yoga stretches. The team's trainer had advised him to keep up with daily massages. If he hadn't booked an earlier flight back to Texas, he would have fit one in here.

"All set, Tanner, thanks!"

Clay Riker sauntered over and another scream erupted from the fans. Next to Tanner, Clay had the highest ranking on the Elite Tour.

"Want to grab a drink?"

"Coffee would be better."

Clay clapped him on the back. "Meet me down in the lounge when you're done with them." He nodded at the waving fans and strolled away.

Almost an hour later, Tanner trekked below the stadium and ducked inside the large lounge. Usually it teemed with riders relaxing before their turns, but in the afternoon before a show, it stood empty.

"Looks like we got an extra dose of crazy today."

Clay shrugged and offered Tanner a mug. "Buckle bunnies. Same as always. Maybe it's you that's different."

Tanner paused mid sip, then finished his coffee and lowered the cup. "How's that?"

"Watched you at lunch. Saw how quiet you were when we started talking about upcoming events. If I didn't know you better, I'd say you don't look excited about coming back."

"That's nuts," Tanner denied automatically, defensive, though he'd been thinking the same thing all day.

"Is it?"

Tanner couldn't hold Clay's eyes and looked away. "What else am I going to do?"

"Well. There's that rodeo school me and some of the guys lent you funds for."

"Jimmy said he'll buy me out once it's running if I don't want to manage it."

At thirty-two, Jimmy Miller's stats had slipped and he didn't qualify for the Elite Tour anymore.

Logically, Tanner's best bet at stopping his financial freefall was returning to rodeo. If he missed many more competitions, his sponsor would drop him and he wouldn't be eligible to compete at the World Championships—career suicide at his age.

Yet the idea of selling the school to Jimmy, leaving the ranch, of not seeing Claire, Jonathan and Martin every day, seemed like a greater loss. They were becoming family to him. The closest to one he'd ever had. More and more he realized the importance of relationships. Another kind of success.

Clay topped off Tanner's cup and added more coffee to his own. He waved the steam away from the surface and studied his friend. "You don't look happy to be here."

"Got a lot going on back at the ranch." He thought of Blossom. He'd hated leaving the laboring cow, despite Charlie's reassurances. Martin had also promised to keep an eye on things when Tanner had mentioned the trip a few days ago. A twinge of regret pulled at his gut that he hadn't told Claire. Between her extreme reaction to the kiss and his worry over Blossom, he'd been too preoccupied to remember.

Clay passed Tanner a bag of chips. "You've got a lot going on there, period."

Tanner ignored the offering. "What are you getting at Clay?"

Clay's lips twisted as if he chewed on a secret. "Isn't that the ranch owned by the family of that gal you dated—the barrel racer? What was her name? Claire?"

Tanner shifted on the compact sofa. "That's right."

"You two were serious."

"A long time ago." He crossed his ankles and spread his arms along the top of the couch. Looked as casual as he could, though every bit of him tensed at her name...and what Clay might be implying.

Clay rested his elbows on his knees and leaned forward. "Let me see your wallet."

Tanner scowled. "Why?"

An amused gleam appeared in Clay's eyes.

"Her picture's in there isn't it? Saw it when you tried paying for lunch."

"Could be. It's a nice picture."

"She's a nice girl. The one that got away?"

Tanner dropped his arms and crossed them over his chest. "I let her go, remember?"

Clay looked sideways at Tanner. "Maybe you want her back."

"She wants no part of rodeo."

"Could be you don't, either." Clay's phone rang and he stepped outside to answer it.

Alone, Tanner thought about his alarm when the team's physician had moved up Tanner's shoulder exam, then his relief when he hadn't been cleared to return to bull riding. He had two more weeks before he'd get rechecked. It felt, strangely, like a reprieve, not a setback.

In fact, he'd gotten the most worked up over selling some of Martin's bucking bulls to the tour manager's main stock supplier. The sense of victory that followed was like winning a bull-riding competition, only more satisfying.

Then this hectic day. How he'd been eager to get through every last bit of it. Rushing. And for what? Because he wanted to get back to the ranch.

Not just out of a sense of responsibility, though that played a large part in it. Sure.

But other things factored in more and more.

Claire.

Could Clay be right?

Was rodeo no longer the right fit for him after all?

CHAPTER TWELVE

CLAIRE STOPPED AT the kitchen table, kissed Jonathan and pointed at his carrots and dip. "Eat your veggies and mind Marie, now." She returned the woman's reassuring smile before heading out to the barns.

And to Tanner.

She felt a flicker of fear that her life had spun utterly out of control.

When she'd spotted his truck after giving riding lessons, anger swiftly followed her relief, her promise to her father slamming her chest. Hard. How would she keep from spilling her secret now that she'd be working so closely with Tanner? Remembering his kiss and how easy it'd been to open up to him, gave her a strangely familiar sort of jolt, deep in her gut.

Beneath it all buzzed the undeniable anticipation that she'd see him again soon.

Jonathan dropped his grilled cheese sandwich and flung himself from the table. "I want to come!"

Roxy scooped up the contraband but halted her backward scooch at Marie's wagging finger.

"Somebody needs to be here in case the hospital calls and Marie's outside hanging laundry." Claire slid her cell phone deeper in her pocket. No need to mention she'd already spoken directly with her impatient father three times today.

The nurses wouldn't let him sleep. The grits were runny. Was Tanner back yet and was she keeping her promise?

A sigh escaped her. Of course Dad wouldn't let that last bit go…

Jonathan strained on his tiptoes to reach the wall-mounted rotary phone and grazed the handle. "I can reach it, Momma! I got taller."

His freckles stretched with his big smile. It filled her full of sunshine. Playing along, she narrowed her eyes, leaned back and rubbed her chin. Pretended to assess him when she knew darn well he'd had a growth spurt. Maybe… just maybe…he'd feel more confident when they sold the ranch and he returned to public school. Hopefully his playdate this afternoon would help.

"You've grown for sure. That's a fact."

Jonathan raced to the base of the stairwell and pressed his back against the molding. "How much?"

Roxy leaped, as if trying to join the height game. Pencil marks started low on the wooden board and climbed along its white paint.

Marie hurried over with measuring tape and Jonathan balanced on his toes.

"No cheating," Claire warned with a grin.

Before she marked the spot with her finger, she pressed down his fluff of hair. Expectant silence filled the room as he stepped away and held the bottom of the tape measure Marie ran up the wall.

"Fifty-five inches! Yes!" Jonathan strutted around the kitchen with Roxy prancing along like a member of his marching band, her bark the percussion section. "I'm going to be a giant! Tanner said he grew six inches one year, so that means I could, too."

Claire turned away and stuffed the tape measure in a drawer, guilt heavy on her shoulders. Jonathan talked about the bull rider nonstop and spent every spare minute after dinner working with him on the truck. How would Jonathan feel about her if he discovered the deception?

She steadied her hand and scribbled the number on the molding. With a flourish, she bowed elaborately. "All hail the Jolly Green Giant. May I play your golden harp?"

Jonathan shot her a superior look. "That's a cartoon on the side of the bean can," he snorted.

"The one with the harp is from 'Jack and the Beanstock' and he's way cooler...so I'll be him. You can play my harp if you promise not to sing."

"Ouch!" Claire clutched her chest dramatically and sniffed. "And here I thought you loved my singing."

Jonathan wrestled his shoelaces out of Roxy's mouth and giggled. "Only when it's in your head."

Marie laughed along with Claire, and for a moment she forgot about her nerves over the unexpected meet and greet with the customer who, according to Marie, arrived an hour ago while she'd been finishing up with her riding students. Tanner had steered him to the barns and they hadn't been seen since. Given her promise, she needed to join them, as her father would have. How would she manage to cooperate with Tanner?

As she slid on her stitched red leather boots, the screen door creaked and in walked Tanner. The moment he spotted her, his lips lifted in a smile that lit up his warm blue eyes.

It was impossible not to stare when he doffed his hat and the thick waves of his hair tumbled across his forehead and curled above his ears. Her stomach clenched with her idiotic excitement at seeing him again. How could she act professionally around Tanner when, inside, she felt like a thirteen-year-old at her first dance? Yikes.

Another man followed Tanner.

"Uncle Larry!" She threw her arms around her godfather, surprised. He wasn't a customer, was he? "I haven't seen you in months. How've you been? How's Aunt Sarah? The kids?"

The smallish man eased back and peered at her through brown, square-framed glasses that matched shaggy hair she'd never been entirely sure was real. He wore a white shirt with stitched points over each lapel and the same eagle belt buckle he'd had as long as she'd known him.

"Good. Sarah's been busy with the library. They're threatening to shut it down again. Mike's unit gets home next month and Joanie's got herself engaged."

"To the insurance agent?"

Her godfather moved closer to the air-conditioning unit and lifted his arms from his sides. "Yep. Sam. He's taking her off my hands and giving me a discount on the insurance for my crop dusters. Not sure what I'm most excited about."

Claire mock scowled at him then laughed. "That's terrible. I know you're most happy for Joanie."

He scratched the back of his ear and shrugged. "Glad not to have her gewgaws clogging up the bathroom anymore."

"What am I going to do with you? Please tell her I said congratulations. No. I'll call her. Would you like a drink? We've got sweet tea or pop."

Uncle Larry rubbed his hands together. "I'd appreciate a cola, if you got it, while we talk business. Getting hot out there."

What business did he have with her father? "Looks like a storm brewing." Claire glanced out the window at the heavy-bellied clouds blanketing the sky. She avoided the temptation to peek at Tanner again. They'd spoken when he'd called from the airport last night, but the awkwardness she felt over their kiss kept the conversation short.

"Sorry to hear about Blossom," Uncle Larry murmured once she'd ushered him into her father's office.

Her eyes rose of their own accord and settled on Tanner. His broad shoulders filled out a blue-and-white plaid shirt he'd tucked into crisp blue jeans that stretched on for days...or at least until they met his boot tips. With his thick lashes shading his eyes she couldn't read his expression. "Thanks. It's a loss. She had a lot of potential."

"She liked dandelions, too!"

Claire strode to the open door. "Have you cleaned your room, yet, Jonathan?"

He crouched down and ruffled Roxy's ears. "I will."

Claire held in a sigh. Counted to ten. Then added twenty. "It needs to be picked up before Austin comes by or no playdate." She really didn't mean the threat, but she'd been nagging him since breakfast.

"On it!" When Jonathan raced after Roxy, and passed the stairs to his room without even a pause, she gave up and turned back to the meeting.

"I didn't know we were seeing you today." She sat at her father's desk and slid the paperclips attached to a horseshoe magnet back and forth, suddenly nervous. Her father ran these meetings. Could she? Lately, it'd been Tanner. Since he stayed silent, she supposed he was testing her. Or maybe he believed in her…trusted that she could pull it off? The thought bolstered her confidence and she suppressed the smile that surged in his direction.

Her godfather glanced sideways at Tanner. "Heard you were thinking of syndicating Revelation. Remembered his sire, Pioneer, and his dam…what was her name?"

"Lady Bug, whose mother, Firefly, was a

breed champion some years back," put in Claire automatically, surprising herself. Pride filled her. She knew this ranch and its livestock better than she'd realized. Then again, why wouldn't she? It was in her DNA. Would she be the same person when she let it go? She'd never imagined herself without the ranch. Even during her years with Kevin, it'd always been her anchor.

"That's right." Uncle Larry tugged his shirt off his paunch. "I wanted to see how much shares were going for."

Tanner slid a cinnamon stick into his mouth after offering one to their guest. "We're in Houston next week. Won't know the price till we show him, but we'll keep you updated as we move through the competition rounds."

"But I thought—" Claire blurted out, then sucked back the words like a popped bubble. Tanner returned her stare steadily when she raised her eyebrows. Far as she knew, losing poor Blossom meant not going to the livestock show, not having to travel with Tanner in her father's place—too close for comfort!—and, best of all, the end of her father's fool's gold chase to save the ranch.

Though now, sitting at his desk, talking about the premium blood lines her family had worked hard to create, she understood why her father didn't want to quit. If only he hadn't had the stroke…and she'd helped him more instead of getting lost in grieving Kevin and focusing on her troubled son. Maybe they could have saved the ranch before it was too late. For the first time, she sensed that she could have managed it. Been the person he'd needed to pick up the reins when his hands couldn't hold them any longer.

"You thought it was the following week?" Tanner interjected smoothly, not missing a beat. "I always make that mistake myself. The show has a way of creeping up on you."

Claire closed her mouth and stared at the two men. She didn't want to deceive her uncle, but they weren't attending unless some other source of funds appeared. What scheme did the bull rider plan now?

Outside, lightning forked and the sky rumbled, a long, deep bass line. Chickens squawked and bulls bellowed in the distance. Her uncle scooted to the edge of his chair. Expression eager. "We never miss it. Seen you ride there the past ten years. The wife and I are big fans. Big."

Tanner half smiled and bowed his head slightly. "I appreciate that, though I'll be there as a rancher this year." His eyes zipped her way. "With Claire."

She gripped her hands fiercely beneath the desk. Days alone with Tanner? Impossible.

"Heard you was laid up. Are you coming back? Can't just hand this year's PBR championship title over to Clay Riker."

Tanner rubbed his jaw and Claire's lungs hung on to her breath. "Not planning on giving up the title, but right now I'm focused on Denton Creek."

His eyes flashed to hers and she exhaled. A curious mix of relief and frustration roiled in her gut.

Uncle Larry shifted his cinnamon stick to the side of his mouth. "Clay had some ride last night. Don't know how he held on when that exhibitor bull—Tamale—got rolling. Wildest bucking I've seen this season. That bull's a clown stabber."

"Martin's been crossbreeding some bucking bulls, too. Could be some champions in there."

"We're selling all of them," Claire declared, not liking where this conversation headed.

Tanner peered at her from beneath his lowered brows. "The ones I'm not using for my rodeo school, of course."

Her godfather whistled. Looked impressed. Missed the tension that flared between them as thick as the weather. "You're starting a rodeo school? Right here? Thought Martin was selling the ranch, but looks like you've got things right in hand. Glad to hear it. Bet Mike might be interested in signing up when he gets home."

"Just have him call and we'll get him in."

"I'm afraid that won't be necessary," put in Claire. "There won't be a rodeo school and we won't be going to the livestock show, either." She'd promised her father she'd work with Tanner but she wouldn't lie, especially to a relative.

Except for a muscle twitch in Tanner's jaw, his expression remained unflustered. Uncle Larry's head whipped between them in the tense silence.

"Claire might not be aware of the latest developments, Larry. We'll be doing both." Tanner rose and her uncle followed him out the door, leaving her to trail behind.

As they passed a loitering Jonathan, Claire gave him her firmest look and pointed up the stairs…which, of course, he ignored.

Outside, lightning cracked again. A black bird skimmed from tree to tree while the bulls in a nearby pasture crowded under their shelter. The heavy air settled around her shoulders. A whiff of rain and fresh earth floated on the misty gusts. As she watched, water began dropping into ground depressions, forming puddles and rivulets.

Uncle Larry settled his hat on his head. "Been

nice seeing you again, Claire. I'll stop by the hospital to visit your Pa next."

She bit her tongue and nodded. No sense quibbling further in front of her uncle. If he reported it to her father, he'd be stressed and think she wasn't cooperating with Tanner.

"I appreciate that. He'll be glad for the company."

After a hug, her godfather turned to Tanner. "Never thought I'd meet you in person, Mr. Hayes. A real treat. Sarah and I'll see you at the livestock show…in the cattle ring, this time."

Claire scanned Tanner's face for disappointment but, to her surprise, glimpsed pride and anticipation. He really believed he would pull this off, she marveled. Wanted Revelation to win. Was fully committed to saving the ranch. Not because he owed a favor or was passing time. He cared…about her father, her home, Jonathan and maybe even her. Joy surged and she gripped the railing.

Leaning out, she let the cool shower splash her face and douse her with reality. Until he convinced her he'd be happy without rodeo and stick around, she'd need to keep Tanner out of her heart.

Suddenly, the rain sounded harder, pelting against the roofs and surfaces, as if someone had increased the volume.

"That's hail," observed Tanner.

"And my cue to go." Uncle Larry held out a hand and Tanner shook it.

"There'll be a couple tickets to the rodeo show waiting for you at the booth. Four if you're bringing your daughter and her fiancé."

Her uncle's eyes brightened and he smiled big enough for Claire to glimpse his fillings. "I wouldn't want to put you to any trouble."

Tanner tucked his chin and shook his head slowly. "No trouble at all."

"Well then! That's kind of you. Thank you." With a wave, her godfather donned his hat and raced to a new truck. No wonder Claire hadn't recognized it.

A streak of white split the air and zapped the weathervane, spinning it. Thunder clapped overhead. Wind whipped through the trees and howled through gaps. When Tanner placed a hand beside her head, she became acutely aware of his nearness. Caught a whiff of his clean, masculine scent.

Their gazes met and clung. All Claire could see were blue eyes under dark brows, the backs of his strong hands and the way his muscles shifted under his shirt. Their passionate wagon kiss flashed in her mind and quick-stepped her heart.

She snipped that ribbon of thought before it tripped her up.

"Why did you tell my uncle we're going to the livestock show?"

"Some other funds came in." His eyes lingered on her mouth and his deep voice set the butterflies in her stomach aflutter.

She laced her fingers behind her back. With his gorgeous face this close, she wanted to trace its hard, handsome lines and touch the cleft of his strong chin. "What funds? The profit on the bucking bulls wasn't enough to cover Blossom's loss. I've seen our books. We don't have it."

"You haven't seen mine."

She ducked under his arm and backed up. "Did you put in your own money?"

"Nothing I won't get back."

"We can't be in debt to you, too."

He shrugged, his face untroubled. "Your dad said he'll comp me a bull for my rodeo school, instead. No debt."

Claire ran a hand through her hair, her fingers tangling in the swelling mass. It might as well be a sponge the way it soaked up the humidity.

"There's no school, either, Tanner. No reason to give you a bull." A twinge of regret took hold as she considered the injunction. Now that she sensed how much he cared, personally, it felt mean, but she couldn't let him bring rodeo to her home.

He hooked his thumbs in his belt loops and peered down at her. "And why's that?"

"I'm getting an injunction to stop the school. Mr. Redmond sent the papers over to the judge this week. We should have a hearing date soon."

He stared at her for a long moment before he finally nodded, his mouth in a flat line. "You've always been a strong competitor, Claire."

The hail eased and turned into sheets of water that sliced the air. "I told you this wasn't a game."

He headed for the stairs, stopped, turned and cocked an eyebrow.

"Maybe not." He slid his hat on and adjusted it over his brow. "But there's still only going to be one winner."

His confident expression left little doubt who he thought that'd be...

TANNER HALTED THE photo shoot they were doing for the ranch's website the next afternoon and flicked his hand. "A little more to the right, Martin. Jon, stop twitching." They'd been at this for over two hours. With an incessantly moving child, and a multitude of photo-op spots to get through, Tanner held on to his patience as tightly as he gripped a bucking bull.

The boy peered up at Tanner and jammed his hands in his shorts. "Can't help it."

Tanner lowered the camera and dragged his gaze off Claire. "Then hold your breath and count to ten."

Jonathan bounced until Martin put a heavy hand on the child's shoulder. "Can I count dragons?"

Tanner felt a grin come on, followed by affection. What a character. "Whatever floats your boat."

"Dragons fly." Jonathan waved a dismissive hand. "They don't ride in boats."

"How do you know? Could be they do."

Jonathan's eyes narrowed. "Have you seen one?"

"Doesn't mean it couldn't happen."

"Yes!" Jonathan squirreled under his grandfather's arm, raced around the group then skidded to a halt. "All you have to do is believe."

"Right." Tanner raised the camera again.

"Are we going to be on the internet, Momma? YouTube?"

"It's for the website, honey." Claire smoothed down her son's red hair. It swirled around his face as irrepressibly as hers, although today she'd trapped it in some kind of side bun. It revealed her delicate jaw and that long, kissable neck. In a turquoise spaghetti-strap sundress, she resembled a colorful exotic bird…bright and rare…one he'd like to capture if she didn't fly from him every chance she got.

"I want Austin to see it!"

Tanner moved the camera again and waited for the boy to twist back around. Looking at hyperactive Jonathan, that inability to focus, his energy, was like seeing himself at that age… only the boy resembled Claire, so it'd be as if he and Claire had had a—

His eyes shot between the two and something he couldn't identify broke over him like a vast, rolling wave. He'd known the timing suggested Jonathan could be his, but he'd believed Martin's story about Claire's whirlwind romance with an old boyfriend. And Claire. She was a lot of things that drove him nuts, but dishonest? The worst trait in his books. He'd asked her outright and she'd said no. She'd never keep something that important from him. Ever.

He brought the camera back up to his eye, but looked through it a little harder now. Jonathan wasn't his son, though it shook him to think how, a moment ago when he'd considered the possibility, anticipation had filled him. Did he want to be a father?

A few more snaps and he ordered the group down off the porch and out to the horse stable. Thick stripes of shadow and sunlight fell across them as they trooped through the mild afternoon. After yesterday's downpour, the day felt freshly scrubbed. Best of all, Martin had come home from the hospital this morning. So far, he'd followed his doctor's orders and let Claire take his place in helping Tanner.

Keep your friends close and your enemies closer...

Which one was Claire?

After their kiss, he'd hoped they'd rekindle their old relationship, but her surprise injunction had thrown him. Then again, that was Claire. A strong woman who pushed back hard. When he leaned left, she rolled right. Better still, she never backed down. It kept things interesting and made him want to stick around to see what she'd try next.

"Claire, would you lead a couple of horses out?"

A breeze teased a curl from her bun. "I don't want Jonathan that close to the horses."

He gritted his teeth and used the counting trick. Claire and that persistent overcautiousness...

"How about bringing them to the front of the stable, tying them up and opening the upper part of the door so we can see their heads in the shot?"

Her mouth worked and he imagined wheels

turning as she tried to figure out how to object. At last, she shrugged and turned for the stable.

"Stay back, son," Martin warned and grabbed hold of Jonathan's arm before he bolted after his mother and Roxy.

"But Guardian's in there. I could give him a bath."

"I gave him one earlier." Tanner chucked the boy under the chin and ducked inside the stable.

The cool gloom enveloped him and he paused to let his eyes adjust.

"Oh, give me a home, where the buffalo roam…"

Roxy howled along with the song and Tanner wasn't sure which "singer" was more off key.

He grinned and ambled farther inside. "Nice tune," he remarked to Claire's trim back.

She whirled and red crept up her neck and colored her cheeks. Her green eyes snapped. Cute and sassy. Just how he liked her.

"Are you spying on me?"

He spread his hands apart, palms up. Looked as innocent as possible, though his thoughts about her were anything but.

"Wanted to help. Didn't expect a concert."

Her lips twisted, and the heat faded from her eyes. "Lucky you."

"I got my money's worth."

"But you didn't pay anything…oh—" A laugh

escaped her and the sound sparkled inside him like fancy champagne. "Clever," she added, giving him a faintly saucy look.

She led Dusty out and handed him the quarter horse's reins. "Think you can handle her?" Claire's dimples appeared and his heart rate picked up steam.

Their fingers brushed when he took the strap. "She's in good hands, darlin'." He didn't take his eyes off Claire until she dropped her gaze and blushed a deeper rose.

When she returned, she led out Guardian.

"Hey, boy." Tanner stroked the horse's white star, the only other color on the mahogany stallion. Guardian nickered and blew as he nudged Tanner's pockets.

"He's looking for a treat." Claire studied Tanner. Her color had faded but her eyes still glowed. She looked so pretty in her element. He glanced around the hay-filled stalls and grew warm thinking about the stolen kisses they'd shared in the stables when they'd been dating. How much he'd like to kiss her again.

"I usually have a carrot for him," Tanner said.

Claire guided Guardian forward and he and Dusty followed.

"Apples," she said over her shoulder.

"Apples?" They stopped together at the door and secured the horses.

"That's my treat for them. I guess we're both suckers for horses." She grinned at him, her eyes wrinkling a bit in the corners, and it was so genuine and unexpected that he found himself grinning back.

"So, what do you think?"

"Huh?" He kept staring and smiling.

"Of this facial expression for the photo. You said we needed to smile more."

His mouth flattened. Right. Of course. Foolish to think her happy look had been for him… but what it'd done to his heart. It thudded hard enough to jump out of his chest.

"It'll work," he muttered and opened the door before following her out and bolting it closed.

After a dozen more shots, he promised Claire he'd put away the horses and was left to himself in the stable.

On a shelf in the back, he discovered a bag of apples and a knife. He set to cutting them.

Claire.

Her good mood today would fade once his contractors rolled in tomorrow.

The injunction, he'd discovered after talking to PBR's legal rep, could stop his rodeo school from operating if awarded. It couldn't, however, halt its construction now. He'd go ahead as planned and use the money he'd raised from his fellow bull riders and his recent sponsor contract payout.

A piece of paper wouldn't stop him. If Claire thought he'd back off because of a threat, she didn't know him at all.

Tanner led Dusty back to her stall, changed her water, added feed and held out an apple once he'd shut her stall door. Her lips whispered across his palm while Guardian neighed from the front of the barn. A few other horses stamped and whinnied, as well, smelling the treat.

The ranch needed the bull-riding school and so did he. It'd be a great additional rental income source if only Claire would conquer her fears and quit obstructing him. It drove him crazy that she'd act against her own interests... and her son's. Her anxiety was her worst enemy and he'd be her best ally if only she'd let him.

He strolled to Guardian, the horse he'd begun thinking of as his own. Just like this stallion, the ranch had transformed into a personal responsibility. It wasn't just a favor to Martin or a backup plan for his future anymore.

After giving Guardian a final pat and an apple half, Tanner headed for the other horses. He imagined Claire and Marie getting supper ready and his stomach rumbled. Like the horses, he wanted his meal but most of all he desired the company.

A family.

He'd never really had one. Maybe that's why he hadn't imagined he'd succeed with one. But now fate forced the issue and he saw things in another light.

How different Tanner's life would have been if he hadn't left for rodeo. He wouldn't wish away Kevin because that'd mean no Jonathan. However, Tanner knew now, after negotiating with buyers, organizing the rodeo school and training show cattle, that there was more to him than a good grip and a flexible back.

Winning Grand Champion with Revelation would show it. Finally, his doubts that he'd ever amount to anything without bull riding would disappear. It'd only taken Martin's call, Jonathan's admiration and his need to prove himself to Claire to make it happen.

The people you loved could bring out more in you than you thought possible.

Seeing Claire resurrected every last feeling and regret he'd had about her. It made him want to repair the dents in her life: her ranch, her truck, her son and even her. What's more, seeing her with Jonathan filled him with an unfamiliar longing. He wanted a son. More than that—he wanted to be a father…to Jonathan… as impossible and crazy as that was.

He poured the last of the horses' feed and doled out the rest of the fruit before securing the stable and heading back toward the ranch house. It was a beautiful home. Easy to see why Martin fought to keep what'd been in his family for generations.

Come hell or high water, he'd make that happen. He just needed Claire's help.

Eventually she'd come along willingly.

As Jonathan said, he just had to believe.

CHAPTER THIRTEEN

CLAIRE STRAINED TO hear Tanner's instructions over the country-rock music booming in their indoor ring. The noise accustomed the show cattle to boisterous crowds, but it'd given her a persistent headache as they'd trained this week for the upcoming livestock competition.

Cupping her hands around her mouth, she raised her voice. "Say that again?"

Tanner leaned against a rough-hewn beam, his boot's heel resting on it. With his long legs filling out worn jeans, his muscular biceps curving below the sleeves of his white T-shirt, he looked devastatingly handsome. Deep blue eyes studied her so intensely she wasn't sure it was legal to be looked at like that. Her chest started humming when he sauntered over to her and Revelation.

"He's still not setting his feet consistently." Tanner passed her a long stick and when their hands brushed she felt the shock of that touch electrify her skin for minutes after.

"Spread his front legs farther and keep his

feet even. For the rear, let's profile so the leg on your side is a couple steps ahead of the opposite one."

"Got it." When she nudged Revelation, his silky ears twitched and his dark eyes rolled back at her. Intimidating as he appeared, to her he'd always be the goofy, affectionate calf she'd bottle-fed because of his mother's mastitis. Who knew he'd grow into such a beauty? Much as she'd like to bypass her father's futile attempts to save the ranch, she rooted for the underdog bull. Once upon a time, they hadn't been sure he'd survive. Now he might become a champion. Incredible.

"Better." Tanner circled the bull, studying every angle while she held the halter.

Overall, it'd been fun fitting the cattle. Tanner taught her fast-turnaround grooming techniques they'd use if they advanced through the show's three competitions: Class. Division. Grand Champion. Helping the animals pose, walk and hold still while being examined filled her with a sense of accomplishment. She could handle this.

Tanner raised the bull's head. "That's the way a champion looks, big guy." Tanner's gaze drifted appreciatively over the animal and he skimmed its ridge line. "Great conformation."

When his hand rested beside hers on the halter, she froze. "I always loved your hands," Tanner observed. His eyes rose to hers.

"Yours, too," breathed Claire and she looked away, remembering his strong, tender grip.

Tanner moved his thumb so gently across her knuckle it was almost imperceptible. She had forgotten this: the way he made her senses explode and pulse race, as if she were properly awake after a long sleep. She had forgotten the thrill, the desire to be close, the melting sensation. How could it be possible after ten years apart and her marriage?

Tanner increased the pressure of his thumb just fractionally, and Claire pulled away before she lost all coherent thought. She ordered her galloping heart to walk...trot, at least...and forced her attention back to Revelation. "He's balanced. Bold sprung. Enough for a good score." Her voice emerged an octave higher but steady.

"And he's got a great top. With that wide chest and deep body, he's a winner." Revelation's black tail whipped at Tanner's appreciative slap on his rump.

She chewed her nail and tried not to notice how Tanner's thick dark lashes and the black ring around his vivid blue eyes made her knees weak. "He might beat his age group."

"Easily."

While Tanner examined the animal's judged areas, Claire pressed a hand to her stomach and steadied her racing nerves. At least Revelation remained placid. What great temperament and disposition. An amazing specimen. The culmination of her family's life work to cull and manipulate breeding lines to their highest quality.

Now they'd test their mettle in Houston with Revelation. Would he stay calm in a huge arena like the Houston Livestock Show? Compete well against bulls from much bigger ranches with more show ring experience? As the largest livestock competition in the country, it attracted thousands of top ranchers.

"You're looking at this year's Grand Champion." Tanner's expression exuded confidence.

"You always think you'll win, don't you?"

His lips quirked. "Until I'm proved wrong. Don't see that happening anytime soon, though, of course."

"Of course." She resisted the smile maneuvering its way around her face. "What was I thinking?" When she stroked Revelation's naturally oily hide, his muscular shoulder shifted. "Guess we'll see, right, little one?" She laughed at her slip. "I mean, 'big guy,' now."

As if in agreement, Revelation snorted and his gold nose ring wiggled.

"Mind walking for me again?" Tanner asked,

more command than question. There was something in his voice, in his gaze, in his whole being, something hungry and insistent, and it untethered her. Rekindled the passion they'd both shared once about animals…about life… about each other. Time to put some distance between them.

"Let's go, Rev."

He stepped nimbly as they circled, head high, gait smooth. Her feet sank into the newly installed AstroTurf Tanner insisted on to mimic competition conditions. Where had they'd gotten the money for it? She eyed Tanner. No doubt he'd loaned more funds, and going further into his debt didn't sit right. How could she keep justifying her secret in the face of so much generosity?

When she observed her chattering son traipse after Tanner to repair her truck each night, the urge to reveal everything clamored and rang. Blew and roared. Harder and louder than ever. Hopefully, once the show ended, he'd feel he'd helped enough, would get medical clearance and return to bull riding. She needed a cease-fire in the nonstop war waged between her conscience and her rational mind.

She met Tanner's eye and dropped her gaze at his measured look. Did he know? On some level? He'd taken such an interest in Jonathan and treated him like a son.

Please let me get through this week without slipping up.

What would life be like when Tanner left? Empty, came the immediate thought. It settled in her heart, compressing her chest.

She missed Kevin so much every day it nearly knocked her off her feet. With Tanner around, however, life swapped its sepia tone for Technicolor. She'd woken each morning lately thinking of the day ahead…with Tanner…instead of listening for echoes of her old happiness.

"Nice pass," Tanner commented as they lapped him. "But make sure that hind foot lands where that front foot takes off. Same track."

"Got it."

She adjusted her pace and kept her eyes on Revelation's feet. Amazing that he followed her so obediently given her lack of experience. Yet from the first day she'd started working with him, he'd been eager to impress. Maybe he remembered her… Animals had long memories, as did humans. Her returning feelings for Tanner proved that time hadn't let her forget him, after all.

"I didn't think I could do this," she marveled. The urge to win seized her, the adrenaline rush as powerful as it'd been in her competition days.

She'd been bold then. Daring. A risk taker. Not an over-cautious woman who put safety ahead of all else...even love.

But shouldn't love always come first?

"He must be putting on a show for you," Tanner called. He studied her beneath the brim of his hat and his whole face, she realized, had sort of opened out, all the hard-edged planes of it softening and lifting. In a heart-stopping moment, he looked like Jonathan. Same face. Identical features. Different coloring but everything else...how had no one else seen it?

Because they trust you. Would never imagine you'd lie. Even Tanner. Guilt pummeled her insides.

Tell him, whispered her conscience.

He'll break your son's heart, her mind hissed.

"Shut up!" muttered Claire.

"What?" Tanner stepped closer and a line appeared between his brows.

She smacked a hand over her mouth and shook her head. "That wasn't for you."

He shot her a teasing look. "So you talk to yourself, or was that for Lottie and Guff?"

She rolled her eyes. "Maybe it was for Guardian. You know, your self-washing horse."

He lifted his hat and cocked an eyebrow. "Touché. Guess we're both a little crazy."

At his grin, it was suddenly impossible to

stop smiling and properly hear anything he said, above this unfamiliar thrumming in her ears. "What?" she asked when his lips moved again.

"I said Revelation wants to please you. Never underestimate what a fella will do to impress a beautiful woman."

Her hand went to her tousled hair before she could stop it. Tanner thought she was beautiful.

Not that it should matter.

She flicked her gaze at him, and her heart thumped against her chest as she led Revelation around one more time.

Oh…but it did. How she wanted to kiss Tanner again.

How crucial that she didn't.

Since the ranch's website had gone live last week, they'd had a steady stream of customers interested in buying stud services, semen, calves, breeding cows, and bulls. That meant spending hours together every day. A gal could do a lot of dreaming so close to a man like Tanner. At first, she'd mostly listened as he'd negotiated, but gradually she'd begun adding her input. Better still, the more she spoke, the less Tanner intervened. Closing solid deals empowered her.

Strange how strongly she connected with the cattle aspect of the ranch now. She'd always been horse crazy growing up. Hadn't paid much attention to the cows and bulls…and now it was too late.

"That's enough for today. Good session." Tanner took hold of Revelation's halter, guided the bull into the cleaning pen and secured him.

"Thanks." Claire unfurled the hose and sprayed the gray bull through the wide-spaced metal rods. From under her curls, she sneaked glances at Tanner, simultaneously berating herself for giving in to his effect on her.

After she drenched Revelation, Tanner squirted the cleaner into the water stream and suds coated the animal from tail to head. They grabbed sponges when she shut down the water. Careful to lay her hand over the bull's ear, she scrubbed behind it then down along his heavy dewlap while Tanner lathered the back half. The music shifted to a tune she and Tanner had once danced to and she caught his eye as he smoothed the sponge over Revelation's flank.

"Tanner, win or not, we'll find a way to pay you back for the livestock show."

His hand stilled and he slowly shook his head. "No need. Like I said, your dad offered one of the bulls for my school."

Irritation rose. How could she fight a man who never accepted defeat? "It won't open."

"Guess that's up to the judge," he replied

easily, and picked up the hose again after she wrung out her sponge and stepped away.

"You don't need the income."

His eyes flicked to Revelation and he shrugged, an uneasy disjointed movement. "If you're going to keep the ranch running every bit helps."

"I couldn't handle all of this." Revelation swung his head to follow the sweep of her arm. "I'd probably fail just as much or more than Dad. Then we'd be back to square one."

"I disagree." He shot water over Revelation again and the air turned to mist. "You've got what it takes."

"I'd only stress my father more in the attempt." Despite her protests, his confidence buoyed her. He believed in her. Always had, she recalled, looking back on their rodeo days and how his cheer had been the loudest when she barrel raced.

He flipped off the water and looped the hose around its holder. "You'd make him proud." He grabbed the comb, turned it upside down and began scraping the smooth rubber edge along Revelation's soaked flanks like a squeegee.

Stung, she stepped back. "I already make him proud." For some ridiculous reason, maybe because he'd expressed her deepest darkest fear, her eyes pricked and she pressed her palms to them.

The comb clattered to the floor and strong hands gripped her shoulders and pulled her close. The heat of him emanated through his shirt and his breath stirred the fine hairs at her temple. He smelled delicious. Leather and soap, sweet hay and an honest day's work.

"Martin couldn't ask for a better daughter. I know you want the best for him. We just don't see eye-to-eye on the approach."

She nodded and rested her cheek on his shoulder. It felt good to let go. Relax. Allow someone else to—no, let *Tanner*—hold her up for a minute. His muscles shifted as his arms came round and his hands slid slowly up her back.

She lingered for a moment then forced herself to step back, her stomach constricting with longing. She had to think about Jonathan. Not let her guard down. She looked away at the sad twist of Tanner's mouth. "We'll never see eye-to-eye. On anything."

When she hunted for the oil conditioner, Tanner released a long breath, then picked up the comb and ran its teeth along Revelation's hair, back to front, all in one direction. Outside a chainsaw whined. The rodeo school. Looked as if her injunction hadn't scared him any. She studied the determined jut of his chin. Why had she thought it would? A construction crew had arrived days ago and made alarming progress. Worse, he'd mentioned someone else taking over the school's management if he left for rodeo sooner than expected.

The thought dropped into her stomach and rolled like a hot coal. She wanted him to stay. Plain and simple…though it was much more complicated than that. And impossible.

With Revelation finished, they headed outside and stopped at the sight of an approaching man. Dressed in a beige, short-sleeved shirt and cream-colored trousers, he had neatly cut, reddish hair, a longish, patrician face and pale gray eyes. He was also tall, and stooped, seemingly out of habit, since Claire knew him to be a Navy man. Submarines he'd said once. Small portals…

"Hi, Mr. Ruddell," she said, trying to keep her dismay at his sudden appearance out of her voice. Why had the ranch's prospective buyer shown up? She pinned on a smile and turned toward Tanner. "This is my father's friend Tanner."

Mr. Ruddell gazed at Tanner with narrowed eyes then turned and spat a wad of chewing tobacco. "I know who you are."

Okay. Not a fan.

"I thought you were visiting your daughter

in Colorado. How's the baby?" Claire asked brightly as she led the way across the pasture.

Her neighbor swatted the air. "Noisy. Couldn't hear myself think."

Tanner unlocked the gate and they passed through. "Nice to see you, Mr. Ruddell."

The man grunted and shot Tanner a disapproving look. "Can't say the same. Heard you were building a rodeo school on my property."

Claire's heart sank. She'd hoped he hadn't gotten word of it... Then again, with so little going on in Coltrane, Tanner's construction project had to be a major headline in the gossip chain.

Tanner slipped a cinnamon stick into his mouth and nodded as they trekked to the house. "Last I heard this land still belonged to Martin."

Mr. Ruddell sputtered. "A formality only."

Claire patted the man's liver-spotted arm. "Of course it is. And Dad's going to sign the agreement soon."

"He's had weeks!" Mr. Ruddell exploded and his voice carried loud in the early evening air.

Tanner looped an arm through Claire's and pulled her away from the agitated man. "It's a big decision," Tanner said mildly, a firm note underlying his words. "A lot to consider." They stepped along the dried mud tracks in the road that encircled the pastures.

"What's to consider? Everyone knows he's being foreclosed on in a month or so. I'll get this property either way. Buying it outright is the neighborly thing to do."

Tanner muttered beneath his breath and Claire struggled to hold her own tongue. Who'd spilled the news about the foreclosure? Her temperature rose as she recalled that Mr. Ruddell's nephew's wife worked as a loan officer. Could that have been the reason for his unexpected, low-ball offer? Claire breathed in the wildflower-scented air and watched the placid, grazing cattle, wishing she felt as peaceful as the idyllic scene appeared.

"And we appreciate it, Mr. Ruddell. We do. It's just Dad's not ready—but he will be soon." Her last words tumbled over each other, shoving to get out first in case she said something she'd regret.

A flock of chickens squawked and scattered as they neared the edge of the driveway. "I promise," Claire continued. "The property will be yours. Just give Dad another week."

The visitor stopped and rubbed his recessed chin. Above him glided birds on wind currents, hunting prey that scurried and crouched in the tall grass.

"So, what happens in a week?" he asked. Tone sharp. Suspicious.

"We're winning Grand Champion at the Houston Livestock Show with Revelation," drawled Tanner. Despite Mr. Ruddell's height, he towered over the man. "Then we'll syndicate him."

A half gasp, half laugh escaped her neighbor. "That's a lot of cash…" He pointed a bent finger. "You're trying to save the ranch."

"What if we are?" came Tanner's quiet words. She felt him tense beside her and she put a hand on his flexing arm.

"This place is mine. I've already made plans. Set things in motion."

A flicker of anger shot through Claire. No. Denton Creek was not his, yet. Amazing how hearing him say it out loud bothered her.

"Are you planning on upgrading the ranch?" Despite her growing irritation, she held on to her manners. Just. She couldn't jeopardize the sale by upsetting their crotchety neighbor. He might withdraw his offer out of spite.

The men followed her as she walked around Mr. Ruddell's truck and along the path that cut through her overflowing flower beds. Wind chimes on the porch rang and bright hummingbirds darted around glass feeders filled with rose-colored water. So pretty…and soon it'd be Mr. Ruddell's. Wistful regret filled her.

How beautiful something looked just before you lost it.

They paused at the bottom of the porch steps and Mr. Ruddell picked paint off the railing. O'Malley, the calico barn cat who came around often enough to earn a name, sat like a stone sentry in the last of the sun. "Upgrade? No. It's an overhaul." His expression turned from exasperation to eagerness as he warmed to his topic. "All of this is getting torn down. Repurposed."

Claire's heart plummeted as she followed the sweep of his arm. "You don't mean the stables." At his nod, she forced out the words. "The barns and pastures?" He nodded again and glanced away from Tanner's hard stare.

"Not the house, too," she continued, her gaze on the geranium flower boxes she and her mother had stenciled years ago. They overflowed with the traditional pink, white and red blooms she planted every year. She pictured Jonathan's height chart...gone, too.

"Yes, yes, yes," Mr. Ruddell exclaimed.

A cold tingling began in her fingers and toes. Spread right to her heart. All of the buildings and her home, gone? Just like that? She shifted on her feet and shivered. When Tanner wrapped an arm around her waist, she leaned against him, glad for his solid presence.

"What's going in their place? Are you rebuilding?" What good was a ranch without its barns? Pastures? She'd assumed he'd keep running the place from his adjoining property, an expansion, and would rent out her house.

Mr. Ruddell craned his neck and pointed to the stables. "I'm going to put the office there." He nodded to the distant show barn. "Might put the commissary there, since we've got electricity and water." He gazed up at her house and shaded his eyes at the sun's glare off the gables. "The gaming house will be built here when we tear this down. Themes. At Halloween it'll be a house of horrors. Christmas, I'll make it Santa's workshop. You know what I mean."

"'Fraid we don't, Ruddell. Elaborate," drawled Tanner. If not for his rigid body, she'd be fooled into thinking he was only mildly curious. As for her, she felt ready to explode.

A house of horrors where her grandmother gave birth to her father? A fake Santa's workshop where her mother crocheted baby clothes as gifts for needy children…a tradition Claire continued. For a moment, it seemed as if she left her body and floated over the property, watching herself nod like an idiot as Mr. Ruddell spouted on. Dani would have a fit if she heard this.

"It's going to be an RV and amusement park. I'm planning on waterslides, tubing down Denton Creek. Maybe even put in a mechanical bull...you know...to follow the tradition of the place."

"You wouldn't know tradition if it came up and bit you in the—"

Ruddell's animated expression faded and his eyes slitted. "Ain't no cause to use that tone with me, missy. Better watch those manners. Your daddy should have reined you in better."

He scrambled down a step at Tanner's sudden lunge. Backed up a few more paces as the bull rider closed the distance.

A nerve throbbed in Tanner's cheek. "Never speak to a lady that way. Got it?" His voice erupted low and menacing.

Mr. Ruddell jerked his head up and down, and beads of moisture popped out on his forehead. "Sorry, there, Claire. Got het up, I suppose."

"Lost your mind is more like."

Claire rubbed her throbbing temples. Losing her ranch was hard enough but imagining this...this mutilation? Rage whizzed banged inside her.

She joined Tanner and laced her fingers with his, needing him to anchor her as her temper spun. "Denton Creek is a working bull ranch with pedigreed animals whose bloodlines would be the envy of half of Texas."

"Half the country," muttered Tanner with an approving look that warmed her to her toes.

"I'm not buying this to keep it a ranch," sputtered Mr. Ruddell. He jingled his keys in his pocket.

Claire dug her nails into her palms. If her father wasn't napping inside, she'd let loose and scream at Mr. Ruddell. The snake. Thank goodness Jonathan had a play date at Austin's house today. "Agreed."

Mr. Ruddell's eyebrows crashed together. "So what's all the fuss then? You won't have any say once it's mine."

She stepped so close their noses nearly touched. "It won't be yours. We're not selling."

He stumbled backward then turned when he reached his truck. "I'll have it no matter what. Cheaper if I take it after it's foreclosed on, anyway."

"Don't get out your checkbook anytime soon," Claire called as the man hauled himself into his truck then revved his engine and raced back down the drive.

When she swung around, Tanner's eyes danced. He caught her hands and gripped them hard. "Claire. What did you just do?"

She swallowed her sudden fear. Pushed con-

fidence through it instead and raised her chin.
Met him eye-to-eye.

"I went all in."

CHAPTER FOURTEEN

"Ahhhhhhh! It's Tanner Hayes!"

For the fifth time since they'd unloaded the cattle and settled them in their spaces at the NRG Center where the Houston Livestock Show was held, Tanner stopped to sign autographs.

"Howdy." He gave the two couples an easy smile and scribbled his name on their outstretched programs. The lowing of cattle sounded in the long, rectangular room, the sweet smell of hay and musky dung mingling. Some ranchers labored over their entrants, combing, washing and blow-drying their cattle, while others stopped to chat with one another and size up the competition. They'd already had a lot of traffic for Revelation.

One of the men, a doughy fellow whose gut hung low and heavy over his belt, squinted down at the signature then back at Tanner. "Didn't really think it was you, but the wife insisted."

His diminutive spouse nodded vigorously, her head no higher than her husband's shoulder. "I knew it the moment we entered the barn. We're your biggest fans."

"Thank you." With his cattle past due for feeding, he hefted a grain bag, hoping they'd take the hint and skedaddle. "Much appreciated. Enjoy the show tonight."

"Shame you're not in it," sighed a middle-aged lady wearing a jade and silver necklace and matching teal boots. She'd joined the growing crowd around him. "We were hoping to see you ride."

Tanner opened his mouth to agree but couldn't lie. Strange. He'd been to this show for years as a bull rider. He should be itching to get back in the ring. Yet he'd been just as happy in the barns hustling to get Revelation and the cows show-ready.

"Soon," he assured them, though his heart wasn't in it. Life on the road had lost its luster compared to his days at the ranch. To his surprise, he liked having daily routines. Had been successful at them instead of restless and unfocused. Instead of grabbing burgers at diners, he liked lingering over meals with a family that felt like his own and Claire...well...he fell for her more every day.

Whenever he recalled her spitfire reaction to Mr. Ruddell, he grinned. The way she'd chased the opportunist off her land...seeing her defend what was hers…it reminded him of the bull-headed woman who'd captured his heart long ago and never given it back. In fact, if anything, she held it tighter now than ever. How could he leave her again?

Then again, what choice did he have? Given the ease of movement her yoga sessions had restored to his arm, he'd be medically cleared to ride in a week. Did he risk giving up his career for her when he didn't even know her feelings? Before they left the livestock show, he'd find out where they stood. Would woo her and charm her until she gave him the answer he wanted.

A well-dressed, gray-haired man stepped forward. "Hey, Tanner. Would you have a minute for me?"

Tanner's gut clenched. His agent. Tanner had been letting his representative's recent messages go to voice mail. "Hi, Mike. Good to see you. Let's talk once I've fed and groomed the cattle. We're showing in an hour."

"Wondered why he was here," mumbled the hefty fan to his wife. He turned back to Tanner. "Didn't know you were a rancher, too."

Once again Tanner's tongue swelled and blocked a false denial. He felt like a rancher. Wanted to be one, he realized with a jolt. He saw the livestock show through different eyes now and liked this view better.

Mike clapped Tanner on the back. "Tanner's just helping out a friend. He'll be back on the Elite Tour soon."

A short teenage boy grinned wide and stared, star-struck, at Tanner. He gave the kid an encouraging smile. Once upon a time, that'd been him. Dreaming big. Not realizing that achieving what you wanted and having what you needed were two different things altogether.

Claire pushed through the small group, handed him a coffee and looked around in surprise. "Y'all here to see our Brahman, Revelation?"

A man with clipped brown hair and piercing hazel eyes stepped forward. "I am. That's a fine bull you got there. Any offers on him, yet?"

"One." Claire shoved a clump of red curls behind her ear and widened her stance. Tanner loved seeing her growing confidence lately. She'd transformed from the overcautious woman who'd warned him off the ranch weeks ago. "We expect more once we start competing."

"Tanner, I'd like a word," insisted Mike. He tapped his cell phone against his thigh.

"You'll have it," Tanner assured him, though he stepped closer to the potential buyer as the rodeo fans waved goodbye and melted away. "Are you interested in making an offer? We're looking for investors rather than an outright sale."

The older man nodded slowly, his eyes running over the bull. "Could be. I'm looking to improve my herd, but perhaps a stake in this one and rights to his offspring would do nicely." He extended a hand to Tanner then Claire. "Stanley Kroenke."

Claire's wide green eyes swerved from Tanner to the well-known billionaire. "You just bought the Broken O," she breathed, impressed.

The man nodded, his chin low and humble. "Montana's beautiful country."

"Tanner," broke in Mike. He shrugged out of his suit jacket and folded it over his arm. "I have another meeting in fifteen."

Tanner glanced between Claire and the potential buyer. Saw dollar signs. Wanted to stay. Funny that he felt more invested in this transaction than talking about his own career.

"I'm sure we'll talk later as the day goes on, Mr. Kroenke."

The man eyed Revelation who, standing majestically in a sunbeam, looked every inch the champion. "This one could go all the way. I'll be watching."

"That'd be an honor. I'll be back shortly, Claire." Tanner tipped his hat and reluctantly followed his agent through the barn's exit.

Outside was a full-on assault of the senses. Shoulder-to-shoulder crowds meandered down thoroughfares of ranching supply vendors, technology exhibits and clothing outfitters. The smell of fried food, sweat and leather permeated the thick air, still humid after this morning's shower. Overhead, clouds hung low and heavy, prompting some of the smaller artisans to raise their awnings over displays of hand-crafted stone and silver jewelry, belt buckles, boots and cowboy hats.

In the distance, a young man hooted and hung on as a mechanical bull whipped him in faster and faster circles. Behind him, a neon marquee attached to the large stadium listed nightly concerts by top country music stars. Maybe he'd convince Claire to step out with him tonight. Since Martin's doctor hadn't approved the trip and Jonathan had stayed home, she was free… and his for the night. A thrill shot through him.

Mike stopped in front of a churro vending truck, plunked his briefcase down on a plastic table and gestured for Tanner to sit.

"How many do you want?" the agent called over his shoulder as he joined the short line.

"Two. Chocolate sauce."

Mike nodded without looking back then stepped to the window. In a moment, he'd returned with the food and two colas.

Tanner popped the can top, releasing a chemical fizz, then drank. Phew. He'd been more parched than he realized and, now that he thought on it, hadn't stopped working since he and Claire had arrived hours ago. He wondered how she was doing with Mr. Kroenke. The big wheeler and dealer had a reputation for tough but fair bargaining, and seeing Claire in action this week proved she was more than up for the challenge.

"Did you hear me?"

Tanner swallowed his bite of churro and blinked at his agent. "Must have blanked for a minute. Say that again."

When some nearby eaters began to point at Tanner and shove back their chairs, Mike waved them away with an uncharacteristic scowl. The guy usually oozed charm but today he looked flat-out irritated.

"I want to know if you're passing next week's medical exam." Mike sipped his soda but left his churro in its wax wrapper.

Tanner nodded slowly. "Guaranteed." His body might be ready to leave but his heart sure wasn't. He wanted to spend more time with Claire and Jonathan.

Mike's shoulders lowered and he picked up the fried dough stick. "That's what I needed to hear." After an enormous bite, he sat back in his chair and stretched his legs, chewing. He pointed the rest of the churro at Tanner. "You'll come back week after next. We'll be in Tulsa."

Tanner nodded absently and studied a young boy and his father as they stopped by a tractor. At the salesman's smiling nod, the boy clamored inside the Plexiglas cab and his father rested a foot on the runner, his face beaming. It did something funny to Tanner's heart. Made him wish he had a son. Jonathan. Before spending time with the boy, Tanner had never imagined he'd be any good at fatherhood. He'd never had one himself—what did he know about being a dad? Yet being around Jonathan felt easy. Natural. Right.

The same could be said for Claire. They had to win Grand Champion today. Get high-rollers like Mr. Kroenke to invest in Revelation. Build their reputation so that they'd not only stop the foreclosure, they'd make the ranch profitable again. Keep it out of Mr. Ruddell's hands so Tanner could contribute with the rodeo school rent.

Tulsa? Who cared about that?

Not him, he realized. Time to stop doubting himself. Using rodeo as a crutch. He could walk just as tall without it. Wanted to march straight into Claire's arms and never let go.

"I'll see you at the rodeo show tonight."

Tanner scooped out more chocolate and took another bite of his churro. Amazing how little the rodeo interested him. "Got other plans," he said after a moment, his mind on Claire. Hopefully they'd be celebrating Revelation's win. A new future for the ranch. A future for themselves, too, if he played his cards right.

Mike stared at him over the rim of his soda can then lowered it. "What's wrong, Tanner?"

Tanner sopped up the speck of chocolate he'd dripped on the round table. "It's more like what I need to make right."

"You're a three-time world champion. Not sure what more you could do right except win this year…but if you don't get back on the road, you won't be eligible to compete."

Tanner shrugged. It felt so far from what concerned him lately.

Mike stared at Tanner for a long moment. "How many years have we been doing this together?"

He breathed deep. Mike knew him too well. "Ten years."

His agent picked up his vibrating phone and clicked it off without taking his eyes from Tanner. "You've never let me down."

"That might be about to change."

Mike cocked his head and his gaze grew sharp. "Are you coming to Tulsa?"

A million thoughts flashed through Tanner's mind, too fast to stop on any except Claire.

"No."

Mike sighed heavily. "You'll lose your endorsement deal."

"I know."

"It'll mean some tough negotiating to convince another sponsor that you're reliable. Not too hurt or impaired given your age." Mike ran a hand over his head, leaving spikes of hair in its wake. "But you're the world champion. I'll make it happen. If you need more time, then take it. It's risky, but you always come out on top."

"I don't need more time." Tanner flicked the can tab back and forth until it broke off. He tossed it onto his churro wrapper.

Mike leaned forward. Elbows on the table. "What do you need? Anything and you've got it."

"I want out." The finality of Tanner's admission shocked them both into silence. Had he really quit bull riding? Looking at Mike's dismayed face, it seemed he had. He waited for panic to set in. Instead he felt lighter. Glad.

There was every chance Revelation would lose tomorrow. A strong possibility the ranch and his shot at the rodeo school would be gone. Claire might not ever forgive him and his imagined happiness could vanish. This wasn't a sure thing. Not like rodeo. But he wanted to take the gamble.

Mike clamped a hand on Tanner's arm as he stood to leave. "What are you doing?"

Tanner gazed at the cattle barn and imagined Claire. Felt himself already working beside her. Sharing a purpose, a common cause that could lead to so much more...

"I'm going all in."

CHAPTER FIFTEEN

"ME?" CLAIRE BLINKED up at Tanner as he led Revelation along the rubber mat walkway toward the show ring. Despite his confident nod, he hadn't relaxed since they'd met in the motel lobby at 4:00 a.m. this morning and raced to the NRG Center to groom Revelation. It was obvious in his intermittently tightened jaw and the way his knuckles showed white on the halter.

He shot her a sideways glance. "He trusts you. Walks and poses better by your side. You're good at this, Claire. Believe it."

Tanner couldn't be serious. With everything riding on this win, they needed an experienced bull handler, like Tanner, to lead Revelation. Not her. But when she glimpsed Tanner's attempted grin, she couldn't help smiling back despite the fear fluttering in her stomach. In a pressed denim shirt tucked into jeans so new they could have walked without him, he cut a handsome figure. If she wasn't so focused on Revelation, she'd give some of the staring ladies a good glare.

"I'll try," Claire ventured. Somewhere in the back of her head a little bell began to chime. She'd started to trust Tanner again this week. Today would be the ultimate test.

They passed cattle, secured in designated areas that stomped and shifted as their owners combed and sprayed them. While yesterday the atmosphere had felt expectant, now a thrum of tension pulsed through the building as competitors labored feverishly over their animals. Above them, television monitors dangling from the rafters broadcast the class competition before Revelation's age group. Her heart lurched as she peered anxiously at judges in navy coats and tan slacks circling the contenders. What would they think of Revelation? Of her?

Fans, attached to the metal bars separating the animals, whirred warm air scented with molasses from open feed bags. Revelation's feet landed evenly on the soft surface and Tanner took care to keep him off the sawdust floor. When the bull's velvet side brushed her arm, her nerves settled a bit.

Now that she'd chased off Mr. Ruddell, they had to win this crucial first challenge: three-year-olds born in Revelation's birth month. To keep the ranch viable long-term, however, Revelation would need to outperform every other bull in this entire show, advancing through eight hours of grueling contests. Impossible…but he couldn't command a high enough offer from investors otherwise.

The same was true of the cows Charlie showed. Luckily he'd come along or they couldn't have focused on their all-important stud. She patted Revelation's freshly combed side and he angled his neck back at her.

"Don't be nervous, Rev," she murmured and the bull blew and picked up his pace. Her heart rate sped, too. "He's nervous, Tanner."

Tanner tilted back his white cowboy hat and his deep blue eyes leveled with hers. "He'll sense your mood, so stay calm. You've both trained for this. Just imagine it's another day back home."

She swallowed down the nerves gathering in the back of her throat as she spotted the show ring's entrance. How convenient to have it located inside the Center. No going outside. No bolting for their trailer and heading home, tails between their legs as she secretly wished. Nope. She had to stay strong. Deep breath in through the nose. Long exhale through the mouth. In. Out. In. Out.

Her father didn't know she'd shot down their only definite chance at avoiding foreclosure, though Dani had been encouraging when Claire confided in her. What would their father think if she came home, defeated, having lost the competition and any chance at saving the ranch? Her heart squeezed as she imagined his saddened face. She couldn't let that happen. What's more, after Mr. Ruddell's odious visit, she didn't want to lose the ranch, either. Would fight for it.

Her shoulders squared and she pictured herself twelve years ago, raring to raise heck on a barrel-racing course. She'd never been afraid then. Couldn't let fear control her now. Not with everything riding on this moment. Time to throw caution to the wind and see where it took her. Hopefully back to a home they'd never be in danger of losing again.

Working with Tanner proved she could manage the ranch without causing her father stress. Better yet, she'd give him peace and happiness in his final years and Jonathan his legacy, a home he'd started enjoying with Tanner. Would that continue when the bull rider left? If she told him the truth about his son, would he come around more, for their boy's sake?

She gave herself a mental shake. Manipulating a man that way was never her style. Still, wasn't that really Tanner's call to make? Given all of the changes she'd seen in him, shouldn't she have more faith that he'd do right by his son…even if he never forgave her for the secret? She shivered, imagining his disappointment in her…losing his trust and good opinion. Before it hadn't mattered, but now, it hurt to think that her reawakening feelings for him would never be returned if…when…he knew all.

As they neared the entrance, other three-year-olds fell in line with their owners. A few of the ranchers slid assessing sidelong glances at Revelation, and she met their stares dead on. Lots of good-looking cattle competed today and Revelation was one of them. He had a decent chance. Had just as much right to be here as any of the big-shot ranchers jockeying for a better entry position. She had to trust Tanner. Believe.

"Where y'all from?" asked a man wearing a ten-gallon hat and a belt buckle emblazoned with "2015 Houston Grand Champion." His face centered too closely around his nose, as if someone had squashed it all together, and his small eyes, beetles under bushes, darted over Revelation as his massive Brahman jerked at its halter.

"Denton Creek Ranch in Coltrane. You?" Claire asked, though she knew exactly who he was. Had watched several news stories about how he and his wife, college graduates with degrees in Animal Science, had used their education to genetically engineer one of the most formidable Brahman herds in the country.

His eyebrows rose and disappeared beneath his hat brim. "I'm Jerry Armstrong Jr., from

Diamond A." He gestured behind him and a middle-aged woman with short aubergine-colored hair joined them. "This is my wife Julie."

Tanner extended a hand as did Claire.

"Looks like our Tempest's got some competition," murmured Julie between bites of an egg sandwich, her gaze trailing over Revelation.

"Lots of nice-looking bulls here, today," Tanner said modestly. "Should be a good matchup." He gripped Claire's hand when she began tapping it against her thigh.

Jerry pulled off his hat and scratched his receding hairline. "Heard of Denton Creek back when we was at university. Isn't that right, darlin'?"

Julie polished off her sandwich and dabbed at her lips as they waited for the bulls from the previous competition to file out. She gazed up at the monitors and nodded absently. "Used to be a respected name in Texas. Haven't heard much from y'all in decades."

Claire's fingers clenched around Tanner's and he winced. "My family's faced some troubles but that's behind us now." At least, she hoped so. God, she hoped so.

Julie patted Claire's shoulder and her red lips pursed. "Well bless your hearts for coming out and trying today." When the bottleneck cleared, they cut ahead of Revelation. "Good luck," she called over her shoulder and disappeared inside with her bull.

Tanner squinted after the couple. "Don't let them get under your skin."

She put her hands into her pockets, took them out again, smoothed her hair, and sighed. "Right." The inside of her mouth felt as if it was covered in powder.

He cupped her shoulders and leaned his head into hers. He felt big and solid and smelled of cinnamon and man. "You've got this."

"I don't have a choice."

Tanner's grin appeared, the sun erasing an overcast day. "No sense worrying about what you can't change."

"Easy for you to say," she muttered.

When a spot opened up, they filed inside the two-story arena. US, state and regional flags dangled from rafters above a long metal railing that ran through the center of the AstroTurf-covered, football-stadium-sized show ring. Spectators pointed and chattered from the packed, ten-tier stands as the competitors led their animals farther inside.

Noise swelled and echoed in the lofted space. Luckily it wasn't much louder than the music Tanner had blared when they'd been training. Revelation didn't miss a step as he lifted his head and walked easily, his muscles shifting with impressive strength and grace. He looked like a champion. Would the judges agree? Acid burned her esophagus. They had to.

They just had to.

A mustached man wearing large round glasses caught Claire's eye and she returned his nod. Bill Sanchez, the Carne Incorporado representative. Alongside him sat Rick Ortis. He leaned forward, knees jiggling, as his eyes darted along the cattle lineup and lingered on Tempest. How many bulls would they offer on today and would Revelation still be one of them? Amazing that just weeks ago she'd wanted to chase them off her land and now she pleaded with them, mentally, to invest in her bull.

Another man, tall and distinguished in an expensive suit, stood behind the partition. When he swept off his hat and bowed slightly with a smile, she recognized Mr. Kroenke. She forced her cheeriest smile in return. Another would-be investor. High stakes. She flicked her eyes sideways to where Tanner stood, tapping his knee, and guessed that he was thinking the same thing.

A livestock committee volunteer wearing a brown suede vest pointed to his left and she took her spot beside the Armstrongs. When all the animals lined up, an announcer climbed on a dais and brought a bullhorn to his mouth.

"Welcome, folks. The Brahman Class Ten is ready to start. Looks like an impressive group. Let's start off with our first lap around the ring."

Claire's heart nearly sprang from her chest. She shook her head, eyes darting. "I ca—"

Tanner pressed a finger to her mouth and his expression softened and grew tender. "You can."

A shaky breath escaped her. "I'm going to throw up."

"You're going to win." He nodded as Jerry Armstrong pulled Tempest out of position and began walking. "Go on and get it, girl." He handed her the stick and she flushed, remembering the familiar words he'd always used before she barrel raced.

She stepped off on the wrong foot, corrected herself and started again, Revelation striding beside her. Hopefully the judges hadn't seen that. Luckily her bull didn't react. If anything, he seemed to be performing better than ever, responding to the cheering crowd with a flexible front line and a raised head as he moved seamlessly around the ring. Unfortunately, Tempest looked just as impressive.

Mr. Kroenke tipped his hat as she passed him and she nodded politely without taking her focus off Revelation. A man in a brown suit paced alongside the moving cattle line, his expert eyes assessing one bull after the other. The senior judge. Claire looked dead ahead. Tried not to let him rattle her.

The bullhorn blared again. "All bulls line up."

She brought Revelation back to his spot, set his feet and back legs and held her breath. Tanner gave her a thumbs-up and the numbness in her fingers receded. Navy-jacketed young men and women strode along the line with clipboards, marking up pages with each bull's name. The senior judge started at the far end and examined each bull. Claire gazed at Revelation, willing him to stand still for so long. To be patient. Wished the same for herself since it took every ounce of willpower not to fidget.

At last the man approached Revelation, nodded briskly at her and set to work. He ran his hands along her bull as Tanner had, the judge's impassive face giving nothing away. When he straightened, he turned without a backward glance.

Bad. This looked very bad. She pressed her trembling lips together when she caught Jerry's smug smile at his wife. He looked as if he had this in the bag with a bow on top. Or a ribbon.

One of the junior judges handed a clipboard to the announcer who peered at it then spoke into the bullhorn again. "Let's have entries 5,

11, 13, 19 and 20 go around one more time. Everyone else, please hold your cattle in the middle, thank you."

Claire watched as owners proudly pulled their chosen bulls out of position, numb. So that was it. Competition over.

"Claire," hissed Tanner from the sidelines. He waved her on, as if shooing a midge fly. "Go!"

"What?" She glanced around, watched Tempest's hindquarters step neatly away as she caught sight of his number badge. Nineteen. And if he was nineteen then she was…

Ah! Late. In all her worrying she'd lost track of her entry number.

Heart racing, she forced a slow pace and brought Revelation around for a second lap. Luckily, he responded quickly when she tugged and they were only a step behind the other finalists. The Carne reps stood now, their heads close as they gestured at Revelation and Tempest. Mr. Kroenke beamed when she passed him again, his excitement so infectious she gave him a genuine smile. Yes. Revelation was getting the attention he deserved, but would he win? She eyed Tempest's long body. Hard to say. Depended on what the judge preferred she supposed. Hopefully it was Revelation.

"Numbers nineteen and twenty, please step

into the center and hold for a final look. Thank you."

She shot Tanner an astonished glance and his eyes lit up. Excitement bubbled inside as she led Revelation to stand beside the Armstrong's bull. When Jerry peered over at her, his face decidedly less friendly now, she mouthed "Good luck," for the fun of it. What did she have to lose? Everything, she thought wildly. But as Tanner said, she couldn't change it now.

The senior judge stepped close and circled each bull. Tempest stood as still as a statue while Revelation looked around. Luckily he didn't pull her. Would his movement lose him too many points? Her clammy hands slid on the halter and she tightened her grip.

The judge stepped in front of both, his head see-sawing back and forth before he pointed at Revelation then held up his index finger.

"And the winner of Class Ten, Age Three, Month January is Claire Shelton with Revelation from Denton Creek Ranch in Coltrane, Texas. Let's give them a round of applause, folks."

The crowd cheered and a hearty whoop erupted from Tanner who grabbed a fistful of air and grinned wide at her.

She'd won.

Revelation was number one.

They'd done it. He'd done it. They could start

thinking about the next competition, all three-year-olds, but she'd worry about that later. For now she'd revel in this moment, then call Dad and Dani. How good it felt to compete again. She rubbed Revelation's nose and he butted her armpit.

"You did it, little one," she whispered, heart full. How many nights had she sat up with the once frail calf, worried if she went to sleep she'd wake up and he'd be gone? Now, here he stood. Magnificent. Awe-inspiring. Victorious.

"Congratulations," murmured the Armstrongs graciously as they moved off and left her and Revelation in the ring alone. The judge pinned a gold-colored ribbon to Revelation's halter.

"Good work showing the Brahman," the man said. "He handles himself well in terms of his lower and center rib shape. Great foot shape and size as he comes down and meets the surface, too. Keep it up. This one could go far today."

His words set her aglow. When she led Revelation out of the arena, Tanner jogged up beside her and squeezed her waist.

"Knew you'd do it."

"I can't believe it," she gasped, her voice full of air.

"Couldn't be prouder of you or this guy." He scratched the top of Revelation's head as the bull walked sedately back to the washing station. They'd need to groom him fast to get ready for the division competition.

"Folks. A word!" Bill Sanchez strode their way and extended a hand. They paused on the walkway as Rick Ortis joined them. "Congratulations. I knew Revelation was a champion."

Tanner tipped his head. "Thank you."

Bill pulled out a cigar and offered one to Tanner.

He frowned. "No smoking in the barns."

With an embarrassed shake of his head, Bill pocketed the cigar. "Of course. Guess I got excited for our bull, here."

"Are you saying you're investing in him? Offering the price Martin named?"

Rick waved his hat in front of his flushed face. "That's a little rich for our blood, but we're willing to come up some."

Tanner nodded, took hold of the halter and began leading Revelation away. "Stop by when we win Grand Champion. Let me know what you can afford then."

Claire peeped over her shoulder at the open-mouthed men, their shocked expressions almost comical.

"Shouldn't we have heard what it was?"

Tanner shrugged. "Nope. We'll do better."

"How can you be sure? Whatever they're offering will help."

"I'm not looking for help. I'm looking to win." He shot her his ready-for-anything grin and winked, looking cocky, masculine and head-rush gorgeous. "You and Revelation are unstoppable."

She studied him, wildly attracted to that super-confident attitude that let him ride the meanest, most dangerous bulls in the world without a care. After her accident, she'd blamed that risk-taking, reckless side of him for urging her to ride the ill-behaved horse that'd nearly killed her. Now, however, she realized that playing it safe would never have given them this shot to save her ranch and family.

She'd been wrong about so much. Especially Tanner.

He was right. Why worry about what she couldn't change? Some things were meant to happen. She glanced at his rugged profile as he turned to acknowledge Mr. Kroenke's hurried congratulations. Another suited man tapped his watch and gave the billionaire a significant look.

After his promise to speak to them later, they waited in line at the washing area. The Armstrongs passed them again with another Brahman, bigger and more muscular than Tempest... if that was possible.

"This is our two-year-old," called Julie with a wave. "Maybe we'll meet up again for the Grand Champion round."

Claire wanted to say something, but her voice had temporarily disappeared. That big and only two? Another strong competitor. And hundreds of them ahead to defeat.

While she fumbled for a comeback, Tanner's lips curled in an easy, unconcerned smile that looked more intimidating than a scowl somehow. "Looking forward to it, ma'am."

Jerry's face fell and he hurried after his wife.

They led Revelation inside when a spot freed up and secured him. "We can't beat them," Claire mused, watching the Armstrongs' graceful animal as he disappeared into the ring.

Tanner picked up the hose. "You got that backwards, darlin'. They can't beat us."

Claire studied him. "I don't have a fallback plan like you. If I lose, it's everything."

Tanner sprayed Revelation from back to front, his eyes on the bull. "We're in this together."

A shaky breath escaped her as she spritzed the cleanser into the stream. What would she do without Tanner and his unshakable faith? She hated thinking of the upcoming day when she'd find out. "Thank you, Tanner."

He put down the nozzle and handed her a

sponge, his expression so sincere it undid her. "No thanks needed. I want this, too."

"I don't understand why that'd be," she exclaimed, her hand scrubbing, mind working twice as fast. "My father was good to you, but we didn't part on the best of terms. No need to go this far to pitch in."

"Martin isn't the only one I want to help." He looked at her. His eyes were exhausted and stubble was starting to show through on his chin. It made him seem curiously vulnerable.

"And you have, Tanner." Revelation stepped sideways as she rubbed his shoulder and she looked down, hiding the tears that sprang beneath her lashes. "The difference you made with my dad. Jonathan…even me, though I didn't appreciate it…" When she peered up and met his steady gaze, she couldn't look away.

She felt simultaneously distant from everything around her and acutely aware of the smallest thing. Like his hands. And his chin dimple. And the way faint creases appeared at the corners of his eyes when he smiled. The last vestiges of her antagonism toward him evaporated and love rushed in to fill the space. Even though she'd thought she'd covered her heart with a permanent porcelain shell, Tanner still found a way to chip through it.

As much as she'd loved Kevin, she'd always

loved Tanner, too. Her feelings for the bull rider, however, had changed. Matured. She could feel it, the way it seemed to have twisted itself into shapes she had never felt before. Could he come to care about her again, too? And if so, would he stay with her this time? Not leave her for rodeo?

"You've done so much for us when you've had nothing to gain."

That uncomfortable expression from yesterday crossed his face again and he bent down to wash Revelation's feet. "There's something I need to tell you, Claire. Tonight. After we're done, will you go out with me?"

At his urgent tone, her heart sped. Would he say he loved her, too?

Hope fizzed inside and her lips quirked. "It's a mighty tempting offer."

He kept his face lowered but his eyes rolled up to hers, amusement and a little insecurity tucked into the corners. He let out a breath. "Is that a yes or a no?"

Her brow arched and she dimpled at him. "I'll take it under consideration. Let you know after the competitions."

He tossed his sponge at her and laughed. Did he sound relieved? "Then get going, woman. We've got a Grand Championship to win."

She set to work, but sneaked glances at him. Tanner had spent every moment with her since they'd arrived and hadn't hung out with his rodeo buddies. In fact, he'd even hurried through fan interruptions to get back to Revelation…to help her. Years ago, she'd thought he'd shattered her life forever, and now here he stood, strong and steady beside her, putting back the pieces after all.

And suddenly she knew. Win or lose, something good would come out of all this.

She'd tell him about Jonathan.

Her pulse sputtered. It could be the end of whatever was developing between them, but she had to take that chance.

His bright eyes caught hers and she flushed. Maybe. Somehow. Could it be a new beginning?

There was only one way to know.

CHAPTER SIXTEEN

"SEVENTY-FIVE THOUSAND DOLLARS!" crowed Claire as they pushed against the tide of rodeo goers and headed, instead, toward a white lattice-work bandstand. Beneath it, a banjo player crouched over his instrument, fingers a blur, notes cascading into the night air that thrummed with electric anticipation. Reba McEntire headlined tonight, as did Tanner's former Elite Tour group...not that he cared much to see, either.

Instead, he kept stealing glances at Claire, noting tiny details. The familiar shape of her hands as she gestured excitedly. Her expressive eyebrows. The way she stood on her tiptoes when she wanted to emphasize her point.

After their tough negotiations today, she couldn't have risen higher in his estimation. Together they'd secured enough funding to stop the foreclosure and forged lasting business connections that'd keep the ranch on solid ground.

"For almost half interest in this year's Grand Champion, I'd say that's not half bad."

"Half bad?" she scoffed and nudged his shoulder with hers. When she smiled up at him, he felt his heart swell against the inside of his chest. "If you'd seen Revelation as a calf, you'd be more amazed."

Tanner forced a casual nod though his body hummed. Standing this close to Claire short-circuited him. "I think Kroenke could have gone to a hundred."

Her mouth twisted sideways and she shot him a skeptical look. With her long red hair twining around her beautiful face and shoulders, a blue sundress gathered tight at her small waist, she took his breath away.

"Incorporado sure wouldn't." An unladylike snort escaped her and he chuckled, recalling the blustering pair. "Plus, if I'd let you keep going, we'd still be negotiating instead of out here."

She threw her arms wide, as if embracing the neon-lit world around them. In the distance, tinny carnival music played and riders screamed as they were thrown skyward in cages that twisted and jerked against the full moon. Carnies hawked chances to win ring tosses and dart games, while popcorn exploded, cotton candy whirred and just about every other food group sizzled in deep fryers. The sweet and salty spiced air felt warm and feather-light against his bare arms.

He'd come to this show for years and imagined her by his side, wishing things could be different. And now they were. It felt as if someone had replaced his old, thrill-a-minute life with this calmer, more satisfying version that squelched his restless need for fame.

If Claire still wanted him after he confessed the truth about his finances, he'd spend the rest of his life making up for lost time. He shoved down the sudden stab of fear. An honest relationship wasn't possible unless they put everything out on the table. What if, deep down, she saw him differently without his success? He'd defined himself that way for so long. Would she still see him as a strong man and a viable partner?

"The band's good." Claire grabbed his hand and he swept her into a slow two-step behind the seated audience.

He breathed in her wildflower scent and pressed his cheek against hers, loving the feel of her soft skin. They swayed lightly, too slow for the rhythm, neither caring. Or at least he didn't. He'd been longing to hold her all day. All month. Since the moment he'd seen her again, actually. His hands rose along her back and she arched against him, her warm breath blowing by his jaw, tickling his earlobe. He closed his eyes and imagined spending the rest of his life with her this way.

The song ended, and he reluctantly let her go when they earned a round of applause from on-lookers. With a tip of his hat, he pulled her down on one of the benches facing the gazebo and laced his fingers with hers. His erratic breathing refused to ease and his pulse kept time with the twanging blue-grass music.

"I think I recognize him." Claire pointed to a middle-aged man plucking a string base held beneath his knees.

"That's Tommy Greene." Tanner nodded to the florid-faced musician. "He retired the year after I began riding."

Claire's hand tensed. "So that's what life after rodeo looks like."

He angled his body toward hers and ducked his head to catch her eye. "I'd like to know what that is."

"What is?" Her foot tapped with the beat but her smile faded.

"Life without rodeo."

Her lashes lifted and her astonished gaze flew to him. "You're not going back?"

"I quit yesterday." It still seemed surreal. Mike had called nonstop since then, offering alternative after alternative to keep Tanner in the rodeo game.

"Why would you do that?" Claire faced the band again as they swung into a slower tune. She shook her head in wonder.

He pressed her palm to his heart. "Because it's not what I want." Could she feel its rapid-fire beat?

"What do you want?" she whispered eventually, her voice as shaky as a newborn calf. He followed her gaze to the oblivious crowd sitting in front of them. Despite the nearby empty benches, it was still too public. He wished they were alone. But for now this would have to do.

"You." The word pulsed out of him, heavy, weighted down by long-held hopes. Would Claire give him another chance? Especially when she learned he'd had selfish reasons for helping her father? Failures he needed to fix?

"I—we've tried this before. It didn't work." Her voice slurred slightly, its edges frayed with pain. She glanced down at her feet as if she were going to say something else. When she pulled her hand away, he felt as if he'd lost something. And then she looked up and hauled her hair briskly into an unnecessary ponytail.

Was he losing her? Again?

He couldn't let that happen.

She shivered when he set his hand on the back of her neck and brushed her cheek with his thumb.

"Don't." She stared blindly into the night.

"Don't what, Claire?"

"Don't break my heart again." There was no anger in her voice, just despair. She turned away and inhaled, closing her eyes and exhaling upward.

At her confession, adrenaline and pain coursed through him. "Come with me."

He tugged her away from the audience, along the line of blinking, flashing and beeping games and wares, and stopped at a ticket booth.

"What are you doing?"

"Taking you on a ride."

Wariness darkened her eyes. "Which one?"

He pointed to the looming Ferris wheel. "We need perspective."

"Oh. I'm not sure—"

Before her overcautious nature hijacked the moment, he hustled her up the riveted, stainless steel walkway, passed over their tickets and handed her into one of the round, swaying cars.

"I forgot these don't have belts." She rose, then settled back against the plastic molded seat when his arm came up, warm, around her.

"I've got you."

Another couple scrambled into the car below them and with a jerk they rose into the black night. Quickly, the show's cacophony faded and when they lurched to a stop at the pinnacle, quiet settled around them.

She looked behind her briefly, which gave him a moment to gaze at her unhindered...that profile, the small tilt to her upper lip, the delicate point of her chin. Something in him constricted, and he knew with a painful pang that he would never again love anyone as he loved Claire Shelton. Ten years had not freed him, and another ten wouldn't, either. When she turned back to him, he couldn't speak, reluctant to reveal everything and spill his guts like someone mortally wounded.

But he couldn't hold back any longer. No matter the consequences.

"I have something to tell you."

He cradled her palm in his lap. With a small shock, he realized his hand shook. When had his grip been anything less than steady?

"I need to tell you something, too," she said, her voice faint. A whisper of a whisper.

"Ladies, first?" He quirked an eyebrow and she shook her head, her fingers ice against his.

"No. You."

"Fine," he said. He had meant to sound reassuring, but his voice cracked on the word. And then, when she didn't respond, he began. "I didn't just come to Denton Creek to help Martin."

She looked at him sharply. Beneath the large moon, the silver light turned her raw beauty into something otherworldly. Unreachable. Unattainable. Yet he had to try.

"I came to save myself."

His ribs felt as if they parted as the long-held confession escaped him, yet her expression didn't change.

"You wanted to rehab your shoulder."

He nodded. "True. But I could have done that somewhere else."

Her brows drew together and she grabbed the metal rail behind her as the ride rocked on another ascent. "You said coming to the ranch had nothing to do with us…"

"It didn't. Not at first. Now, it's every reason I want to stay."

At the surge of happiness in her eyes, he gripped her hands and frowned. She needed to know everything. "I'm broke and I wanted to find another way to make money. The ranch seemed like the best opportunity."

When they sped past the ride operator and rose again, he stared out at the bright world below, imagining her disgust. He hadn't paid attention to important business matters while on the road and had failed.

She jerked her hand loose and laced her fingers in her lap. Slid a short distance away.

"Don't you make millions a year? Why do you need us?"

A short, mirthless laugh escaped him. He'd expected her rejection, but it didn't lesson the blow. "My investor put my money in a Ponzi scheme. I lost everything."

A breeze ruffled her dress hem when they yanked to a stop at the peak and teetered. It felt as if his hopes and dreams for them hung in the balance, too. How would she ever see him as a man worthy of her love?

Doubt clouded her voice. "Everything? Don't you own a home? Property?"

In the distance a carousel circled, its riders waving to cheering onlookers. He'd chased after attention like that all his life and what had it gotten him? Metal trophies but not a permanent place to store them. Or a family to share them with.

"I never stayed put long enough. It didn't make sense to buy one so I lived like a vagabond. Sounds like my father." His tone took on a rough, jagged edge, each word slicing his tongue on the way out. Without even knowing it, he'd grown into the same self-centered man he'd vowed never to emulate.

"So you thought you'd come to my home and open a rodeo school to make a buck? You should have known better given our past." Her voice heated, searing him.

"Rodeo is what I'm best at."

Claire snorted. "So? It doesn't mean that's the only thing you can do. You've nearly single-handedly saved our ranch and you helped me train for and win a Grand Championship. If that's not good enough for you, then I'm sorry for you."

Her pity backhanded him across the face, sucker punched his gut so that the wind was knocked out of him. The ride revolved again before he could speak. He'd expected her anger, but her sympathy? It cut him through.

Still, she had a point. Why was being the best so all-important? Shouldn't good be good enough? Who was he trying to prove himself to? His mind raced back to his teachers who'd told him he'd never amount to anything, a mother who hadn't cared enough to check in on him for days at a time.

"Don't be," he blurted at last, looking her dead in the eye. "Hitting the bottom brought me back here and it was worth losing it all to be with you now. Only I don't expect you to think much of a broke, out-of-work cowboy."

He stared up at the bright stars bearing down on them. Felt the weight of their judgment, too.

"How could you think that?" came her soft

voice, surprising him. He leaned closer, straining to hear her over the creaking ride.

The shadows inside gathered in his throat, making it hard to speak. He forced out the hardest admission of all. "Because I'm nothing now."

She scooted closer and placed a hand on either side of his tense face. Compelled him to look at her. "You're strong, caring, dedicated... what every man should be."

He lost himself in her expressive eyes. "You're everything to me, Claire."

When she traced the bare skin of his arms, his stomach tensed. "I feel the same way."

He scanned her face, sure he'd heard her wrong. "But I'm—"

"Broke." Her lips twisted in a wry smile. "At least you're not in debt like we are."

"You *were* in debt," he corrected automatically, dazed that she took his admission in stride. If anything, her expression softened, that veneer of hardness she wore around him was stripped away. She didn't care about him being a big shot. She just appreciated him as a man.

Why had he chased after fame to affirm his worth and left behind the one person who'd valued him simply for being himself? Amazing. Finally he felt free to just be.

She snuggled closer. "I wish you'd told me

up front. Then I might not have given you such a hard time."

His chin lifted. "About the rodeo school?"

When the Ferris wheel slid to a halt, they exited and maneuvered through the press of attendees.

The light of a nearby ride cast a hectic flush on her cheeks. "No. I still oppose that. But there are worse things than being poor. You didn't kill anyone. Steal. Cheat. You're a good man. That's what counts most and all that ever mattered to me."

He swallowed. Hard. "I didn't think you'd respect me." He pulled her into a private picnic area between closed-down breakfast vendors. The dark made it easier to speak. "Want me."

They sat at a picnic table and Claire pulled a napkin from a dispenser and began shredding it. "I loved you for who you were, not what you accomplished. I just couldn't bear being around rodeo. It hurts that you're trying to bring it here with your school."

"What are you so afraid of?" When she flinched, his mind flashed to her barrel-racing accident. "You can't live your life in fear."

"I'm living it safely."

He drew her close and their feet tangled beneath the table. "But it's pulling us apart. You're too cautious."

She tensed against him then, with a nod, rested her head on his shoulder. "I can't help it."

"But I can help you. I should have gotten you back on the horse after your accident. If you'll trust me, give me that chance now."

She sucked in a harsh breath and they stared at each other. Tanner gripped her shoulders and held her steady, willing her to have faith in him. In them.

"Yes," she whispered, at last, into his neck.

His shoulders lowered and he pressed his cheek to hers, touched. She trusted him and he had to deliver. He had to help her reclaim her bold, brave self.

CHAPTER SEVENTEEN

A COUPLE OF days later, in the stable, Claire hefted a saddle onto Dusty and the gray mare sidestepped. There was a faint ringing sound in Claire's ears. She shook her head, trying to get rid of it. Why had she agreed to Tanner's crazy plan?

Because she wanted to be the girl he'd once loved…a woman who didn't let fear rule her life. She wished her first ride could at least be in full daylight, but given their now-busy work schedule that would be near impossible.

"Settle now, girl." She slipped an apple half from her pocket and Dusty's lips whispered over her palm, leaving it empty save for a damp streak.

"Doing okay over there?" called Tanner. Only the top of his head was visible as he bent over to grab Guardian's dangling cinch.

She wiped her hand on her shorts. "Peachy," she replied, striving to sound as normal as possible which meant it immediately rose an octave and wobbled. Dusty's ears flattened.

Great.

Her horse looked as spooked as she felt.

The memory of her last, wild race rushed back: sudden, explosive bucking and her desperate attempt to keep the horse's head from getting too low. Leaning back, holding on with her legs. Air. Falling. Then hard ground rushing up to meet her. A horrible snap. Crushing of bones when her saddle horn smacked her chest as the horse crashed backward. And pain. Excruciating pain that'd obliterated everything until she'd woken in a hospital bed, her legs casted from foot to hip, ribs taped and bandaged, gauze around her head.

Warm arms gathered her from behind and pulled her close. "You can do this."

She nodded and let herself be consumed by the simple pleasure of having Tanner's body next to hers. The fresh, outdoorsy smell of him distracted her, making her wish suddenly that they were not in this stable at all, but back home. Alone. "It's been a long time."

"Too long." He squeezed her waist then finished saddling Dusty before he handed her the reins. "Go on now. You'll do great."

She smoothed her hair and looked absently around the stable. "I don't know."

Out in the corral, Claire walked Dusty in a slow circle as she did with her beginner students. The words she used to reassure them came back to her, but none of them settled her racing heart.

The sky had purpled and a quarter moon rose slightly above the tree line, competing against the last of the sun. To the north, a star shone faintly and she made a wish.

Please let me get through this. Face my fears instead of run from them.

Tanner was right. She shouldn't have let anxiety control her all these years.

But if she really wanted to change…be brave…why hadn't she told him about Jonathan yet?

She shoved down the persistent thought. After his confession at the show, she'd wanted to savor their togetherness before she risked blowing it apart with *her* revelation. They'd held hands on the way home, much to Charlie's brow-raised surprise, and it'd felt too good to spoil just yet. Still, time was running out. Once she overcame this long-held fear, she'd feel strong enough to make her horrible admission tomorrow. Would he still want her? Forgive her?

Guardian's head appeared next to Dusty and the two old friends touched noses.

"Ready?"

A cat streaked by Dusty and her tail swooshed. Guardian blew. "Yes." Claire's voice crackled like a dry log in a fire, and her hair seemed suddenly electrified, springing free from its two clips.

"Up you go then."

Before she could back out, she stepped into the stirrup then settled in her seat. Dusty scuttled backward and Claire's pulse pounded in her eardrums.

"Breathe, Claire."

Tanner's reassuring smile shone up at her and she exhaled. He held both horses' reins and looked in no hurry to hand them over.

He waited.

She waited.

He waited some more.

At last the pressure in her chest eased and she reached for the leather straps.

"All set?" He absently rubbed her calf, as if she was a jittery filly. Maybe she was.

"Best as I'll get."

In a flash, he swung up into his saddle and lightly nudged Guardian's side so the stallion stepped briskly. Dusty automatically followed and suddenly Claire's initial lurch of fear was displaced by a sense of mounting excitement as she followed Tanner around the corral.

She rocked steadily, and the familiar rhythms returned to her. Not fearsome enemies but old friends. She patted the gray's muscular neck and smiled, feeling her face relax for the first time. Her shoulders, she realized, had risen up around her ears with tension.

Tanner pulled up beside her and grinned, his eyes warm and appreciative. "Looking good up there."

The corners of her lips rose and stuck. "Thanks."

"Ready to break out of here?"

"You mean take the trail?"

She glanced down the tree-lined lane that lead along Denton Creek and up a small incline that looked over the ranch. A sudden desire to see it all seized her.

"Yes."

"Attagirl." Tanner winked at her as he vaulted off the horse in a move so smooth, so polished, it vacuumed her mouth dry with longing. There was something infinitely attractive about a man who rode well.

Tanner pushed the gate open, tapping his horse on its side so that it pirouetted around him, and Claire rode through, Dusty's hooves making soft plodding noises on the clay-packed soil.

In a moment, Tanner and Guardian joined them on the wide path, the horses' noses occasionally touching as they walked sedately. Mosquitoes whined around Claire's face and Dusty's tail slapped her rump.

"Feels like old times."

Claire met Tanner's eyes in the dimming light, recalling their rides together. Stolen kisses on horseback. Leaving the world behind for moments alone...like this. Her cheeks heated and she was glad for the shadows that hid her blush.

"In a way," she ventured, and stared at her horse's ears. Back and forth went the right one.

"A lot's changed since then. We've changed. For the better," Tanner said, from the greater height of the quarter horse beside her. He held both reins in his right hand, while his other arm hung loosely down his left side.

"Sometimes I wonder."

"What do you mean?"

"I could do a lot better with Jonathan," she confessed.

Tanner's mouth pulled down. "You're a great mom."

"I've made him afraid. Infected him with my fear," she said, sharing her darkest doubt.

He ducked under a low-hanging branch. "Seems like he's coming out of that."

"Yeah. Thanks to you," she blurted. Tanner would be a great dad. Probably a better parent than she was. She had to tell him...

His face whipped around and she shook her head, realizing that must have sounded surly. "I mean, thank you. Truly." Her throat closed and she struggled to get out what needed to be said. "He's a different kid now that you're here and I can't tell you what that means to me. It feels good to have help. A—a partner."

She glanced furtively at Tanner, unsure if she'd gone too far. Revealed too much.

He studied her for a long minute then nodded. "I'd like that."

Heat rose up her neck. At least twice she had blushed tonight, his habit of staring at her very directly when he spoke leaving her unable to concentrate on what he was actually saying.

The little gray horse moved obediently under her, its ears flicking backward and forward as she and Tanner spoke, her neck arched like that of a rocking horse. Dusty hadn't tried to buck her off, bite her, kick her, swerve into a tree or bolt into the distance, as Claire had feared despite all her experience with the gentle mare. Dusty hadn't eyed her with that expression of malevolent intent Claire pictured whenever she recalled her accident, but instead seemed satisfied to simply be out enjoying the crisp early summer evening.

And why had Claire expected any different? She had handpicked the mare. Trusted her with the youngest of students. Riding Dusty felt as comfortable as donning a favorite pair of slippers.

They entered a long clearing with a ridgeline in the distance, clearly visible under the setting sun and rising moon.

"Ready to let them loose?" Tanner slid her a sideways glance. "Let's race to the ridgeline."

"What do I get when I win?" Claire taunted, diverting frightening thoughts of a speeding horse beneath her.

"Nothing, because I'm winning."

Claire felt her face break into a wide smile at his teasing and Tanner grinned back at her, his eyes flashing beneath the glimmering stars. Dusty immediately began trotting at Claire's clucking noise and excitement surged.

Guardian picked up the pace and stepped quickly beside them. "Ready?" asked Tanner.

"I haven't named my prize."

"I know what I want." The side of his mouth rose and her breath caught as she flicked a glance at his rugged profile. "A kiss."

Her heart raced. She wanted that, too. Did she dare admit it? Especially since she hadn't come clean about Jonathan, yet? "Too bad you'll be cleaning my stables instead." She made a smooching sound and Dusty broke into a lope.

Claire opened the inside rein back toward her hip and peered at the ridgeline.

"Hey," protested Tanner, and Guardian came up fast on Dusty's flank.

Claire, squaring her shoulders, found her mouth bubbling wide with laughter. "Sorry, sucker." With a little kick, Dusty transitioned into a gallop and with a frightening suddenness, Tanner was at her side, Guardian charging.

"Ya!" he hollered and the horses sped across the grassy field, kicking up clods of dirt behind them.

Guardian gained slightly and Claire nudged Dusty harder to surge ahead. Yes! She'd win this…a week without stable chores…but that kiss sounded more tempting, even if she didn't deserve it. Not until Tanner knew the truth.

The ridgeline loomed closer as they galloped faster and faster and, just as they neared its base, Guardian, with a mighty leap, took the lead by a head. But before he got too far away, Claire pushed her hips forward and squeezed her legs more. Dusty bounded ahead and they shot to the top, gaining the pinnacle and winning by a nose.

Her pulse clamored and rushed as she eased Dusty to a halt, patting the little horse beneath her, unable to believe what they had just achieved. "Good girl, good girl," she sang joyously. "You clever, clever girl." Her blood infused with adrenaline, she wanted to shout and exclaim and race again and again.

She'd done it. She'd overcome her fear of riding, but it felt bigger than that…as though the collective weight of her worries had dropped away, left behind somewhere in the field. She could do anything. Even deal with Tanner's wrath when she confessed her terrible deception, perhaps. She hoped…

"Nice, Claire!" Tanner leaped off Guardian, tied him to a nearby tree and offered Claire a hand as she dismounted. The corners of his mouth lifted into a smile. Claire found that her own met it. She swelled with pride when she thought about her win.

With Dusty secured, they strolled to the top of the knoll and peered out into the growing gloom at the ranch's sprawling pastures below.

A sudden suspicion seized her. "You didn't let me win, did you?"

Tanner's eyes were soft, hinting at amusement. He cupped the brim of his hat into a neat C. "Do you honestly believe I'd ever lose on purpose?"

She laughed. "Not a chance."

"Too bad I won't get that kiss now." Tanner stared for a disconcertingly long time into Claire's eyes, so that she felt temporarily unbalanced. She had to tell him about Jonathan, but this moment felt too perfect to spoil. Tomorrow, she thought, her mind growing foggy at his closeness...she would tell him tomorrow. Surely she could allow herself this one moment of stolen happiness...

With a step, she drew close and traced the shape of his face, her fingertips so light they barely touched him. "Who says?"

TANNER'S BODY TIGHTENED at Claire's question, her proximity wreaking havoc on his senses.

"Are you sure?" He'd never been one to hesitate with a woman before, but with Claire, this was different. Forever. Or he hoped it'd be. He didn't want to rush her. Mess things up. Had the horse ride worked and helped her conquer her fear of him...or them?

Her gorgeous mouth curved up and his heart slammed against his chest. "Yes. I'm sure. I can't seem to stop thanking you, but thank you. For Jonathan. For my dad and for me."

"Still afraid?"

She shook her head fiercely and her red hair swung around her face. In the soft light, he'd never seen her look more beautiful. "No. Not of the past or the future...with you."

He imagined what would have happened if he'd simply ridden after his rodeo dream again and left the ranch as he'd planned. What he would have lost. Time to open up completely. Take the ultimate gamble.

"Claire. I've been in love with you a long time. A real long time. And I've been out with other girls since—great gals with lots to offer. But the more I went out with, the more I realized that if something's missing at the core of it, if you don't feel that—that—thing, the thing that is just right, then there's no point."

Her mouth fell open and he took off his hat, raked a hand through his wavy hair. "And then our trucks crashed, and I knew it straight off. I knew from the first time I saw you in that truck, when you stood up to that police officer, told me off and tried walking home on a bruised ankle, and something in here—" he thumped at his chest "—something just went 'Ahh. There it is.' And I knew."

"Oh, Tanner," she murmured, and there was sweetness in the way she said his name, an unbearable tenderness that spoke of all the love and loss he, too, had felt. Her body leaned against his, and he heard the sigh that traveled through her, then felt her breath on his lips. The air stilled around them. Her mouth touched his and something broke open in his chest.

He pressed his lips to hers more urgently, elated, unable to believe this turn of events. Time became a blur, the kisses more urgent, and he knew he was trying to tell her the depth of how he felt. Even as he lost himself in her, felt her hair sweep across his face, her lips meet his skin, he understood that there were people for whom one other was their missing part. She set him alight.

He kissed the scar from her barrel-racing accident that ran across her clavicle, ignored her flinching reluctance until she accepted what he was telling her—this silvered ridge was beautiful to him; it told him she had loved him and trusted him once. It told him she might feel that way again. He kissed it because there was no part of her that he didn't want to make better, no part of her that he didn't adore.

He watched joy grow in her as if it were a gift shared between them, and felt blessed. Some part of him had always known, even though he had chosen not to believe it, that there must be something that could make him feel like this. More than bull riding and glory. And to have it returned to him was more than he could have hoped for.

He kissed the top of her head, let his fingers rest in her tangled hair. A perfect peace had descended on him, spreading to his very bones. *This is it. I'm home*, he thought.

CHAPTER EIGHTEEN

"HERE'S YOUR MILK, TANNER."

When Claire's fingers lingered on Tanner's, he shot a quick look at her father who scribbled a word in Jonathan's crossword puzzle. Tanner surreptitiously stroked her knuckles with his thumb before she released the glass and batted her eyelashes in a flirty, funny look—the best combination in his books.

He held in a chuckle. It'd been a hectic day since last night's horseback ride. With the livestock show ending, they'd had a surge of calls and drop-ins, the influx of business exceeding even his wildest expectations. Yet every moment he could, he'd pulled her aside for stolen kisses, unable to get enough of her. To believe his good luck.

With the rodeo school construction completed on existing buildings while they were away, he would open next week and become self-supporting. Surely Claire wouldn't go through with the injunction now that she'd conquered her fears. With his financial future secure, he'd be ready to ask Claire for her hand. He couldn't wait to make her his wife and Jon his stepson. As for Martin, he'd been the only real father Tanner ever had. A wedding would just make it official.

A yelp sounded from the other end of the table. Jonathan hopped and cried, holding out his brown-stained T-shirt from his stomach. "Hot! Hot! Hot!"

In a flash, Tanner raced around the table and yanked Jonathan's shirt off while Claire mopped up her father's spilled coffee, dabbing at the stain on his pants.

"Sorry, Jonathan," Martin exclaimed, raising his shaky hand. He'd increased his range of motion recently but still lacked coordination.

"Are you burned, honey?" Claire crouched beside her son, and he buried his face in her shoulder and shook his head, looking more shocked than hurt. She brushed back Jonathan's wet curls and eased him away. "Let me look at you."

Tanner's gaze fell on Jonathan's exposed ears and froze. Attached lobes. Like his. They weren't so rare that they couldn't have been inherited from Kevin…

Tanner fingered his own attached earlobes and met Claire's stricken look. She glanced between him and Jonathan, a fearful expression darkening her eyes to emerald. "Tanner. We need to talk."

His blood rushed to his head, made him dizzy. What did she have to say that couldn't wait? And did it have to do with Jonathan and him?

"Let's go outside," she said, her voice so low he barely heard it. Without waiting to see if he followed, she stalked out the front door and down brick-tiered steps. She stopped at the bottom and put a hand against the cool stone sculpture of a bucking bull on the edge of a formal rose garden as if bracing herself. But for what?

Overhead, heavy-bellied clouds hung low and threatening, and the air swarmed around him, thick and moist.

Tanner shut the door behind him and joined her. She could barely look at him.

When a brisk gust ruffled her hair, she sat on the steps, a loose-jointed collapse as if someone cut the strings holding her up. Her voice was so quiet he strained to hear it. "Tanner, Jonathan is your son."

He stared down at her familiar features, questioning if he knew her at all. His heart was doing something strange. He placed his palm against his chest, wondering if this was what it felt like to have a heart attack. "Say that again."

"I wanted to tell you." She reached up to him

but he pulled away. Her sad eyes dropped and she shook her head. "No. I didn't. Not at first. I thought you wanted to be famous. Didn't want me, let alone a baby. Maybe I was also mad that you'd left. Didn't think you deserved to know… but I was wrong. I see that now. I'd planned to tell you and I'm sorry I waited so long."

He ignored the pleading note in her voice and held still, a silent howl building in the back of his throat. When thunder shook the sky, he wanted to growl with it.

He had a son.

Jonathan.

Claire had never told him.

Had lied.

Did Martin know?

As if reading his thoughts, Claire said, "Only Kevin knew. We told my father I got pregnant after our first date, although it wasn't really a date. When Kevin found me crying over the pregnancy, he offered to take responsibility. Said he'd always loved me and I needed to hear that."

"*I* loved you!" came Tanner's low, anguished cry. The words ripped loose a piece of his heart and carried it away. He paced along the brick walkway as plops of water intermittently splattered at his feet, darkening the stone.

"You left."

He found himself holding his stomach with both hands, as if he had been punched. The magnitude of what he'd given up for rodeo nearly felled him. All that he'd missed. All that she'd kept from him.

Under the bright flash of lightning, her pale cheeks turned ashen. She gestured to a screened-in gazebo at the end of the walkway and bolted to her feet.

Furious, he followed and hunkered on the bench across from her. His knees jittered and his back teeth ground against each other. How could she have kept this from him? He'd loved her for so many reasons, especially her honesty. Now he didn't know what to think.

"Did you always love him?"

Was I just a fling?

"No. You were my first love. I came to love Kevin, but it was different. Deep down, I think I loved you both."

"Just not enough to tell me I was a father." In his mind's eye, Jonathan's face flashed. Why hadn't he known, deep down, the boy was his?

Because you trusted Claire.

The sky growled again.

If he'd left the ranch earlier, would she have let him leave without the truth? Let him go his entire life never seeing his son grow up? Never tinkering on mechanics with him? Never teaching Jonathan how to ride? How to be a man?

Claire plucked a petunia blossom from a hanging flower basket and shredded its petals. "A baby would have ruined your dreams and I didn't want you coming home out of obligation. Didn't want my son to have a father who saw him as a burden."

"He would never have been a burden," Tanner ground out through his locked jaw.

Claire tilted her head and another lightning surge illuminated the dim day and her wet cheeks. "So you would have been happy staying home with us? Working as a ranch hand? Been fine losing your shot at rodeo?"

He shifted on the edge of the attached seat, imagining his young, ambitious self. "I would have done right by you. Provided for my family."

"But you wouldn't have been happy about it."

"What does that have to do with anything? Jon was mine. My responsibility." Fire torched his blood cells. Singed his bones.

In the distance, a siren blared, growing closer and louder as it screamed by the property.

"I wanted you to love him for who he was." Her laced fingers dropped to her lap.

"You never gave me the chance." He looked skyward. Tracked the storm's light show until, after another ear-splitting clap, the clouds dropped a flood of water that pelted the gazebo's roof.

"Would it have made a difference?" The confusion on her face didn't move him. She should know the answer to that.

"I guess you'll never know since you made that decision for both of us."

When she reached for him, he hurtled to his feet and strode to the gazebo's screen door.

He needed space. Distance from the woman who'd betrayed him so deeply. It was as if someone had reached in, grabbed his heart, and ripped it out through his ribs.

"Ten years, Claire." He took a breath and forced his clenched hands to unfurl.

"I know," she choked out.

"And you let Jon and I get close. We worked on his father's truck. *His father*. You didn't feel that was even a little bit wrong?"

She pinched the bridge of her nose, her face contorted. "Every day. Why do you think I tried to stop it? Didn't want you spending time together?"

"To keep me from discovering the truth!"

His voice thundered along with the tempest and she wept into her hands, not denying his accusation. What kind of woman would do something so low? Despite everything, a part of him wanted to reach for her and dry those tears. He couldn't bear seeing Claire hurt.

"I'm heading back. Tell Jon…tell Jon…" His brain kept skipping over the phrase, tumbling over the word *son* that pounded through him. He rubbed his throbbing temples. "Tell Jon we won't be working on the truck tonight."

"Are we going to tell him about you?" she whispered, her words barely audible over the pounding rain.

"It's overdue."

She nodded bleakly. "Tomorrow, though. Okay?"

It made sense. They couldn't approach Jonathan with everything so raw. With emotions this intense, it'd only scare the boy. "Fine."

When he jerked the door open, she rose. "Please. Stay. Let's talk this out."

He studied her shadowed shape in the gloom, unable to make her out clearly…if he ever had. "I've heard enough. Goodbye, Claire," he said, meaning it, as he spun around and strode away. Time to let go of the fantasy woman who'd haunted his thoughts and dreams these past ten years.

She didn't exist anymore. Maybe she never had.

CLAIRE WOKE THE next morning, her limbs heavy, her heart sore. A high-pitched scream echoed in the distance and she tossed back her covers and leaped out of bed, pulse pounding.

Jonathan! It sounded like Jonathan.

She swerved into his room, spotted his empty bed and bolted back out. As she ran by her father's door, she slowed when she heard him call.

"What's going on?"

"I don't know. I'll be back."

She hurtled off the bottom step and sprinted through the back door and down the porch steps. Where was he? Her heart raced so fast her breath couldn't keep up and spots appeared around the edge of her vision.

At another blood-curdling yell, she swung toward the newly constructed rodeo school and a massive lump lodged itself in her stomach, like something bad was about to happen.

No! Jonathan would never...

She followed the shrieks, her mind in overdrive. Could Jonathan have gotten inside? Tanner wasn't ready to open yet and the bulls...her heart lurched...he'd chosen the orneriest ones to populate it. Could her son have broken in and messed with the dangerous, untamed animals? They shouldn't be out of their old pasture, though...

Tanner galloped up on Guardian, jumped off

and threw the reins over one of the fence posts. "Jon?"

She nodded and they exchanged horrified glances as they raced to the staging area.

"He's not at home?"

"He wasn't in his room," she gasped.

They rounded a bend and there, lying in the middle of the riding ring, was a small, crumpled heap, a snorting bull kicking and trampling beside him. Roxy raced up and down, a gray blur, barking like mad, nipping at the ornery bull's heels and drawing it away from Jonathan as she valiantly dodged its horns.

Panic washed over Claire in an icy wave, tightening her throat. She opened her mouth to scream, but Tanner clamped a hand over her mouth.

"Claire," Tanner said quietly, his eyes on the bull. "I'm going in the ring. Once I draw off the bull, haul Jon out of there."

Her heart hammered against her ribs like a bird in a cage and she nodded fast, her breath coming in fits and starts.

Claire unlatched the gate and tiptoed inside while Tanner sprinted ahead, waving his hands and hollering. The bull grunted and swung its massive head away from Roxy and Jonathan who, to Claire's horror, looked unconscious. Was he breathing?

When the bull lowered his horns again, Tanner charged, slapping them away from Jonathan then sidestepping fast when the bull swerved and gave chase. Roxy stayed by her boy's side and began frantically licking Jonathan's face.

"Claire, now!" Tanner yelled and raced ahead of the bull.

She dashed into the ring but skidded to a halt when the massive animal reversed course and charged her and Jonathan again. Before she could react, Roxy dashed forward as Tanner ducked in front of the bull then threw himself sideways at the last possible moment. He rolled away as the bull stormed after him, fast and deadly.

In an instant, she scooped up her son and jogged as gently as possible out of the ring, Roxy trotting fast beside them. The moment she set Jonathan on the ground, she slammed and bolted the gate behind her. She waved to Tanner who, once he spotted them, darted to the fence and vaulted over it as the beast missed him by an inch or less. It pawed at the ground and butted its head against the metal rails, scraping them with its long horns.

Claire crouched beside her son and ran her eyes over the still child, noting his oddly angled arm and the bone protruding from a deep gash. Tanner yanked off his shirt and wrapped it around Jonathan's cold body while Claire held him tight.

"I don't want to move him any more in case…" she looked down at his drooping limbs "…in case…" Her throat seized. Could he be paralyzed? Why was he so still?

Tanner shook his head. "No. No. Don't move him. I'm calling 911." He whipped out his cell phone and they waited an agonizing fifteen minutes for the ambulance to arrive, their attempts to revive Jonathan failing, his breath growing more shallow until, through streaming eyes, she could barely discern his chest rise at all…

HOURS LATER, CLAIRE huddled in a molded hospital seat. "No more updates, Dad," she murmured into her cell phone. "He's still in surgery. I'll call you as soon as I know anything."

She clicked off the call and stared at the pacing cowboy.

He'd rescued her son, but Tanner's obstinate decision to build the bull-riding school had nearly killed Jonathan, too. Why had she gone along with Tanner's remonstrations that she was too cautious? She'd matured. Grown older. Thought like a parent now. Wasn't a reckless daredevil who refused to grow up, like Tanner. She wasn't wrong. He was.

"He should be out of surgery by now."

She raised burning eyes and shot Tanner a flinty look. "He shouldn't be in surgery at all."

"Claire." He dropped into the seat beside her, his face gray. "I had nothing to do with this."

Anger boiled in her blood like poison. "You had everything to do with it," she cried, her voice loud in the private waiting room. "That rodeo school. Accessibility to those bulls...none of that would have been possible without you."

"I never suggested he try to ride one."

His refusal to take responsibility made her want to scream. "You didn't have to. With those bulls so around..." She froze as a thought occurred. "And why were they in the school instead of out to pasture? It wasn't open, yet. We have a hearing."

He stared hard out the window. "I moved them over last night after our horse ride and Jonathan watched me from his window." Tanner thrust his hands in his pockets. "I thought you'd drop the injunction."

A short, ominous silence. "Please tell me I'm hallucinating through my ears."

When he shook his head, her mouth fell open until she recovered her wits. Was he insane? "I never said that and I shouldn't have gone along with all your talk about me being overly anxious. Look what happens when you don't take precautions. If I'd known he'd seen them,

I would have given him a warning. Kept an eye on him in case he got tempted to investigate. That's what a parent would have done."

Tanner's head whipped around and pain flashed in his eyes at her accusation. "I may not have been around all these years, but that wasn't my choice. I'm not any less of a parent than you. Or I won't be."

"Then start thinking like one!" she exploded, all of her pent-up fear and fury pouring out of her. "He looks up to you. Wants to follow your example and look at the one you gave him. Daredevil rodeo champion Tanner. No wonder he wanted to ride…to be like you."

He watched her carefully, his whole face an apology. "The nurse said they're going to reset his arm and the CT scan showed a severe concussion but no brain swelling. He'll recover, Claire. You'll see."

She breathed a sigh of disgust. "What I'll see is a child in pain. A kid who'd just started to get out in the world only to have it hurt him worse than a hundred school bullies. Concussions that severe can have lasting effects. Could impair him. If the ambulance hadn't arrived when it did…"

She shuddered as she recalled the outright terror she'd felt watching her injured son strapped to the large black gurney and hefted into the shrieking emergency vehicle. How small he'd looked. How still.

"I know that, Claire. But he's in good hands now."

"That's supposed to comfort me?" She wanted to shake him.

"Yes." He shot to his feet and paced the short length of the tiled room. Overhead, one of the fluorescent lights blinked on and off.

"And what if it happens again? Are you going to close the rodeo school to make sure he's not in danger?" She rubbed her temples, her brain afire.

Tanner thrust a waxed paper cone under a water dispenser then gulped down the drink. "He'll have learned not to go near the bulls now."

A bitter laugh escaped her. "Some way to learn a lesson, and you still didn't answer my question."

Her eyes stared daggers at him until a soft cough interrupted them.

"Mr. and Mrs. Shelton?"

"I'm Mrs. Shelton." She jolted to her feet and Tanner joined her as they hurried across the room to the white-coated woman wearing hospital scrubs and a hair covering.

"I'm Dr. Blackstone. My apologies for not

speaking to you before surgery, but there wasn't time."

Tanner nodded and Claire wanted to holler *hurry up*!

"How's Jonathan?" she asked, striving and failing to keep the tears out of her voice.

The woman's lined face looked grave as she studied Claire and Tanner from behind wireless spectacles. "He's in stable condition and the injuries to his arm should heal nicely." Claire dipped slightly at the knees and grabbed hold of the door.

Tanner stepped forward. "Is he conscious?"

The doctor tucked her chart beneath her arm. "Not yet. Given the severity of his concussion, we have him on our ICU floor for closer monitoring tonight."

Claire swallowed hard and then let out a long, shuddering breath. "Will he have brain damage? I heard there are sometimes problems with memory loss. Paying attention. And he already has enough trouble in that area."

After a moment, the doctor sighed. "We'll have to see. Luckily we intervened quickly so his chances are fair to good. He also sustained an injury to his *longus colli* muscle, which is what we typically see in severe cases of whiplash. He'll need to be in traction for a month."

Claire covered her face with her hands.

"When can we see him?" she asked after a moment.

"A nurse will bring you back within the hour." The doctor placed a hand on Claire's arm. "This is a difficult time, but know that your son is getting the best possible care we can give him."

When the door swung shut behind the surgeon, Claire collapsed back into a chair and wept into her hands. She pictured Jonathan chasing circles around the table with Roxy. Jonathan gluing model airplanes together. Helping her make cupcakes and eating more batter than he placed in each holder. Would a normal life be hampered now? The thought slashed her deep. Ripped her through.

"He's so young," sobbed Claire.

"He'll recover. Beat the odds," Tanner insisted, his automatic assumption feeling like salt rubbed hard in her wound.

She stared up at him through her fingers. "Life isn't some game. Not everyone's born bulletproof like you." Her hands drifted to her own scar and she thought of how she'd tried to impress him, too, by taking the dare to ride the horse that'd nearly killed her. Now her son paid a similar price. She should have fought harder to chase Tanner off her property and out of their lives. Not given in to old feelings that should have stayed in the past.

An overhead page sounded and Claire tensed until security guards, not a code team, rushed by. "Tell me you'll close the school."

Unbelievably, Tanner shook his head. "I promise you, Jon will never go near it again."

"Why is that?" she burst out and her gesturing arm overturned a coffee he'd gotten her hours ago. The brown liquid spilled across the table and dripped to the tiled floor. "Because you'll build twenty-foot walls around it? Make sure they can't be climbed? Keep Jonathan under lock and key? Or maybe that won't be necessary because he might not be as coordinated now." Her last words ended in a watery gulp.

"Stop thinking that way, Claire."

"What way? Like a mother? A parent? It's clear that's something you don't know how to do."

He staggered back a step, as though she'd shoved him. "We don't have all the facts yet. Everything could change in the next twenty-four hours. Have faith in the professionals."

She went out to the nurses' station and returned with napkins. He squatted beside her, helping to mop up the spill.

"One thing won't change, Tanner. You."

He lurched to his feet and tossed out the sodden paper. "What do you mean?"

"I was wrong to think you were different.

Like you said, you came to the ranch to help yourself as much as us and look what that got us…a rodeo school that benefits you and injured Jonathan. You still put yourself and your success first, no matter how many people you hurt to achieve it. Even your own child."

He opened his mouth then shut it. The air crackled, electric with regret and anger. "I didn't mean to hurt anyone."

"That's the thing, Tanner. You never do, yet your recklessness harms others. You're a danger to Jonathan."

"No." He shook his head, his chest rising and falling fast.

"Yes. You're not cut out to be a dad. A friend, yes. The kind kids like to pal around with. But the people who make good parents make sacrifices, put children's well-being ahead of their needs, know how to protect kids and make their lives safe. That's not you, Tanner."

She smothered a flare of regret that followed her harsh words, knowing it was unfair to expect him to act like a parent when he'd never had the chance to be one, or had one himself… Still, if he thought he could be a father to Jonathan, she had to be straight with him.

"So, what are you saying?"

She gazed at him, deeply troubled, her bottom lip pushed out. "I want you to leave for good.

I'll tell Jonathan you went back to rodeo. You still have opportunities there, right?"

He nodded slowly and she imagined how easy it'd be for a champion like him to get back into the bull-riding world. It was where he belonged. She shouldn't have imagined otherwise, no matter how much she'd hoped it could be different.

"I won't leave until I know he's out of danger."

Claire crossed her arms. If only she was like that old-time TV character, Jeannie, and could nod her head, blink and wish him away. "But after that, leave. If you truly love Jonathan, the best thing you can do for him is stay out of his life."

He stepped close and peered down at her, his face grave. "You've denied him to me all these years. I'm not staying away."

"My injunction will shut down the school."

"If it does, then I'll cut back on my schedule. Rent a place in town. Sue for custody so that he's with me during the off-season."

The implication of what he said sank in followed by actual pain, something like a punch, just under her ribs. She wouldn't share Jonathan, especially not with Tanner. "Then we'll have two days in court. I won't ever forgive you for this."

"If he takes a turn for the worse and I lose

him before I ever get to call him my son, I'll never forgive *you*." His words were quietly said, but held the powerful kickback of a firearm, and Claire, wounded, pulled her knees to her chest.

Without another word, he turned on his heel and marched down the hall, probably to the public waiting room they'd passed on the way in. She stared at the empty doorway long after he'd disappeared through it.

She couldn't think about losing Tanner when her son's health hung in the balance, but the pain of watching Tanner walk away shredded her. They'd been so close to finally having the love, and the family, they should have had all those years ago. Now it'd fallen apart. Her future felt like a bleak, empty road.

They were wrong for each other, plain and simple. She buried her face in the arms resting on her knees...and just that complicated.

CHAPTER NINETEEN

"COWBOY UP, TANNER!" hollered Pete Wilkes, the chute boss who stood bowlegged on the Montana rodeo's catwalk. His long moustache hung low on both sides of his mouth and deep grooves ran from the corners of his eyes down his leathery cheeks. The smell of his cherry chewing tobacco grew stronger as Tanner approached.

"Got it, Pete."

He buckled on his helmet and instantly the cheering crowd, along with a thumping Garth Brooks tune, grew muffled. Out in the arena, bullfighters chased off a rowdy bull while a safety rider circled a lasso overhead then tossed it neatly around the animal's neck before leading it out. A barrel man executed back flips and other tricks to entertain the crowd while Tanner got ready.

In the bucking chute, Yellow Jacket, a younger bull considered to be the tour's rankest bucker and spinner, jerked his head and stamped, butting against the narrow metal chute slide. Tanner reached down, grabbed the tail of his rope and handed it to his chute helper, Armand, a talk-ative Cajun who'd been with Elite for twenty years.

With one hand on the opposite rail, Tanner put his foot on the bull's back to let it know he was coming, then crawled over and slid his legs down until he sat atop the restless animal. Careful to keep his spurs from touching Yellow Jacket's heaving sides, he pointed his boots forward.

The familiar adrenaline rush zipped through him. He rolled his shoulder as he warmed up his rope, working the slack out of it. His muscles felt as strong as ever, his torn rotator cuff fully healed as the doctor had promised when he'd cleared Tanner before his return to rodeo a month ago.

If only his heart had mended that fully. Despite Claire's lies and their fiery exchange at the hospital, he missed her. Wasn't satisfied to hear bits about her through Martin when Tanner called daily to check in on Jonathan. Luckily the boy had been released from the hospital two days ago and, according to his grandfather, was up and around, though not out much. Tanner would fix that when he returned from the PBR tour. As for him and Claire, he didn't see how they'd ever repair what those last two days together had torn apart. Still, his heart wouldn't quit her.

Unable to talk with his mouthpiece in, Tanner pointed at the rope then up, signaling for Armand to grab it. Using his gloved right hand, Tanner rubbed the rosin-coated rope section, getting it hot and sticky, the motion firing him up to ride this sucker.

It'd be his first time on Yellow Jacket, though he'd watched enough to expect some hard bucking and a quick turn back. Should be a wild, high-scoring ride if he hung on for eight seconds. A win today would earn him enough to pay off the rest of the loans he'd gotten for his bull-riding school.

Since Claire had postponed the hearing until Jonathan left the hospital, though, it still hadn't been approved to open. He'd get the judge's decision day after tomorrow, when he and his lawyer attended the rescheduled hearing. Anticipation jolted through him. He wanted the way cleared to open the school, but deep down he knew he was most excited to see Claire again.

Was opening the school a good idea considering he might not be around to keep an eye on Jonathan? And if he went ahead with his plans, would he hire a manager to oversee it while he continued bull riding, or return year-round to Coltrane if Claire's injunction failed?

The million dollar question.

It felt good being back at rodeo. Easy success. Yet, despite earning more in eight seconds than he could make in a month selling cattle or giving bull-riding lessons, he found that work more satisfying. Unexpectedly, he felt more restless at the rodeo than on the ranch, his mind preoccupied with Claire and Jonathan.

Using the back of his hand, Tanner tapped the rope, signaling for Armand to slack it up. Tanner set the block against his knee and warmed the handle before rolling it up and under to get the attached bells to slide farther toward his knot. He peered around Yellow Jacket's brown sides to make sure the bells were shook down and centered under the bull. Too many guys got their feet caught in the bell-strap and dragged around when they didn't perform that three-second check.

Armand nudged Tanner's spotter, Zane, and said, "Light de grill, boo—cause the ribeyes is about to fly."

Zane nodded and winked at Tanner. "Get 'em, ruffie!"

Tanner grinned up at them and rolled his rope back over into position, letting it settle around the bull. When Yellow Jacket lunged against the gate, Zane braced Tanner's shoulder, but he shook the man's hand off. He had this. Looked like the infamous bull was raring to go. Well, let her rip. He wasn't taking no for an answer on today's second go.

One of the best parts of bull riding was taking charge. Assuming complete control. Unleashing his aggressive nature as he bested champion bulls. Tested his mettle and won. No other achievement could beat the thrill, save one. He thought back to Claire's beautiful, beaming face when Revelation won Grand Champion. He'd never felt more excited in his life. Would she keep competing? He hoped so. For her sake and the sake of the ranch, though given her attitude at the hospital, he guessed she'd retreat back into her cautious world and never emerge again.

Damn. It bugged him.

Waste of a spirited woman. She might have the kind of temper that'd burn a man's hide off, but her passion…he recalled their kiss atop the ranch's ridge…it couldn't be beat. He could handle himself against the toughest bulls in the world—why had he let her chase him off? Sure, he'd felt guilty. Responsible. But he should have stayed at the ranch longer, worked on Claire until she came around again. Of course, that didn't erase her lies about him and Jonathan. He couldn't forgive deception like that. But the time away helped him get a better handle on his emotions.

When he stuck his hand through his handle, he curled his fingers, making himself comfortable. Armand pulled the rope tight while Tanner wrapped the tail around his hand to secure it in his grip.

Raising his free arm, he slid up and nodded. Yellow Jacket snapped his neck back, already looking hooky. Yep. It'd be a wild ride.

When the latch popped and the gate swung open, the bull rushed forward, raring to go, his back legs kicking high. He spun away from Tanner's hand not five feet into the arena, pulling Tanner's shoulder. His back and neck jerked, but he held on as the bull changed directions, twisting, his belly rolling as he bucked harder still.

A ringing sounded in Tanner's ears, but he hung on, battling to keep his seat as the whirling, outraged animal tried everything to kick him loose. He kept his knees slightly bent and his calves and spurs set in position, clenching the sweating bull's sides when it faded, moving backward as it spun in both directions. With Tanner's feet ahead of the bull rope, he got up on his legs a bit and kept his center of balance as the devil beneath him yanked right then left, up and back down again, its tricks lightning fast and hard-hitting.

It bellowed loudly and Tanner used the thigh beneath his riding arm as leverage to hang on as

Yellow Jacket went flat out sunfishing, leaping off the ground and kicking out with all four feet.

"Get around, get around, get around," chanted the crowd, some waving signs with his name, though he barely noticed. With his chin tucked, he kept his eyes on the spot just ahead of his riding hand and leaned forward, his back straight... or as straight as he could keep it given the jarring, jolting, spin-dry of a ride Yellow Jacket served up.

Woo-hoo what a bull!

A buzzer sounded and Tanner looked up at the score board. Eight seconds! He'd covered Yellow Jacket! Tanner waited until the bullfighter distracted the bull. When it spun left, he freed his riding hand with the other and dismounted off the right side as the bull kicked. The momentum launched Tanner a small distance from the animal, which immediately spun around and charged. Tanner sprinted to the fence, leaped up and threw himself over the side. His Elite traveling buddies slapped him on the helmet and cheered while Tanner pulled off his gear and spat out his mouth guard.

Yes! A qualified ride! Was it a winning score?

When the number flashed on the board, the group roared again and Tanner nodded, grinning. Another win. One step closer to his old financial security. But if he hadn't lost it, or his health, a voice whispered, would he have discovered other talents—like ranching? Would he have reunited with Claire? Found out he was a father? Nothing, not even his three gold buckles, beat that, though things hadn't ended well with Claire.

After shaking hands with the event coordinator and waving to the arena, he headed off to his hotel room, feeling strangely beat instead of elated. He checked his watch. Nine o'clock. Too late to call Jonathan? They'd spoken briefly every time Tanner called the hospital for updates on his condition. Now that Jonathan was home from the hospital, Tanner itched to have a long talk with his son. He wondered what, if anything, Claire had told Jonathan about Tanner being his father. She couldn't lie forever.

He grabbed a slice of pizza, part of last night's to-go order, from the minifridge and placed it on a paper plate. After starting it up in the microwave, he headed back to the living room with a cola. His phone buzzed in his hand and he fumbled to punch the answer button, suddenly clumsy when he recognized the Denton Creek number. Claire?

"Tanner?" quavered a young voice.

He grabbed the back of his couch and sat, his knees unsteady. "Jon?" Fierce pride gripped him. This was his son…his son…

A bark sounded through the phone. "And Roxy," the boy said.

Tanner smiled, warmth spreading through him as he pictured the pair. How good it felt to hear Jonathan's voice.

"But are Lottie and Guff around?" Tanner murmured, low and furtive.

"I think they're hiding behind my bookshelf," Jonathan whispered back. "Roxy keeps sniffing there."

"She'll get 'em."

"Roxy's brave."

Tanner closed his eyes and recalled the small dog ferociously defending Jonathan from the bull. "Yes. Yes, she is. How are you feeling?"

"Good. Got my cast off."

"I didn't get to sign it." Though what would he have written? From Tanner or Love, Dad?

"I'm sorry, Tanner." Jonathan's voice suddenly rose and cracked, making Tanner's chest constrict.

"It's okay," Tanner began.

"No. I mean about riding. I saw you put the bulls in the new school and wanted to show you I was big enough to learn to ride."

Tanner held the phone away from his mouth and let out a breath before he brought it back to his ear. "You proved you're brave, that's for sure."

"But I couldn't ride the bull. I used the prod to get him in the chute but I didn't get the rope tight around him like you showed me."

Tanner leaned his head back and stared at the ceiling. The microwave dinged and the smell of pepperoni wafted his way. Suddenly he didn't feel like eating.

"That was on a horse."

"But you said that's what you did on a bull."

Tanner nodded, regretting giving in to the boy's pleas to teach him a little about rodeo. Maybe Claire was right; he'd opened Pandora's box and hadn't thought to warn anyone, not Jonathan and not Claire.

"Are we going to finish working on the truck?"

Tanner's lungs searched for air, gave up and quit. He shook his head mutely in answer, unsure how to act around the child. He'd only spoken to Martin about it since finding out Jonathan was his son, and had been surprised at the man's encouragement.

"Kevin was a good dad," Martin had said, "but you would have been a good one, too. It's not too late. I know things aren't right between you and Claire, but don't let that stop you from claiming what's yours. Jonathan could do with a father in his life."

Tanner had nodded though he hadn't worked

out all the logistics. He'd already spoken to a real estate agent about renting a place in town. Something with two bedrooms. One for him. One for his son. He imagined weekend visits. Jonathan following Tanner's safety guidelines and helping with the rodeo school during the week if the injunction failed. A family. The kind he'd dreamed of, growing up. It filled his every last thought when he didn't dwell on Claire's betrayal.

"Tanner. You still there? Roxy. No! Toes aren't for eating. That's what French fries are for."

Despite his dark thoughts, Tanner smiled and propped his feet on the coffee table. He imagined lots of conversations like this in the years ahead with his child.

"Still here, son. We pretty much finished the truck before you got hurt and I had it painted while you were in the hospital. They were supposed to deliver it back to the barn. Might want to check and see if they did."

"Yippeeee!" Jonathan hollered so loud Tanner had to pull the phone from his ear. "We did it. That'll make Daddy happy."

Tanner smiled. "I hope so."

"Momma, too."

Tanner stayed silent, recalling Claire's outrage when he'd plowed into the truck months ago. He'd thought so much had changed since then, but here they both were, back in the same spot: Tanner away at rodeo and Claire home raising a child without him. He gritted his teeth. He'd at least make a difference on the last part.

"Don't you like me anymore?" asked Jonathan quietly.

Tanner sucked in a fast breath, his pulse starting to pound. He wished he could reach through the phone and hug his son. "Of course I like you."

I love you.

Jonathan sniffled. "You don't ever spend time with me anymore. You didn't visit me in the hospital except the first couple of days."

The words lassoed Tanner's heart and yanked. Hard. As soon as he flew to Texas, he'd make a beeline for Jonathan. That was more important than the hearing. "Of course I want to spend time with you. It's been…a little crazy lately," he temporized.

"I know," Jonathan sighed. "I've been watching you on TV. Saw you win tonight. Hey! I didn't know bulls could fly."

Tanner laughed. "That one could. Guess he's magic."

"I'm too old for magic," Jonathan muttered and the *thwack* of a ball thrown against a wall sounded, followed by Roxy's bark. "Mrs. Purdy told me."

Biting back what he really wanted to say about Coltrane's uptight florist, Tanner said, instead, "No one is too old for magic."

Jonathan let out a relieved-sounding breath. "Good. I always want to believe. It's fun."

Tanner opened his mouth to answer but Jonathan rushed on. "Can I tell you another secret?"

"Okay," Tanner remarked absently, walking back to the kitchen, his stomach deciding on the pizza, after all. It felt incredible talking to his son. He couldn't stop marveling over it.

"I was spying."

"Mmm-hmm." Tanner grabbed the plate out of the microwave and set it on the small counter.

"I heard Momma tell Grandpa you were my dad. I was supposed to be asleep but I came downstairs for water."

Tanner's mouth opened. Closed. Opened again. What? He'd wanted to be present when Jonathan learned the truth. His first co-parenting act.

"Momma said Daddy wasn't my real father." Jonathan's voice sounded waterlogged. "Can I still call him Dad?"

Tanner leaned forward and the fingers wrapped around the counter grew white. "Always."

He heard Jonathan swallow hard. "He was the best dad."

"I don't ever want you to forget him."

"Sometimes," Jonathan's voice broke. "Sometimes I can't remember what he looked like."

Tanner's chest burned. "Do you have a picture?"

Jonathan was silent for a moment then said, "But he's not laughing. His face looked funny when he laughed. I miss that."

"Does your mom have any videos?"

Jonathan blew his nose. "I don't know."

Tanner spun his plate in circles, thinking fast. "I bet she does, and I would also guess your dad is laughing in them."

Jonathan cleared his throat. "He liked to laugh a lot. Sometimes he pushed up his nose, went cross-eyed and snorted." Jonathan was silent for a long moment. Then, "He's not ever coming back."

Tanner shook his head slowly, wishing like anything he was in Coltrane. "No. But he's always watching over you."

"What's the difference between a real father and a dad?"

"None," Tanner said firmly, thinking of Kevin. How he must have loved Claire and Jonathan…what a debt Tanner owed him for stepping up to take care of them when Tanner hadn't stuck around.

Jonathan's breathing drifted through the line.

"There is a difference, though. Like how you like horses and Daddy liked cars, and how you tap your hands when music's playing while Daddy sang. But you're both the same to me, in here." Jonathan laughed then said, "Oops. You can't see me. I pointed at my heart."

A baseball-sized lump formed in Tanner's throat. "Same. I love you, Jon." He lifted his soda and took a cold, sweet gulp.

"Wow!" Bedsprings creaked and Tanner envisioned Jonathan jumping up and down. Roxy must have joined in the fun because she barked and yipped. Then, suddenly, silence, followed by, "I love you—" Jonathan's voice trailed off. "Do I call you Dad, too?"

At the boy's frightened tone, Tanner thought fast. "How about I'll be your Pa?"

"I like that… Pa."

Tanner blew out a long breath. "Sounds good." And it did. He was a pa. Responsible for this boy who he'd raise to be a man. No matter how much Claire disapproved of him, he wouldn't abandon what was his. Here was the chance to be the father he wished he'd had, and he wouldn't mess it up. Everything else, everything but the feelings he'd had for Claire, paled in comparison.

"Did you know you were my Pa?"

"I found out when I saw your ears. We have the same kind."

"Pixie ears," gasped Jonathan. "The kids in gym class made fun of me for that."

"Then they're jealous because only a special few have them."

Jonathan made a humming sound. "I was in a special group at school. Gifted and talented."

Tanner nodded, impressed. "I'm proud of you."

"Austin says I should go back to school next year. Here, Roxy. Fetch." The dog yelped, a loud joyous sound. "Do you think I should go back?"

"I think you can handle yourself."

"Tucker apologized and he's the biggest, baddest bully."

Tanner chuckled. "I wouldn't mess with a tough guy like you, and if Tucker tries anything, just remind him who your Pa is."

The bedsprings creaked again. Tanner imagined Jonathan springing to his feet. "So how come you don't live here anymore? Did you leave forever?" Jonathan's voice wobbled and he rushed on before Tanner could reassure him. "Because Momma told Grandpa she didn't tell you because you only wanted to be famous and cared more about rodeo than people. Is that true?"

Tanner opened his mouth to deny everything but something stopped him. The truth.

Ten years ago, he had wanted fame and fortune. Left the love of his life in pursuit of it. Was it any wonder Claire believed he wouldn't want a son?

Suddenly he saw her secret-keeping differently. It wasn't so much lying as it was protecting. Maybe even protecting him. She'd loved him. Misguided as it was, she could have thought she'd done them all a favor by letting Tanner chase his dreams. What reasons had he given to make her believe he'd want to stay?

If he'd given up his bull-riding dream, he might have always wondered what he'd missed. Could have resented, rather than appreciated, Jonathan and Claire. What a strong woman. Until Kevin had come along, she'd planned to raise a baby on her own rather than haul back a reluctant father. After Kevin's death, she'd tried to keep things going on her own when she'd needed support most. If she'd called, he would have dropped everything for her and Jonathan.

Suddenly, he discovered that he could forgive Claire. How would she have understood his real reasons for leaving when he'd never explained them? After he'd outright rejected her ultimatum? He'd been deceptive and selfish, too, and played a role in this, he now saw.

Well-intentioned lies. They'd both paid a price for them these past ten years. Wasn't it time for this to be over? For them to have another chance without the mistakes?

"Tanner?" Jonathan asked. "Will you write me?"

Tanner stood and dumped his cold food in the trash. "No need to write. I'm coming back." He'd tell Mike to stop the negotiations with a new sponsor and he'd retire. Swallow his pride and take a job working for someone else if the injunction stopped his school. Anything to be with his child and, hopefully, Claire.

"Yes! I knew it. Or I wanted it. That's the same thing, Pa. Are you going to live on the ranch again? Ick! Roxy stop licking me." After a scrabbling scratching sound, Jonathan shouted, "Puppy time out!" and the dog's frantic panting quieted.

Tanner stared out the window and watched the same quarter moon he'd kissed Claire under a month ago. "I hope so," he replied, wishing for it as hard as Jonathan. He saw his future unfold like a newly paved road, leading him to a family, to Claire, if she'd hear him out. "I'll let you know day after tomorrow."

"You're coming home!"

"I've got business." Tanner smiled slowly,

planning the words he'd use to persuade Claire at the injunction trial to give them one last shot. "Family business."

CHAPTER TWENTY

Claire watched Jonathan as he trekked back upstairs after dinner. He'd shot down her offer of a drive-in movie.

"He's withdrawing again," mumbled her father around a piece of pie.

"I know, Dad." Claire gave him a weary smile. "I'll think of something."

"Get Tanner back. That'd be something," snapped her father.

She flinched and watched as he set down his fork with his once-afflicted hand. Improved mobility, for sure. Better yet, with the increased income they'd been making from sales, she'd hired an in-home therapist to work with him every day. The assisted living facility wasn't needed after all, and Jonathan wouldn't lose his home…though it didn't bring her the happiness she'd expected…not without Tanner. Her dad had a point.

Despite everything, she missed the cowboy. Caught herself looking for him at meals or in the barns. It felt as if he haunted every corner of the ranch, yet she'd been the one to banish him. Had she made a mistake? She eyed the extra arm sling lying on the counter and gave herself a mental slap. No. Tanner brought danger.

But he brought love, too. Had helped Jonathan come out of his shell and made her conquer her fear.

A sudden thought stilled her hand and it hovered, holding a dirty plate over the sink. She could do the same thing with Jonathan. After hurrying through the dishwashing, she kissed her surprised father, hustled upstairs and burst into Jonathan's room.

He looked up at her from a comic book, startled.

"I've got a surprise for you!" Roxy, hearing the excitement in her voice, leaped from the bed in a bound and began chewing and licking Claire's sandal tassels. "Stop, Rox." She nudged the aggressively affectionate dog away. "What do you say, Jonathan? Want to find out what it is?"

He cradled his casted arm. "Do I have to go outside?"

She nodded and pasted her most reassuring smile on. "It's the only way the magic happens."

Jonathan closed his comic book and sat up straighter. "Magic?"

"The best kind, but hurry or we'll be too late."

She turned and clomped down the stairs, hoping, praying, he'd be right behind her. She could force him, but like horses, it was best if he came willingly.

In a moment, Jonathan slipped his hand into hers. "Grandpa, we're going outside to do magic."

Her father squinted at Claire over the top of his newspaper then gave an approving nod. "That's the best place to find it, young man. Go to it!"

Roxy streaked out the door ahead of them and Claire led Jonathan to the horse stables. The summer sun still shone and grasshoppers bounded ahead of them as they stepped through the grass. The wind chimes spun and tinkled as they passed, the sound her mother had always loved. It filled Claire with peace now. This was her home and she wouldn't lose it, thanks to Tanner. Looking at the big picture, she owed him so much. She had overreacted at the hospital, she realized now. It'd been a terrifying time.

"Are we going to give Guardian a bath?" sang Jonathan. He stopped to pick up a stick and winged it far. With a gleeful bark, Roxy bounded after it and disappeared around a tree.

"Nope. Better."

"What is it?"

She pressed the freckle on the tip of his nose. "You can't rush magic, buster."

He gave an exaggerated sigh, grabbed the stick from a returning Roxy and chucked it again.

Roxy, distracted by a couple of squawking sparrows, didn't follow the trajectory and turned in circles as they walked, searching. "Over there, Rox." They caught up to the spot where the stick had landed and the dog pounced on it, trotting beside them with it held in her mouth like a prize.

At the stables, Claire saddled Dusty as Jonathan watched her, wide-eyed.

"Are you giving someone a lesson?" He scratched at a scab on his knee and looked down—probably to hide his disappointment, thought Claire.

"Yes. You."

Jonathan's head snapped up. "Me?" he squeaked.

"It's time."

"What if I get hurt?" He held out his arm.

"I'm riding with you."

"You don't ride," he gasped, absent-mindedly giving Roxy a head scratch.

"I do now. Watch." Claire swung herself into the saddle and took Dusty around the ring. She swerved her around a couple of barrels she'd set out for her advanced students and smiled broadly at Jonathan's loud cheer. She pulled up beside him. "Want to come?"

He jumped up and down, and Roxy did, too. "Yes."

Claire dismounted, then handed Jonathan up. "Hold on to the saddle horn."

"I am!" He gripped the large knob and grinned down at her. "Can I do it by myself?"

Claire studied docile Dusty. She'd carried many young children, even ones with disabilities, and had never had an off day. "Okay, but I'm leading the horse."

"That's okay!" Jonathan started to scooch forward and Claire put a hand on his leg. "You can't fidget on a horse. Stay perfectly still while I lead you around."

Jonathan's cheeks bulged and he froze.

Claire laughed. "You can breathe, silly."

He exhaled. "Phew. Okay. Let's go. To infinity and beyond!"

Dusty's ears flicked but she willingly followed Claire around the ring. "I'm doing it," shouted Jonathan. "I'm riding like Tanner."

"And me," put in Claire. Roxy wove in and out of her legs but steered clear of steady Dusty.

"Who taught you?"

"My momma."

"But you stopped." Jonathan peered down at

her, his body swaying with the horse. A natural. "How come you started again?"

Memory of her night riding with Tanner blew through her, whirling in the empty spaces he'd left behind. "Tanner helped me."

"He did something else, too. Can I get off now? I feel a little dizzy."

"Of course!" Claire helped her son down and hugged him against her while Dusty moved off to graze on some grass springing up by a fence post. "What did Tanner do?"

Jonathan cut her a saucy, sideways look. "It's a surprise. Follow me!" He marched for the gate.

"I have to put Dusty away!" she called and he swung back around.

"I can help!"

She smiled as her little man bustled back, ready to work. What a rancher he'd make. The real deal. Thank goodness she hadn't sold out after all. Taken the safe route. She thought of all the things she'd said to Tanner at the hospital as she unsaddled Dusty and put her back in the stall. She wished she could take half of them back...maybe more.

After they closed up the stable, Jonathan hustled her over to the old barn that held Kevin's truck. Roxy had swerved away and left when they'd passed the house, lured by her feed bowl, no doubt.

"Momma, can you open the door but keep your eyes closed?"

"Okay," she ventured, anxious. Last she'd seen the truck it'd been in parts—scattered on the particle-board floor. The smell of fresh paint hit her as she pulled the door back on its rollers.

"Ta-da!" called Jonathan. "Magic! You can open your eyes."

When she did, Claire stared, hardly believing the sight. There, sparkling as if it'd just come off the assembly line, was the truck...glossy teal paint and all.

"How did you do this?" she gasped, wandering into the lofted space. Sunshine angled through the large windows, its beams a spotlight on her pickup as if she'd just won it on a game show. It felt as if she had.

Jonathan raced ahead and ran a hand over the chrome fender. "Tanner did it. I mean we did it. We had it almost all together before the accident and Tanner finished it up and had it painted while we were at the hospital."

Claire drew close and pressed her palms on the front hood. Stared through the windshield, her giddy heart skipping along her ribcage.

Tanner had done this? Even after she'd said all of those mean things? Tossed him out of their lives?

Her insides curled as she remembered telling

him he needed to act and think like a grown-up. Doing this for her, despite the secret she'd kept from him, showed maturity. He'd done right by her, and looking at Jonathan's glowing face, his sense of accomplishment and pride, she realized how much he'd done for her son in seeing this restoration through.

She eased open the truck door and sat behind the wheel. Her fingers traced the steering wheel and she glanced in the rearview mirror. With her eyes closed, she tried bringing up Kevin's face, but Tanner's kept intruding. As much as she'd always love her husband, for the first time she felt ready to move on. And then something amazing happened. Kevin's smiling face leaped to mind. He wore the look he'd always given her when he was proud of her.

"Should I forgive him, babe?" she murmured, and imagined his approving nod.

Jonathan knocked on the window and she unrolled it. He leaned his freckled face in. "Are you still mad at Tanner, Momma? It's not his fault I rode the bull."

She smoothed down Jonathan's cowlick and smiled when it sprang back up. You couldn't suppress what was meant to be, like her and Tanner.

"So why'd you do it?"

"Because I wanted to be like my Pa."

Her fingers stilled in his hair then dropped. "What did you say?"

Jonathan tugged on the door handle. She pushed it open and helped him climb into her lap. "Don't be mad, but I snooped on you and Grandpa."

"What did you hear?"

"You said Tanner would never care more about me than rodeo, but you're wrong because he's coming to see me tomorrow. He said we have family business."

Claire's hand half rose to her mouth. She recalled her and her father's late-night conversation. How they'd paused, thinking they'd heard something, then continued when it proved to be nothing.

But it had been something.

Huge.

Panic swept through her. Would Jonathan forgive her? He rarely listened to her as it was. Would this put their mother-son relationship on even shakier ground?

"I'm sorry for not telling you."

Jonathan twisted around and gave her a disapproving frown. "Lying is bad."

Claire nodded. First Tanner, now his son. And they were both right. "I know. After your daddy died, I should have told you."

"Will I get to drive his truck someday?" Jonathan scooched down and tried to touch the pedals.

Claire pulled him back up and hugged him tight. "Yes."

"Can Tanner teach me?"

Her head began to pound. "Yes. So, you told Tanner you know he's your father?"

Jonathan nodded and leaned across her to turn dials. "I decided it was my secret to tell, too, so I called him last night."

The world bucked and rolled beneath her. She'd planned to broach the subject of telling Jonathan with Tanner after the injunction hearing.

"And how do you feel about this, honey?"

Jonathan twisted in her arms and kissed her jaw. "Great. Tanner said there's no difference between a dad and a real father and that I don't have to call him Dad. That's why he's Pa, so I won't ever forget Daddy."

Claire marveled at the tact Tanner used in dealing with this difficult conversation. He'd probably done a better job than she would have. Who said he couldn't think like a parent?

Stupid, stupid her.

She pulled Jonathan close and his head rested on her shoulder, weighty and satisfying. Her son. Her son with Kevin…and Tanner. Both incredible men.

"We won't ever forget your daddy."

"Do we have any videos of him?"

She leaned back and looked Jonathan in the eye. "Of course we do."

Jonathan smiled and dropped his head back down. "Because I told Tanner I missed Daddy's laugh and he said to ask you for a video."

"I love you, Jonathan."

"I love you, too, Momma."

Tears stung her eyes as the close bond they'd shared before Jonathan had withdrawn, snapped shut around them and held them tight.

She'd avoided watching those videos since Kevin passed. Now she saw what she'd missed and Tanner hadn't. Her son needed a father. Living and deceased. Both Kevin and Tanner would play vital roles in Jonathan's life. And if she handled things right tomorrow, Tanner would be a part of hers again, too.

Her mind formed a plan and her fingers gripped the steering wheel as she asked Kevin to wish her luck, hoping he'd give her that as he had so many things—the sun, the moon, the stars...and maybe even Tanner.

"YOU'RE SURE THIS is what you want to do?"

Claire held in a sneeze as Mr. Redmond leaned forward and passed her back the document she'd prepared last night. His expensive cologne mingled with the scent of some kind of hair product that'd been used to sculpt his comb over into some retro fifties look.

"Yes. And thank you for all your help." Claire smoothed down the front of her suit jacket and plucked a couple of Roxy's hairs off her skirt.

They'd arrived at the courthouse at nine thirty, a half hour before their scheduled injunction hearing, and been ushered into this private meeting room. A long table dominated it and a counter held a percolating coffee machine. Bright green potted ferns hung in front of windows overlooking downtown Coltrane.

"Women." An exasperated snort escaped him. "Do you ever make up your minds?"

She forced a nervous smile as Mr. Redmond adjusted his silk tie, a bright slash of pink against an otherwise conservative shirt and tailored suit. Claire sensed eccentric Carol Lynn's influence and smiled. A happily-ever-after for her lawyer. Would she have one, too?

Her fingers drummed on the underside of the table. At Mr. Redmond's disapproving glance, she laced them in her lap instead, damp palms touching. Would Tanner hear her out?

Mr. Redmond eased back in his chair and stood. "If you're sure, I'll see if Tanner and his lawyer have arrived yet."

At her nod, the door swished closed behind

him. Claire pressed her hands to her eyes and tightened her jaw until she could think about nothing other than the feeling of her back teeth pressing against each other. Outside, a faint breeze rushed through the window screens, trees rustled, and a car door slammed.

After several excruciating moments, the door opened and in the entrance stood Tanner, looking devastatingly handsome in a fitted gray pinstripe suit that deepened his eyes to a startling blue. His face held a curious expression. Not anger, as she'd expected, but something else.

"Your lawyer said you wanted to settle out of court if I agreed to your terms."

She nodded and, shaking, passed the paper to him as he sat down across the table from her, his back to the door.

"These are the terms?" He turned over her daisy-embroidered stationery paper and she flushed. Not very official looking.

"Yes."

Tanner leaned across the table and a sudden intensity darkened his eyes. "There's something I'd like to say, first."

Claire shook her head, but to her surprise Tanner strode around the table and pulled her to her feet.

"I want to apologize."

"You do?" Despite herself, she squeaked. "I thought you wouldn't want to see me again."

"Sometimes a man needs time to think."

At his earnest expression, her skin prickled. "And what's this man been thinking?"

"That he was wrong." His nose flared as he breathed deep. "I'm sorry, Claire. I let my temper get the better of me and didn't hear you out."

Relief loosened her joints and his chest rose steeply when she set both hands on his shoulders for balance. "I'm sorry, too. You had a right to know when I first found out. Just because you wanted rodeo more than me didn't mean you'd feel the same about your child."

"I'd like to think that's true." His voice lowered and his arm came around her waist, solid and warm. "But I was a kid. Immature. Maybe I would have resented being a young father. I didn't want to stick around Coltrane and be a failure like my folks."

"I thought you left to be famous."

"I wanted to prove to myself and the town that I wasn't the loser everyone thought I was. That I could succeed and be someone important." He looked up at the ceiling, blinking rapidly as if he'd gotten something in his eyes. "But now I see things differently. You, Jon and Martin are all the success I need. Family. Love. What more is there?"

His words unfolded in her heart, made its walls stretch, filled it with wonder and joy. "Nothing. Absolutely nothing."

He cupped her chin and gazed down at her. "Jon's my son," he said, as if testing out the words, each one rounding and lingering in his mouth before he released it.

"He's just as twitchy," she ventured, and he smiled slightly.

"I know how to handle twitchy."

She leaned her cheek into his palm. "Seeing you two together proves what a great father you'll be. I was dead wrong to have said otherwise and I'm sorry for what happened at the hospital."

When his face broke into a wide smile, she stood on tiptoe and let her lips graze his chin. It carried the faint trace of stubble. "And you never had to become a star to impress me."

He loosened the pins holding her low bun and ran his fingers through her curls as they fell around her face. "No. You cared about me before that."

"I still do. I love you, Tanner." Her small, breathless laugh carried in the quiet room.

He held her gaze, fierce happiness setting his eyes aglow. "I love you, too, Claire. You're the most incredible thing I've ever encountered. You've haunted every waking hour. Every feeling, every experience I've had in my life up to this point was flat out unimportant compared to this. Us."

She held her breath as he traced the bare skin of her arms, and her stomach tensed pleasurably. Her legs became oddly weak. Then he placed the flat of his hand on the small of her back, so that they were as close as they could decently be.

Joy lit a fuse in her heart and it burned straight to her toes. She threw caution to the wind and tilted her face so that her mouth was inches from his, then moved closer still until their lips met. She almost jolted when she felt the pressure of his mouth on hers, the sweetness of him. And she no longer cared about anything. She wanted him. Now and forever. Her cowboy. Her partner. Her son's father.

What's more, the anxiousness that'd plagued her these past ten years dried up and blew away, carried by the slight wind curling through the window. Never to return. Her old boldness took its place. She felt like the kind of daring woman she'd once been, a woman who'd kiss a man in an unlocked room beside a window for all of Coltrane to see.

His kind of cowgirl.

And the strong woman she wanted to be.

She smiled as he nibbled the upward sweep of her mouth, gently at first, and then with a fierce, gratifying passion that quickened her breathing. Her hand stole up to his neck, her eyes closing—and he lifted her off her feet and fitted her tight against him, kissing her so hard that her head fell back. Her body hummed with pleasure, with rightness, with a bone-deep knowing that the missing part of her had finally come home.

The room spun and a sense of satisfaction deeper than their kiss consumed her. Tanner would always support her. She'd never go it alone again. A partner for life. Her train of thought was broken by his kissing her jaw, her neck, her shoulder with intense concentration.

With effort, she pulled back and studied him. "You still haven't agreed to my terms."

His mouth hitched and he picked up the girly paper, his arm molding her to his side. She watched his eyes scan the page then rise to meet hers in wonder.

"Do you mean this?"

"With my whole heart."

His brow furrowed. "Number One. Tanner Hayes must always follow his own path," he read, then stopped. He continued at her solemn nod. "Number Two. No matter where it leads,

Claire Shelton will support and love him if he'll let her."

"Sounds right." Claire smiled back at him, his growing excitement infectious.

"So, no injunction?"

"Not if you agree to my terms."

"I want to be with you, period. No matter the terms." Then, as if he couldn't help himself, he captured her lips again and she lost herself in his arms. Never before had she felt this happy and complete.

"I want to see what we can add up to, Claire Elizabeth Shelton. All of us. What do you say, will you marry me?"

She reached up and pressed a kiss to his chin dimple then his mouth, peace stealing through her, filling in the cracks and holes left by her past. Only their shining future lay ahead of her, so bright it brought tears to her eyes when she pictured it. No more fear. Only love.

"Claire," Tanner murmured between kisses. "Is that a yes?"

Claire laughed. She couldn't help it. "It's a definite yes, although I already know what we add up to."

Her fingers laced behind his neck and pulled his lips to hers again before she whispered the words that meant everything to her. What she'd lost more than once and now, like a miracle, had found again.

"A family."

* * * * *

LARGER-PRINT BOOKS!

GET 2 FREE
LARGER-PRINT NOVELS
PLUS 2 FREE
MYSTERY GIFTS

Love Inspired®
SUSPENSE
RIVETING INSPIRATIONAL ROMANCE

Larger-print novels are now available...

YES! Please send me 2 FREE LARGER-PRINT Love Inspired® Suspense novels and my 2 FREE mystery gifts (gifts are worth about $10). After receiving them, if I don't wish to receive any more books, I can return the shipping statement marked "cancel." If I don't cancel, I will receive 4 brand-new novels every month and be billed just $5.49 per book in the U.S. or $5.99 per book in Canada. That's a savings of at least 19% off the cover price. It's quite a bargain! Shipping and handling is just 50¢ per book in the U.S. and 75¢ per book in Canada.* I understand that accepting the 2 free books and gifts places me under no obligation to buy anything. I can always return a shipment and cancel at any time. Even if I never buy another book, the two free books and gifts are mine to keep forever.

110/310 IDN GH6P

Name _____ (PLEASE PRINT)

Address _____ Apt. #

City _____ State/Prov. _____ Zip/Postal Code

Signature (if under 18, a parent or guardian must sign)

Mail to the **Reader Service:**
IN U.S.A.: P.O. Box 1867, Buffalo, NY 14240-1867
IN CANADA: P.O. Box 609, Fort Erie, Ontario L2A 5X3

Are you a current subscriber to Love Inspired® Suspense books and want to receive the larger-print edition?
Call 1-800-873-8635 or visit www.ReaderService.com.

* Terms and prices subject to change without notice. Prices do not include applicable taxes. Sales tax applicable in N.Y. Canadian residents will be charged applicable taxes. Offer not valid in Quebec. This offer is limited to one order per household. Not valid for current subscribers to Love Inspired Suspense larger-print books. All orders subject to credit approval. Credit or debit balances in a customer's account(s) may be offset by any other outstanding balance owed by or to the customer. Please allow 4 to 6 weeks for delivery. Offer available while quantities last.

Your Privacy—The Reader Service is committed to protecting your privacy. Our Privacy Policy is available online at www.ReaderService.com or upon request from the Reader Service.

We make a portion of our mailing list available to reputable third parties that offer products we believe may interest you. If you prefer that we not exchange your name with third parties, or if you wish to clarify or modify your communication preferences, please visit us at www.ReaderService.com/consumerschoice or write to us at Reader Service Preference Service, P.O. Box 9062, Buffalo, NY 14240-9062. Include your complete name and address.

YES! Please send me **The Montana Mavericks Collection** in Larger Print. This collection begins with 3 FREE books and 2 FREE gifts (gifts valued at approx. $20.00 retail) in the first shipment, along with the other first 4 books from the collection! If I do not cancel, I will receive 8 monthly shipments until I have the entire 51-book Montana Mavericks collection. I will receive 2 or 3 FREE books in each shipment and I will pay just $4.99 US/ $5.89 CDN for each of the other four books in each shipment, plus $2.99 for shipping and handling per shipment.*If I decide to keep the entire collection, I'll have paid for only 32 books, because 19 books are FREE! I understand that accepting the 3 free books and gifts places me under no obligation to buy anything. I can always return a shipment and cancel at any time. My free books and gifts are mine to keep no matter what I decide.

263 HCN 2404   463 HCN 2404

Name	(PLEASE PRINT)	
Address		Apt. #
City	State/Prov.	Zip/Postal Code

Signature (if under 18, a parent or guardian must sign)

Mail to the **Reader Service:**

IN U.S.A.: P.O. Box 1867, Buffalo, NY 14240-1867
IN CANADA: P.O. Box 609, Fort Erie, Ontario L2A 5X3